The Louisiana Beauty Queen

Dr. Karl Hedman

Published 2021 by Karl Hedman.

Karl Hedman, Alstromerg. 14, 50343 Boras, Sweden

Names: Hedman, Karl, 1967-, author.

Title: The Louisiana Beauty Queen / Karl Hedman.

Identifiers:
ISBN (ebook) 978-91-985241-8-5
ISBN-13 (pbk) 978-91-985241-7-8
ISBN (hardcover) 978-91-985241-6-1

Subjects: Biography. Cancer. Dementia. Louisiana.
Mental Illness. Romance. Women.

Cover photos of Mary Jackson Guillory and Maria
Guillory Hedman. Permission by Mary Jackson
Guillory and Maria Guillory Hedman to use the
images of them.

Cover design © Karl Hedman

In loving memory of Maria Guillory Hedman (1973-2020) and Mary Jackson Guillory (1940-2021)

CONTENTS

CHARACTERS

Mary – Teacher and beauty queen

Maria – Daughter of Mary, writer and married to Karl

Karl – Married to Maria, university professor and author

Bianca – Elder daughter of Maria and Karl, fashion designer and artist

Heidi – Younger daughter of Maria and Karl and IT specialist

Juliet – Mother of Mary and chemist

Mami (Willie) – Grandmother of Mary and deli clerk

Daddy (Claude Sr.) – Father of Mary and blacksmith

Claude Jr. –Mary's brother, welder and rock'n'roll band member

Ruby – Mary's sister and mathematics teacher

1 FALLING IN LOVE

Mary is born in 1940. She becomes an educator and wins a Louisiana beauty pageant. Mary falls in love with the handsome brother of another beauty pageant contestant. They get married and have a baby girl named Maria.

Mary and her husband divorce after having trouble. He moves to California. The separation from her father is a great loss for two-year-old Maria. She grows up with her grandmother Juliet and Mary in Louisiana. Occasionally Maria visits her father. Later, Maria and I meet as graduate students at UCLA in Los Angeles and fall in love.

Los Angeles, September 5th, 1995

I discover Maria suddenly in the graduate house where we live. She opens the balcony door. I am in the cafeteria below her. I look up. Maria catches my eyes and smiles at me. Her sensual eyes radiate. I can't take my eyes off her. Her lips are pleasing. I want to kiss her. She has thick eyebrows and adorable black hair. Her skin is pale. I look at her lovely shoulders. Maria dresses in an exquisite way with warm colors and fine materials. I fall in love with her as I watch her. She opens her book in the balcony chair. Maria is very studious reading all the time.

I see Maria the next day. She walks down the stairs looking gorgeous. I look up at her with total attention. Maria smiles at me. I'm blushing. She has kind eyes. Maria is very flirtatious towards me. I am mesmerized by her. She's so hot, calm, and sophisticated. She puts her lips together in a sensual way. I love the burgundy velvet skirt and the blouse that she wears like a divine queen. I can see her breasts through the blouse. Her legs are shapely. Maria is wearing black stockings. I fall in love with

1

her.

We watch each other for days. It's the end of my first week at UCLA. Maria approaches me at the international graduate student party. I'm wearing an exclusive black shirt from Paris and black pants. Our eyes meet. I love her warmth.

Hello. I'm Karl, I say.

I'm Maria, she says.

It's lovely to meet you, I respond and smile the warmest smile I can.

You, too. I've seen you in the cafeteria, she tells me.

Her voice is kind-hearted and serene. I love her for her beauty and sweetness inside and outside.

I've seen you on the balcony, I reply.

We make each other laugh when we look at another.

As we start our first date time stands still. We are in love. She looks at me intently and listens to me. I listen to her and smile.

Where are you from? Maria asks.

I'm from Sweden. I'll be here for a year, I tell her.

I've never been to Sweden, but I would like to go one day, Maria replies.

We talk about leaps of faith and the existentialist philosopher Kierkegaard from Denmark. Maria has studied art history and English at Louisiana State University where she received a full scholarship. She worked at the dean's office. Her dad lives in California. She was separated from him when she was a toddler. Maria wanted to be closer to him. She applied to The UCLA School of Law and was admitted.

I spot Maria in the corridor in the morning. She is spellbinding. We flirt with glowing faces. Her love reaches my heart. Maria's brown eyes are warm. I gaze into her eyes for a long time. She has cute eyelashes. I invite her for lunch. I adore her.

I walk back to my room after my classes. I'm awake in my bed thinking about Maria. I need her and have a strong desire to be in her arms. I leave my room,

2

turn, and walk down the hall to hers. I'm so excited. My body is shaking. Her roommate is gone for the weekend. I knock on the door. She opens.

Come on in, she says.

Maria gives me a warm hug.

I love you, I say warmly, extending my hands to her.

I love you too, Karl, Maria responds.

We have fallen in love with each other. It's love at first sight. She takes my hands, smiles, and laughs. I take Maria into my arms. She kisses me on the mouth. Her lips are soft and chapped. We look into each other's eyes and caress each other. We share things that we had never told anyone else.

We kiss gently with wet mouths. Her tongue moves into my mouth a little. We are drawn to each other like magnets. I push my lips softly on Maria's lips. It's a delicious taste. Her breath is warm and sweet. Maria's fingers dig into my hair. We take off our clothes and kiss passionately for hours. Our bodies touch. The delights of kissing are amazing. We lie naked next to each other. I kiss Maria's neck and touch her waist tenderly. She is so beautiful. I can feel her eyes on me.

It's almost 9 a.m. on Saturday morning. Maria wakes up first. I'm waking up slowly. We are tangled together and curled in each other's arms. I love being with her.

I'm falling in love with you, Karl. I love everything about you, she says.

I love you. I have loved you since I first saw you, I reply.

After the year in Los Angeles, I return to Stockholm. Maria has moved back to Louisiana. We want to be with each other.

Lille, France, fall 1996

In the summer of 1996, Maria tells me that she is going on exchange to France for a year.

I want to be close to you, I say.

I love you, Maria replies.

Maria goes to France. She begins her art history studies at a university in the North French city of Lille.

She invites me to stay with her.

I'll come to you, I say.

I call Maria. I tell her that I have bought a train ticket and will be with her the next day.

I'll come to meet you. I'll wait for you on the platform, she says.

We meet again. Maria is instantly recognizable. I run towards her, take Maria in my arms, and kiss her.

I have missed you so incredibly much, I say, laughing of joy.

I give her red roses and chocolates from Brussels.

I'm so happy that we're together again, Maria replies.

The evening air is warm. We dine romantically at a lovely restaurant. The oysters taste wonderful with the rich and deeply colored white wine from Alsace with exotic aromas of lychee and rose petals. Maria's eyes glitter in the lights from the candles on the table. We kiss and laugh.

To the love of my life, I say.

I love you, Maria replies.

We walk back to Maria's apartment. She gets onto the soft bed. I sit down beside her. We kiss.

I missed you so much, I say.

Maria smiles and kisses me.

You look so beautiful. It's so wonderful to be with you again, I say.

We are fully in the moment. Maria and I lay on her bed half dressed. We hug warmly and kiss each other's noses, eyes, and foreheads. We caress and touch each other's necks, backs, ears, chests, bellies, and hips. We make love for the first time. Our bodies are shaking with pleasure. We lay naked next to each other all night.

The next morning Maria and I go to a Tunisian coffee shop with delicious almond cookies. I love the way that Maria is speaking with the eloquent vocabulary of an art historian. Before I came to France, Maria made a friend in a local French girl. The French girl showed Maria around Lille.

In the afternoon, Maria takes me around the city and to her university campus. She walks majestically on the campus with her dark burgundy skirt, floral blouse, and sexy black stockings. Most people look at her with admiration and treat her with politeness. Maria loves to be in France. I'm so happy with her.

It's late fall. The morning is cold and grey. Maria and I walk over many bridges in the mist. We say bye for now.

I love you, Maria. See you soon, I say when Maria's face is wet with tears.

Stockholm, December 1996-January 1997

I am crying on my way back to Stockholm. I'm sad that Maria is not with me. I tremble and miss her so much. A couple of days later, Maria decides to move to me in Stockholm. Our love story continues. I want to marry her. I show my love for her with every part of my body and soul.

Will you marry me, Karl? I love you so much, Maria says with a voice full of love.

I love you, Maria. Yes. I want to marry you, I respond.

We have genuine feelings for each other. We start to cry with joy. Maria and I get engaged after visiting an Icelandic wedding ring designer. He makes handmade rings according to our design wishes.

The wedding day is a very big day for us. We have a lovely wedding ceremony in a church in a posh neighborhood in the center of Stockholm. Maria's wedding dress is golden beige showing her sensual

5

shapes. Maria and I promise each other love, commitment, and honesty. We will stick together no matter what.

You may kiss the bride, the priest says.

We laugh and kiss each other.

You look so beautiful, I tell Maria.

Maria is now my wife. We are so happy together. Maria's smiling lips are blood red. Her hair is styled in a French roll.

I love your hair that way, I say.

Thank you, Karl, Maria replies.

We have both needed someone to trust and lean on. It's so wonderful to be close to each other. We promise to be there for each other. The wedding party is at a Japanese restaurant close from the church. The guests are family and friends.

Welcome, everyone. First, I'd like to say, I love you Maria, I say.

Maria smiles.

I wish you all a fun party, I conclude.

All the wedding dinner guests seem to be having a wonderful time. Maria and I leave in a taxi. We spend the first night as a married couple at a romantic hotel next to the Royal Castle in the Old Town of Stockholm.

Maria has changed into a black velvet dress. The bed is covered with red rose pedals. The rose scent fills the bedroom. Maria turns her face to me. I feel Maria's soft skin against mine. We hold each other close. I am totally hers. I move my mouth closer to hers. We kiss passionately. We desire each other. Our bodies and souls become one when we make love.

New York City and Connecticut, February 1997

We celebrate our honeymoon on Manhattan. Maria and I visit the Consulate General of Sweden in New York City. She applies for a Swedish residence permit. The officer says that the decision will take about a year. Maria will be in the United States when she waits for her Swedish residence permit. She will stay with Louisiana friends in Connecticut. After a lovely honeymoon, I kiss Maria goodbye and return to Stockholm.

Stockholm, March 1997

I live in the embassy district of the capital. Most
weekdays, I go to an opera café with live opera
performances. At the café, I meet a Frenchman
named Leo. We become good friends. Leo tells me
that he used to live in Louisiana. He has connections
at the Embassy of the United States of America in
Sweden.

The next day, one of the American officers calls the
Swedish Migration Agency. A few days later, an
officer at the Consulate General of Sweden in New
York City calls Maria. She tells Maria that her
Swedish residence permit is available. We're
eternally grateful to Leo for making it possible for us
to be together again so soon.

Maria returns to Sweden. She says that she wants to
have children. Maria wants us to live in the
countryside to have a peaceful environment for the
children.

West Sweden, summer 1997

We move from Stockholm to my childhood
community in West Sweden. This is a small river
community in the South Swedish Highlands with
rare flowers, wild animals, and beautiful waterfalls.

Maria and I go biking on romantic rides in the birch
forests. We always bring picnic food. We have red
wine, cheese, bread, grapes, and figs. Our lips touch
when we sit down on the soft blankets. The leaves
shiver gently in the wind. We lean our heads together
– it is heaven. We can hear the sparkling stream of
the river. We are so aroused. We take off our clothes
and make love among thousands of flowers. Later,
Maria becomes pregnant. We're looking forward to
the baby. One day, Maria has sharp cramps and
bleeds in the bathroom.

Love, come here, Maria says quietly.

I walk to her. We realize that she has had a miscarriage. We cry. I kiss her forehead. I leave my lips on Maria's forehead for a long time to comfort her. Maria and I experience a strong loss of our love baby. We name the baby Liv which means life in Swedish. The miscarriage is too much for Maria. She wants to have her family around. We move to her native state of Louisiana.

2 THE FAMILY

Louisiana, 1997-2000

Maria and I fly from Paris to New Orleans. We wake up when we land at The Louis Armstrong New Orleans International Airport. This is the first time I visit Louisiana. Most people that I meet are friendly and have a sense of humor. I feel comfortable here.

My dad used to play Louisiana jazz, blues, rock'n'roll, soul, and zydeco music to me when I grew up. He had over 8000 vinyl records and a huge sound system. Our house was like a New Orleans dance club. I danced with my friends to Queen Ida and The Bon Temps Zydeco Band, Fats Domino, Big Chenier, and Clarence Frogman Henry.

Maria's family lives in the capital Baton Rouge 73 miles northwest of New Orleans. Native Americans lived on this Mississippi River land when French explorers in 1699 named the place red stick or Baton Rouge. The name of the place referred to the reddened cypress pole that Houma and Bayagoula Native Americans had staked in the ground to mark the boundaries of their hunting territories.

Maria's aunt Ruby drives us to the family house with pecan trees and fig bushes. Mary answers the door when we ring the bell.

This is my mother, Maria says.

Hey y'all. Come on in, Mary says.

Mary has a flirtatious personality. She praises my appearance, Oh, you're a good-looking man, Karl.

Thank you, Mary. You're so pretty, I reply.

Thank you, Mary says.

Maria tells me that her friends were always surprised when they first met her beautiful mother.

That's your mom. She's so pretty, and her cooking is amazing, they said.

I realize that giving compliments to Mary about her

beauty is the key to her heart. Mary invites us to sit in the living room sofa. A piano is placed next to the sofa.

Where's Granny? Maria asks.

I'm coming, Juliet says with a radiant smile.

Juliet and Maria hold each other close. Maria loves her granny more than anyone else. She is the light of her life. Maria has missed her granny so much. Juliet walks up to me.

How do you do? Juliet asks me with a curious and caring voice.

I am fine. How are you?, I ask.

I'm fine. Thank you, Juliet says.

She is so kind.

Do you play the piano? I ask Juliet.

Juliet sits down by the piano. She plays the classic rag *The Entertainer* by Scott Joplin. I'm amazed. I laugh and cry feeling I'm in music heaven. Maria tells me that everyone in her family plays musical instruments. I am astonished and admire her family.

Brilliant, Juliet. That's so incredibly melodious, I say.

I feel the warm emotions that Juliet and her music performance radiate in the room.

Thank you very much, Juliet replies.

I love to listen to you when you play the piano. You're so gifted, I say.

That is so sweet of you to say, Juliet says and smiles.

Juliet and I form a strong friendship from the beginning. Maria has told me that Juliet was always there for her when she grew up. Juliet was one of the first women to study mathematics at Louisiana State University. She has been an independent and strong woman her entire life. When I listen to her life story I see that she is a pioneer feminist who has realized her identity, full professional potential, and cared and been there for her three children.

I'm so happy that you are the same Karl who was talking to Maria on the phone, Mary says.

11

I throw my arms out to hug Mary and Juliet. I smile fondly at them.

Thank you so much for welcoming me into your family. I feel so accepted. I belong here with you, I say.

Mary knows that I love Maria and them. This family is caring and fun. They play musical instruments, sing, cook food and they all love me. I'm so blessed and grateful.

Someone knocks on the house door. Mary opens and I can hear a joyous male voice.

Is Maria home? Maria's uncle Claude says.

Maria's face lights up. Claude walks into the living room. Maria runs to hug him. I can see that she loves him so much. Claude loves Maria back. I'm so happy to see them together. They both cry.

Claude is very nice to me. He becomes a role model for me in terms of dressing cool in Louisiana. He always wears elegant clothes and shoes. Claude drives a fancy car and plays the bass and clarinet. He has been playing in blues and rock'n'roll bands and teaches me about music.

We walk back into the kitchen. Mary has cooked a chicken and sausage gumbo.

Please give me some gumbo, Juliet says.

The gumbo is divine, I tell Mary.

She glows.

I'm so excited to have a Louisiana family. I look at Maria when she is interacting with her family members. They are all about faith, love, beauty, music, and spiritual motivation. They praise and encourage each other in a way that I have never seen before. It feels wonderful to hear such uplifting words expressed with the South Louisiana accent and charm.

The women in Maria's family live in the moment. Mary is a constant party. We dance, joke, play and act silly all the time. Juliet is quiet and more serious. She is deeply reflecting about life, and so lovely.

Maria's dad is Cajun-French from the Lafayette area of Louisiana. Cajun-French culture is born of the tradition of the Acadians who settled in southern Louisiana after their expulsion from Nova Scotia, Canada, by the British in 1755. Maria's dad works as a mechanic at the Los Angeles International Airport. I haven't met him and know very little about him. He went on one tour to Vietnam. He got out in 1968. Maria loves and misses her dad.

Maria's father was a farm boy like me taking care of animals and growing crops. We lived on the family farm with my maternal grandfather who was a farmer and carpenter. My dad is a banker. My mom works in a care home. I have a younger sister. Later, we moved from the farm to a bank house that my father bought.

Mary's maternal family are Louisiana Creole. Black Creole culture in southern Louisiana originates from integration over three centuries between African slaves, free people of color, French and Spanish colonists, Native Americans, Cajuns, and others. Creole culture includes French Creole language, New Orleans jazz and zydeco, the Mardi Gras festival, jambalaya and gumbo.

Mary is so proud when she tells me that she is related to the world-famous sisters Debbie Allen, choreographer, actress, dancer, singer-songwriter, director, and producer, and Phylicia Rashād, actress, singer, and stage director. She has met them a couple of times at funerals in Louisiana.

Maria has a vast music knowledge. She introduces me to gothic and industrial music that she used to play as a student union DJ at Louisiana State University. I love Maria for her warmth.

At home that evening, we lock the bedroom door. We light candles and make a bubble bath. We undress and step into the warm water. I feel so close to Maria. We start to kiss passionately. She tastes so good. I kiss the side of her neck and feel her sensual breathing.

I love you, Karl, she whispers.

I always want to be with you. I love you, Maria, I whisper.

We love the affection that we show each other. We let our hands lightly rest on each other's hips, on our bellies and make love.

We sip an incredibly full-bodied dark red wine. It has a hint of dark cherry.

I get up in the morning when Maria is still asleep to make coffee for her. She loves it. I brew coffee with bold, chocolatey flavors and fruity notes.

Good morning, I say when I kiss Maria and serve her coffee.

Karl, you're always so sweet, Maria replies kissing me.

Another passion for Maria is chocolate. I surprise her with her favorite ones that melt smoothly on our tongues. We live a wonderful life in Louisiana.

Mary and I sit on the porch and drink lemonade. Mary says that she is a devoted Catholic. She was named Mary after the blessed mother. Mary recites the rosary. She explains that the repetition in the Rosary is meant to lead one into restful and contemplative prayer related to each Mystery. She tells me that praying helps us to enter the silence of our hearts, where Christ's spirit dwells.

Mary and I go inside the house. We dance to and sing Hank Williams' song *Jambalaya (On the Bayou)*. We make a crawfish pie for the family. Mary is very spirited. We sing the song repeatedly and scream, CRAWFISH PIE every time the words come in the lyrics. We make the pie shell and fill it with crawfish tails, bell peppers, green onions, garlic, stock, parsley, milk, cornstarch, butter, and seasonings. The ingredients are cooked until it thickens. We pour the filling into the pie crust. The pie is baked in the oven until the crust becomes golden brown and the filling is bubbling.

Mary was brought up by Juliet and her grandmother called Mami. Mary's dad visited on Saturdays. University educated Juliet studied mathematics and chemistry and later worked in a laboratory.

Juliet, Mary, and Maria lived in a shotgun house or a Creole house on 823 Europe Street in the historic district Beauregard Town in downtown Baton Rouge. A shotgun house has long, narrow layout, typically one room wide. It lacks a front yard and has a short street-front stairway. The layout features one room opening into another, without hallways. They had banana trees and vegetables in the garden.

Mary loves her mother Juliet Agatha Aguillard who was born in 1914. Mary called her Mama. Juliet was born between Lincoln's Birthday and Saint Valentine's Day. Her Creole father's name was Westley Goya. He was a sugar chemistry professor at Louisiana State University. He came from Cuba to Louisiana. He was kin to the famous Spanish painter Goya and died when Juliet was very young.

Her mother taught her to pray and love God above all things. Juliet's mother made learning fun for her. She played games that taught concepts. Her first lesson was, Juliet, be a good girl always.

There were no shopping malls in Baton Rouge when Juliet was a girl. The department stores were located on Third Street and Main Street only. A blacksmith's shop was located on the corner of Royal and Louisiana Avenue. Men rode big, beautiful horses on the street. Juliet was a little afraid, thinking what if one of those big horses panicked and ran her over.

Juliet didn't realize that the rider was controlling where the horse went. She was always more comfortable when she was out its way. During that time there were more horse drawn vehicles than cars. Most of the cars were early model Fords. Some of the wealthy citizens owned imported cars from England. The Pierce Arrow is one that Juliet remembered seeing. Others owned early model Buicks.

Juliet was very smart and way ahead of anyone in her class. She stayed out of school sometimes to take care of her aunt. Juliet finished high school and college with honors. When she finished college in math and chemistry, Juliet washed glassware for the laboratory technicians so they could do their scientific tests. The head of the laboratory said that she was so smart. He promoted her to do lab tests on blood. When some of the technicians didn't draw enough blood, she did ratio and proportion problems so the tests could come out right. Juliet worked in the lab for 28 years.

In 1937, Juliet married Claude N. Jackson Jr. II. They had three babies: Claude, Ruby, and Mary. When Juliet worked in the laboratory she also took care of her mother after she broke her hip. Every time Mami wanted to pee Juliet had to get up. Juliet had worked all day long washing bottles at the laboratory. People were nasty to her sometimes and she needed a break. Mary went to Juliet's job for three days and did her work so she could rest at home. Mary took the test tubes and put them in the drawers.

When Juliet retired from the laboratory she started working at the Catholic Life Center. The job required someone to set up a library for The Institute of Early Learning with the books that were already there. Juliet was not a librarian and so she had to do some research. Teachers brought their classes to the library. One day, visitors from the State Department of Education came to the library. They made a telecast to show the operation of the library. A documentary of the library was shown over LPB TV Station. Juliet received an award for excellent work.

When her supervisor was transferred from the library to the Dr. Leo S. Butler Center in Baton Rouge; she asked Juliet to go with her. She accepted and there Juliet took lessons in computer literacy. She bought a computer for her home and studied diligently. By the time Juliet's computer teacher left for another IT role, she was prepared ready to replace her as a teacher of computer literacy at the Butler Center. She enjoyed working there until she fell and broke her hip. Juliet continued her computer work at home.

Juliet was deeply spiritual and full of love, patience, and kindness. She was blessed with determination, courage, and a love of learning. She was a passionate advocate toward higher education and is showed in her beloved children, her work, and her students.

Mary's daddy Claude Nathaniel Jackson II was a blacksmith. He had two families to take care of. He gave money to Mary and her siblings. He paid for his mother, father, his two sisters and their children in the community of Sunshine outside Baton Rouge. It took a lot of money to take care of two families.

Juliet wanted Claude to save for their children's education. Claude just wanted his children to finish 8th grade. He didn't want them to go to high school or college. They argued late at night about this. With this arguing the family couldn't sleep. Mami and Juliet got tired of the fighting. They packed Claude's clothes, put them outside and locked the door. He had to take his clothes and walk away. Juliet and Claude got a divorce after that. He had to pay the three children 15 dollars every two weeks. Claude loved his children. He came to visit them every weekend. They were happy to see him. Several times Claude wanted to marry Juliet again. She refused to marry him because her cousin said that he had a bad disease called syphilis.

Mary's maternal grandmother was Willie Bates Aguillard. They called her Mami. She was married to the professor Westley Goya. Mami lived with Juliet and the three children in Beauregard Town. Mami was very sweet to Mary. She loved her so much. Mary loved her too. As a little girl Mary did everything Mami said. She showed Mary how to sweep with a

17

broom. Mami washed clothes and taught Mary how to hang them up. They ate dinner. She taught Mary how to wash dishes. They were very happy together.

Mami was proud of Mary when she got confirmed in the Catholic Church. Mary was dressed in a white dress with a veil, white stockings, and shoes. She had a white handbag and candle. Mary smiled when she stood by the altar and held her rosary.

When Juliet was young, Baton Rouge had two dairies. Mami clerked for one of them. She went to the branch dairy every morning at 5:00 o'clock. Mami churned whole sour milk until it was separated into butter and buttermilk. She washed the butter by pressing ice into it with a large wooden spoon and pouring off the liquid. She chilled and molded the butter. Mami bottled and capped the buttermilk and put it into the refrigerator.

In those times, milk was sold in glass bottles with round cardboard caps. When milk was first purchased a deposit was paid for the bottles. The bottles were washed and returned when the customer purchased more milk. Mami rewashed and sterilized the returned bottles which were refilled with milk. The disposable cartons of today are quite an improvement. Thick clabber was put into tin molds, that had holes to drain the whey, which when finished makes a soft smooth solid. When sweet cream was poured over this solid, it was called cream cheese. This made a delicious breakfast treat.

Mary wonders what happened to the smooth creamed cheese? The closest thing that Mary has seen in the stores is cottage cheese. Mami opened the shop at 9 o'clock. Mami took Juliet to work every day. Juliet has told Mary that she felt like she was part of it all.

Mary was always loyal and obedient to Mami. She only disobeyed her one time and that is when she got into a car accident. Mary was 26 years old. She was very sorry that she disobeyed Mami. Mami didn't want her to drive that day. Mary had a terrible crash.

Mami had a sister named Aunt Ching. Aunt Ching loved her family and neighbors. She was getting sick. When Mary and Mami got about half a block away from her house they could hear her neighbors howling:

She's dead! She's dead! She's dead!

This upset Mary and Mami. They didn't cry and held up strong. Mary held Mami and balanced her so she wouldn't fall. They went into Aunt Ching's bedroom. She was lying flat on her back with her eyes closed. Mami stood at the head of the bed. Mary went to the foot of the bed. Mami felt her face. Aunt Ching was turning cold. Mami was certain that she was dead. Mary called Juliet's work. She told Juliet that Aunt Ching had died. This was a big shock to Juliet.

Mary and Mami went to the laboratory to pick up Juliet. Juliet had already walked about half a block when they picked her up. They went by the house to see Ruby and Claude. Claude was sick with the measles. Mami told them that Aunt Ching had died. They were shocked.

Mami and Juliet went to Aunt Ching's house to see her. The neighbor took Ruby to Aunt Ching's house and dropped her off. The coroner came and pronounced her dead. The coroner said that she had died of a heart attack. Mami called the funeral home and they picked up her body. Juliet and Mami went to Aunt Ching's bedroom and found her bankbook and marriage license and put them in Juliet's purse. Juliet, Mami and Ruby returned home. They told Mary and Claude what happened.

I ask Mary how Mami died. Mary looks sad and filled with love.

Mami took sick with a stroke in the end of her life, Mary replies.

The next day, Mary and I make homemade southern fudge. She talks about how much she loves her brother Claude. He played the clarinet and the base in several rock'n'roll bands. Fats Domino was his favorite rock'n'roll star. He loved how Fats Domino sang and played the piano. Claude has always been nice to Mary.

Ruby has not always been civil to Mary. They often fight. Mary remembers when they were girls and played on the street outside their house. They played with their chickens. One time, Mary played rough with one of the chickens and it died. She felt very guilty after this incident.

The Jackson sisters grew up together and supported each other most of the time. Ruby had two master's degrees, one in administration and supervision and the other in guidance and counseling. She encouraged Mary to work on her second masters in guidance and counseling. Mary thought it was very sweet and thoughtful of Ruby to help her. Ruby was there for her when Mary went to school each summer, took her exam, and got her second master's degree.

Besides her focus on higher learning Mary loves playing the trumpet. She has played the trumpet most of her life. Her band director thought that Mary was gifted on the trumpet because she could play all the high notes. He wanted Mary to go on TV and play with him. The band used to go on trips. Juliet and Mami didn't let Mary go because they felt the children who joined behaved badly.

When Mary was in the ninth grade she joined the school band. Previously, Mary was in another school band in another school from sixth grade to eight grade. When Mary was in the new band the band director put her on solo trumpet. Mary played well. She loves to play the trumpet. Her brother played clarinet. He loaned Mary his trumpet to play. Ruby used to go on the band trips. When Claude and Ruby graduated Mary couldn't go. The band director let Mary play in the band in parades in town.

When Mary finished college she started a job and

taught school. She gave a demonstration to the faculty with her students. The demonstration was on woodwind instruments. Mary needed instruments for the demonstrations. She went to see her high school band director. He told her that she could borrow instruments from music mart. Mary got the instruments there. Her principal praised her demonstration. She was very happy.

In the beginning of September 1998, Maria gives birth to our baby. We shine of happiness.

A baby girl, the midwife says and turns to us.

The midwife puts Mary's first granddaughter on Maria's chest. Maria and I love our beautiful baby girl. She's our heart. We call Mary and Juliet from the hospital and tell them the good news.

What is her name? Mary and Juliet ask.

We will call her Bianca Isabella Jade, Maria says.

Maria and I bring Bianca to the anniversary concert celebrating Baton Rouge's 300-year-old history. The concert is held next to the Mississippi River in the warm night. I have six-month old Bianca on my shoulders. We listen and dance to the live performances by Kool and the Gang and the Neville Brothers. This is one of the happiest family moments ever.

March 8th, 1999

Most days, Maria and I bring Bianca to a playground in a park after we return home from work to swing and slide. Bianca loves her baby walker. I work for Louisiana's Secretary of State in the castle-like political history museum Old Louisiana State Capitol, a 160-year-old Gothic Revival building. The U.S. Senator of Louisiana in Washington D.C. helps me to get a work permit. Maria works in the Louisiana Arts and Science Center across the street in downtown Baton Rouge. Together we support the family. We're having so much fun at work and at home.

21

One exception to the family harmony is Ruby. The Jackson sisters used to support each other in love relationships with boys and men, at school and when fighting for civil rights at Southern University, Baton Rouge's historically black institution of higher education. They both embraced campus life as a source of personal awakenings. They survived encounters with racism and sexism. Now, Ruby is always fussing and fighting with Mary. They are getting worked up about all kinds of things. I'm always happy when Ruby leaves the house, and the peace returns.

Ruby and I don't have the best relationship. Ruby was only nice to me once when I first arrived in Louisiana. After that day, she frowns at me. I feel that she wants to have Maria all for herself. She wants to take Maria to the hairdresser, the restaurants and everywhere else. Ruby doesn't understand why Maria wants to spend any time with me and Bianca. She thinks I'm not from Louisiana and that's true. I'm Swedish. I'm a foreigner to her. She wants me out of the family.

Maria has told me that it was mainly Juliet who cared for her and acted as a mother figure when Mary was in the mental health hospitals during her girlhood. Ruby was there for Maria when Mary was depressed or delusional and sometimes hitting Maria or putting her at risk. Maria stayed with Ruby from time to time. Later when Ruby was teaching mathematics in high schools she used to invite Maria to have pizza and grade math examinations together. I'll love Ruby even if she treats me bad.

Ruby likes manly men. She doesn't respect a tender and caring Swede like me. Ruby likes to chat with tall and muscular police officers. She thinks they are sexy in their uniforms. When Mary and I go to the small corner grocery store Calandro's on Government Street in Baton Rouge we often meet Ruby. She flirts and chats with police officers stopping for coffee.

Ruby is charming with them because the police officers give her a lot of attention. Ruby ignores us and pretend that she doesn't know us.

Ruby is very strict as a math teacher. She has been teaching in notoriously dangerous high schools with shootings and other violence. Maybe that is why Ruby is so harsh on people, but she is not only harsh. She is a good educator who knows how to explain complex math problems. I often meet people in Baton Rouge who had Ruby as a math teacher. They tell me that Ruby opened their worlds to mathematics. They see her as a math legend and are so grateful for what she has done for them or their family members. I respect Ruby for that even if she is impolite to me.

3 THE LOUISIANA BEAUTY QUEEN

Louisiana and Minnesota, 1960s-1970s

Mary attends Southern University which was at the time the largest public black college in the United States. Southern University became home to the Civil Rights Movement in Baton Rouge. Mary's professors promoted equal right and justice in Louisiana and the South.

After graduating from Southern University, Mary attended Louisiana State University. The material difference between student life at Southern University in the black part of the city and Louisiana State University in the white part of Baton Rouge city was striking. Southern University had a black president and black administrators but was under the control of the white elected officials in Louisiana. They spent much less per student at Southern University as they did at LSU which had so many more resources.

Mary and Ruby went to the University of Minnesota to study their master's courses in education. In contrast to the daily fights between Mary and Ruby now, the Jackson sisters lived together in Minnesota supporting each other. They returned to Baton Rouge. Ruby married an engineering student from India that she later divorced. She never remarried.

When Mary finished college there was an opening at a Catholic school. Mary met with Father Wood. She said that she finished her BA degree in lower elementary school teaching, 1st to 4th grade. Father told Mary that she could have the teaching job. He also asked Mary to be his secretary after school. Mary gladly accepted both jobs. She was making more money working as a teacher and secretary. Mary could save the money.

Before Mary got the job with Father Wood she doubted if there was a God or not. She was thinking about if the devil brought doubts into her mind. Her atheist professors at Southern University were communists. They talked like communism was right. Mary started thinking that there was no God. She gave up on God. Mary explains that was when the devil took over her soul. She got tormented for three days and three nights. Mary was tormented so bad. She felt like she was burning in hell with the devil. Mary threw up her hands and went to confession. She told father about her doubts. He told her to come to his office and talk to him. Father Wood told her to go.

Thanks to God she felt better. During this time Juliet helped her. Juliet took Maria to Montessori school and picked her up from school in the evening. Mary's parents were very proud of her earning her first money. Mary was very pleased. She paid Ruby for gas. Ruby came to the church each evening and drove her back home. Juliet took a small salary every month. Mami received a small check that she saved.

Later, Mary was getting tired of working two jobs. She lost weight and got very skinny. Mary was not used to being that small. She started sleeping more. Mary went to bed at 8 o'clock and got up at 6 o'clock in the morning. She remained small. Mary ate cookies and drank cold drinks when she worked with Father Wood. This didn't help Mary to gain weight. Father Wood laughed at Mary eating so many cookies.

This will make the grocery bill higher, he said.

Several priests at the church said that Mary was a beautiful lady. She thought that all the other church secretaries in the parish were not as beautiful as she was. The priests were very respectful towards her.

She enjoyed working for Father Wood. A short period after she worked for him they became close friends. He started to call her a close friend or chum.

Mary had lots of work to do in father's office. She had money from personal envelopes, amounts to record on church members record cards. Some members paid $5 or $10. Mary didn't know why he left the money in the envelopes. She didn't know if Father Wood missed it or if he was just testing her if she was honest. She returned every dollar. Father Wood also had birth certificates. Mary typed the birth certificates for him to sign.

At lunch time, she had to walk a few doors down to the kitchen to get her lunch. The lunch consisted of sandwiches, cold drinks, and cookies. Mary liked the lunch. There were four priests that lived in the house.

When it was time for Father Wood to pay Mary on Fridays, he paid her from cash he had taken from the safe. Father Wood kept cash money for the church and school. He kept all the money from the collections in the church they made on Sunday. It was like $10 or $20 from each envelope. It was in a cash box from the bank. Mary was happy because it was her first job. This was the first money she had earned since she was an adult. She saved some of it.

One night, Mary had a wonderful dream about Jesus. She was walking on the sidewalk. On each side there were little cottage houses. She looked around and saw Jesus walking beside her. Jesus had a black robe on him and oblong holes on his hips. Mary asked him if she could kiss him on the cheek. Jesus said yes and so she did. She was very happy. Mary didn't want to wake up, but she did. Juliet was standing by the bed. She told her that she had a delightful dream about kissing Jesus. Juliet smiled.

I make some coffee for us. When we drink the coffee Mary talks about her teaching job in the Cajun community of Church Point in south-central Louisiana 130 miles west of New Orleans. Church Point is a charming town rich in French culture with courteous and hilarious people. The town is close to Lafayette in the heart of Cajun Country with a colorful culture.

Mary enjoyed living in Church Point. She loved her

job teaching at the school in Church Point because the teachers, the principal and everyone else were very nice. Mary's colleagues at the school wanted her to register for the upcoming beauty pageant. In this beauty contest she would compete with other women. The judges would rank the physical attributes of the contestants. They would look at the inner beauty, personality, intelligence, talent, character, and charitable involvement. Mary was flattered and excited. She registered for the pageant.

Mary charmed the judges and the audience. She won the beauty pageant. Mary was now a Louisiana beauty queen. She giggled and was overjoyed. Mary celebrated. The awards of the beauty contest were the title, the money, and the tiara. One of the contestants was the girlfriend of one of the judges so even if Mary won, the tiara was given to that girl. Mary felt so disappointed. She was still happy about the title and the money.

After the beauty pageant, Mary participated in the local parade in Church Point. The other woman gave the tiara back to Mary. Mary wore the tiara at the parade. She waved at the cheering crowds and smiled. Mary was happy to be a symbol of beauty and community ideals. She loves to talk about that and views herself as a beauty queen.

After winning the beauty pageant Mary returned to Baton Rouge. She worked in a new school led by principal Mr. Burnt. He was very skinny. Mr. Burnt looked so worried. At the end of the school season, he called on the Intercom for all the teachers to meet him in the library. Mr. Burnt told them that that a whole caravan of teachers had told another principal that he had treated a teacher bad. Mary didn't complain about him. Mr. Burnt invited her to his house. Mary drove to his house that evening and met his wife. They talked about Mary's aunt who they knew. He showed Mary his daughters' pictures. Mary thought they were beautiful ladies. Mary thanked Mr.

Burnt and his wife for a lovely evening and drove home.

Another day at school Mary was on duty watching the children play. It was in the morning. Mr. Burnt drove up in his car. He came on the breeze walk and walked by Mary to go to the office. Mary told him that he looked very nice. He thanked Mary and smiled. Mary was 22 years old. She wasn't married and she was gorgeous. Mary told him that she didn't want to be an old maid. Mr. Burnt told Mary that she could wait until she was about 30 before she got married. Mary waited. She was 27 years old when she got married.

Mary went on to teach in a new elementary school. She had to leave the school that she liked so much. Mary was going to miss the previous principal and all his praise. He knew the principal in her new school. The new principal told her that she would have a nice time at his school, and Mary did.

The children were quiet and very peaceful. Mary checked their papers. They were smart. She knew they were honest. Mary would go around in the class and see if they were checking their papers correctly and they did. This took all the work off Mary, and they could all learn from this. Mary's work was done for the day, except she would work after school, and do her lesson plans for the next day.

The principal wanted Mary to also take care of Maria. One day Mary stayed after school. The principal came into her classroom. He told Mary to go home and be with her baby because it was being forecasted to be a tornado. Mary left and went home. He went home, too. Mary liked that he cared about her family.

After the tornado, Mary ordered tests for the students to find out their grade and reading levels. She would listen to them read and find out their problems in reading. Mary would give them work according to their problems. This would correct their problems and go to another grade level. Sometimes in one school session one student would rise one or two grade levels. The teacher would provide materials for that student on that grade level.

After the school session was ended at this school, Mary was sent to another elementary school. It was supposed to be a promotion, but it was a big letdown for her. Mary was happy with the progress at the other school. She went to the new school and talked to the principal. Mary knew that she had impressed him positively. She went home. Mary told Juliet about her new principal and the new school. It was Friday evening. On Sunday evening her husband took her to find the direction to the new school. He was good at directions and finding a new place. Mary learned the direction to the new school. She was confident that she could find it the next day and she did.

Mary writes a letter to the parents about her stand concerning discipline of the children in her school class:

All children are basically good. The desirable behavior should be recognized and reinforced with praise. The undesirable behavior should be corrected and sometimes ignored. Eventually it will be extinguished.

A child should possess a positive attitude toward doing the correct thing. I encourage self-improvement. It's okay for the children to make mistakes. The children grow from that and learn new things. It's necessary for the children to recognize their mistakes and take positive actions toward correcting them.

Forcing children into doing the correct thing and not teaching them to want to do the correct is not learning. If they are forced, they will only do the correct thing when observed. We want intrinsic motivation to take place. They will become interested from within. They will eventually learn to discipline themselves and become independent and self-directive. This is our goal. We want the expectations for our children challenging, but not frustrating. The classroom discipline is not complete without the support of the parents. My success depends on your help. We must work together and support each other.

Mary introduced herself to the parents at her elementary school. She said that she received a M Ed. Degree in Elementary Education, and a M Ed. Degree in Guidance and Counselling from Southern University. Mary did her graduate studies in education at Louisiana State University and a certification in reading at LSU. She did graduate work at the University of Minnesota in educational psychology.

Mary asked the parents to share information about their children with her. She asked for details about what kind of school subjects, sports, and hobbies the children like and dislike, the children's strengths and weaknesses in school, sports, character traits, attitudes, and behaviors, physical or emotional problems and any recommendations from the parents.

It was close to Thanksgiving. Mary made and decorated a puppet box in her classroom. She taught off words on flash cards. She was amazed that the children had learnt all the words. Mary had cut out the face of the Jack o' lantern and had it in her classroom. They didn't have school the next week because it was Thanksgiving.

When Monday came home she didn't get out of bed. Mary laughed in bed all week because it was Thanksgiving. Juliet cooked the Thanksgiving dinner. Mary didn't eat any of it because Juliet left the turkey out all night.

Mary tells me that when Maria was two years old, she brought her to a home to see the parents of one of her pupils at school. The situation at the house turned violent. The two men could have murdered

Mary when taking out their guns. The only reason for not killing Mary was that she had the baby with her. Maria and Mary survived. After that incident Mary took her retirement.

4 SEXY BOYFRIENDS

New Orleans and Baton Rouge, 1960s-1970s

Mary knows the nature of men. She has loved so many. Mary is flirtatious and knows how to get their attention. She constantly talks about all the hot men in her life; from the boys in her class to the teachers, graduates and even the professors who had fallen for her.

Karl, why did so many men fall in love with me? Mary asks.

It was because I was sweet, smart, and stunning, Mary answers.

I nod and smile.

Mary used to love a teacher when she was in 11th grade in high school. His name was Beau. She loved him tremendously. Mary loved Beau more than all the other men because he was so smart and handsome. Mary thought about Beau all day. After school and in the evening she couldn't wait for the next day to come so she could look at him. She thought about Beau walking to school. During summer school Mary daydreamed about him.

Mary married and didn't get along with her husband. They divorced. One of Mary's boyfriends was David. He was a very sweet boyfriend and loved her a lot. David was so sweet to Mary. When she went to the mental health hospital he used to come and see her every Sunday evening for a whole year. He only missed one Sunday when his sister died. He even came in severe thunderstorms. David took Mary to clothing stores several times and got her clothes. He bought Mary pant suits, dresses, shirts, and blouses. They looked at a beautiful pant suit though it costs too much. Mary didn't want him to buy it. About a few minutes after Mary got home, she heard a knock on the front door. There was David with the pant suit in his hand. Mary was so surprised. He had bought the pant suit anyway. She thought it was very sweet of him.

David was the best boyfriend that Mary ever had. She loved him very much. Mary got out of the mental health hospital and went to a halfway house. David continued to come and see Mary. He later took sick. Her brother Claude came over and told her that David had died. She was very sad and missed him so much.

Mary went into the mental hospital and Juliet came to stay with her. Mary realized that she did not get her period that time and advised Juliet so. They decided that she should see Dr. Hannah who confirmed that she was pregnant. Mary was overjoyed and really wanted a baby girl. When Mary was pregnant with Maria the doctor told her to stop taking her medication as it could affect the unborn baby. Nine months later she gave birth to Maria.

5 MENTAL HEALTH HOSPITALS

Louisiana, 1960s-1970s

Mary has suffered from anxiety, delusions, depression, hallucinations, and suicidal thoughts. She tells me about her experiences that she had in mental hospitals that she was admitted to in Louisiana. Mary has suffered tremendously and was admitted twenty-nine times, but she has difficulty accepting her illness. She stays in denial most of the time.

When Mary went to the mental health hospital the first time her husband and brother took her to the emergency room. The nurse rolled her in the room. There was a magazine on the table and a cross with Jesus hanging on the wall. Mary was so happy to see Jesus. She saw his suffering. Mary believed he was telling her that she was to suffer like Jesus. Mary thought she was going to go to the mental health hospital only one time, but she was mistaken. She saw the Blessed Mother picture on the wall and kept looking at it. The picture kept flashing. It changed several times. Mary woke up the next morning and saw that God had come in. Mary asked God if he believes in God. God told her, yes.

Mary and I go walking in downtown Baton Rouge. The weather is lovely. Mary greets and chats with most people we meet. I buy some ice cream for us. We sit down outside the ice cream stand. Mary talks about the second time she went to a mental health hospital.

She was doing a wonderful job at an elementary school. Mary had problems and she wanted to see a psychiatrist. She chose to see Dr. Westover.

Jesus talked to Mary. He told her to go to another car place and buy a new car. Mary drove her wrecked car to this place. The salesman took her to see the cars. She saw a wonderful blue car. Mary knew that this was the car she wanted to buy. She bought the blue car and left her wreck car at the car place.

The spirit of Jesus told her to go to a clothing store and get about five pant suits and she got them. The spirit of Jesus told her to go to a beauty parlor and get her hair fixed and styled. Mary did these things and went home late in the evening. Mary was very happy. She called her boyfriend Will. They got a date for that night.

Before that date, two policemen came in a car, picked her up and drove her to the mental health hospital. Mary became so sad and heartbroken. She was so unhappy. Mary believed it was a big miracle she had accomplished so much that day.

The policemen took her to the emergency room of the mental health hospital. As she was entering the room, the television was on. There was a movie on. A crucifix with Jesus hung on the wall. She knew that she was at the mental health hospital. Mary felt so much better because she was going through suffering like Jesus.

In the mental health hospital, Mary was monitored through observation and medication. They observed Mary to see if she acted normal or not. After being discharged after a few weeks she drove her new clothes back home. Mary also took the old clothes that her mother had brought her to wear in the hospital.

Mary went to the mental health hospital a third time. She started off sad before she went to the mental health hospital. It was close to the Christmas holidays. The principal in the school where Mary was teaching was in his office. He would make fun of her and insult her in different ways. He said something to her. Mary couldn't hear him. She knew that it was something mean because he usually said nasty things to her. Mary knew it wasn't nice because when he had something to say it was always mean. He came to Mary's classroom that morning. He came to observe

35

her teaching. He laughed at her and made a few ugly remarks. Since it was close to Christmas Mary thought she would teach about Jesus and his birth. He called her to his office to talk about his observation of her teaching. He said it was against the United States government to teach about Jesus. A lady came the next day and talked about the birth of Jesus. Mary felt alright. A little bit later she told Mary that one of the supervisors had said that she was teaching about Jesus. The supervisor told Mary that it was alright to do so. This made her happy.

Mary was being taken to the hospital again.

Calm down, Ms. Jackson, the police officer said.

The police officers led Mary to their car and drove her to the psychiatrist. Mary signed herself into the mental health hospital. This meant that she could sign herself out. She went to a large building. The nurses were very nice. One of the nurses asked her if she was mental from the way she acted. Mary didn't view herself as mental.

The patients could walk around the grounds. Mary liked that very much. She met an elderly guy. He was very nice and became her boyfriend. Now she had two boyfriends. She thought that it was good to have two boyfriends giving her things and helping her in different ways. One of her boyfriends was at the hospital and the other one was in Baton Rouge.

Mary would go on the grounds and see her boyfriend at the hospital. She had lots of fun with him each day. He would buy her cold drinks. He would walk around the grounds with her. They used to sit on a bench and eat potato chips. They went to the canteen and ate there for a while. Later, he got discharged and went to live in a nursing home in Baton Rouge. Mary missed him. He was a very nice man.

I ask Mary about the other boyfriend David from Baton Rouge. He would bring picnic lunch of ham and bread, and cold drinks. They sat on the bench, talked, and ate lunch. David got Juliet's house fixed. When Mary was in the hospital Juliet took care of Maria. He took Juliet and Maria to places they needed to go to. I can see in Mary's eyes that she loved David so much for all the things he did for her.

Mary talks about another time she was admitted to the mental health hospital. She didn't think she acted mental. Mary started talking to her family about Jesus. She picked up a large crucifix that a Catholic priest had given her. Ruby, Claude, Juliet, and Mary's husband were there. She told her family about the suffering that Jesus had done for mankind. Mary told the family that Jesus had suffered for this family too. Then, a flash had gone through her eyes of saints and angels. Juliet called the ambulance to take her to the mental health hospital. They rolled Mary to her room. She went to sleep.

Mary woke up in the morning. A doctor came. He was very sweet. She asked him if he believed in Jesus. He said yes. The doctor said that Mary didn't need to go to the mental health hospital. She wanted to go. He said that he would psychoanalyze her. Mary was very happy that he wanted to do this for her.

She was discharged a few weeks later. Mary was married then and went home to her husband. Juliet came, cooked, and stayed with her. They had a nice time.

Mary tells me about when she went to the mental health hospital in Mandeville, Louisiana. This was the fifth time she had been sent to the mental health hospital. Mary's father-in-law said that she needed to go to the mental health hospital. Juliet had told him that Mary wasn't taking her medicine. He told Mary to do so. Mary told him that she didn't need to take medicine. She was fine. Her psychiatrist told her that she didn't need to take medicine.

The next day, the policemen handcuffed her and took her to the mental health hospital without telling Mary anything. When she got to the mental health hospital, Mary talked to the coroner. He gave her an order for her to go to Mandeville. Going to Mandeville was a surprise to her. She refused to go. Mary was pulled by a man by force and put in a car. They drove her to Mandeville. Some of the mental patients at the psychiatric ward in Mandeville were standing up and sitting down. They told Mary that she was going to a regular hospital. When she looked at the patients, they looked mental. A nurse took her pantsuit off her and put a gown on Mary. She didn't like that. Mary liked to dress nice and not wear mental health hospital gowns.

Mary looks sad.

Are you okay, Mary? I ask.

Karl, can you make me some coffee? Mary asks.

I make coffee for us and hug her. We drink the coffee and eat hazelnut milk chocolate.

Karl, you're an angel. You're like Jesus. You want to help everyone. You care about and think about how people feel. You do what you can to help. You're not a selfish person. You're a sweetheart, Mary says.

At the mental health hospital, Mary talked to Juliet on the telephone. Juliet wanted to get Mary in the mental health hospital in Mandeville. Juliet said that Ruby told the psychiatrist that Mary didn't speak to the neighbors anymore. The psychiatrist called the governor and said that they wanted them to get a state car to drive Mary to Mandeville. Mary didn't understand why Ruby and Juliet did that to her.

Mary didn't go home after leaving the mental health hospital. She moved to a halfway house. The halfway house was a home for psychiatric patients who stayed there for a limited period of time to get used to life outside the hospital.

Juliet didn't let Mary come home to the house. Juliet and Maria used to take her to her house on Saturdays. Mary thought that that was nice of them, but she had rather lived with them. She didn't like the halfway house at all. There were too many rules to follow. If they were sick at the halfway house, they couldn't stay there and rest. They had to go to the doctors and get an excuse. Mary's time at the halfway house was up. She had to move to an apartment. David, her boyfriend came one night and moved her to an apartment.

Prior from moving from the halfway house, Mary had to go to a program. Mary got a check from there. The check was based on how many hours she studied. They usually paid Mary $50 a week. That was nice. Mary studied there and turned in lessons. She practiced her typing skills. There were too many demands on Mary. David kept coming to see her.

Juliet sent $7 from her retirement check. Mary thought this was very nice. Then, Juliet asked her to move to the house with her and Maria. Juliet started talking about them buying a house together. Mary went for that. They started looking for a house. The down payment was too high. Mary had gotten money from the Teachers Retirement System of Louisiana. She received $5000 which they could use for the down payment. She was very happy about that.

Juliet and Mary had a lot to do after they fixed the house. They went to a clothing store and bought dresses for Maria. The dresses were so beautiful. One of the dresses was orange with a ruffle around the neck and sleeve and a ruffle around the hem. Maria wore the orange dress to a party at one of the parents' houses. She looked so pretty that a parent at the school told her in the door, Maria, you looked so beautiful at the party. Mary was standing across the street waiting for Maria. This made Maria very happy.

Mary had to stay in the mental health hospital for a whole year one time. Before her hospital stay, she had weird thoughts in her mind such as the world was coming to an end.

6 SUICIDAL

Baton Rouge, 1975

Mary was going through a rough patch in life and started to fall apart. She was highly distressed. Her life was too much of a struggle. Mary had recently experienced divorce from her husband a second time. She had difficulties at work. Everything was horrible. Mary was hurting inside with feelings of lifelessness and hopelessness.

It got worse when she felt that her life had no meaning. The deepest needs of her soul were not satisfied. She was depressed. Her emotional pain was unbearable. Mary couldn't cope with life any longer. Mary had dark thoughts most of the time. When her mind stayed in the darkest places, she thought that she would be better off dead. She started to plan how to commit suicide and bring her toddler Maria with her in death.

When Mary was suicidal without hope one evening she made the most impulsive decision of her life. The inescapable bonds between Mary and Maria were disastrous. Mary brought Maria to the bridge over the Mississippi River between Baton Rouge and Port Allen. The streams ran deep and dangerous below.

Mary would throw herself off the bridge into the river and take her baby girl with her. When they are about to fall into the river and die her boyfriend David drive up unexpectedly and sees them standing at the bridge.

Mary, STOP! David shouts out.

I'm gonna do it, Mary replies.

Don't do it, David says.

I'm gonna do it, Mary replies.

Don't do it. Think about Maria, David says.

Maria looks terrified.

Mary listens to David and looks at him.

I'm gonna do it, Mary says.

Do it then, David replies.

David stands there giving hope and support to Mary and Maria with his eyes and face. Mary shows hesitation in her eyes.

I can help you and Maria, David says.

Mary decides to not go through with the suicide.

I got you, David says.

David holds Mary and Maria. They start to relax.

Mary turns around. She brings Maria into David's car.

Maria was a little girl when this happened. She grew up in a harsh world. I think about why Mary didn't give Maria to Juliet when she thought of killing herself? Why did Mary not ask for help from her family, her boyfriend, or her psychiatrists? I'm not blaming Mary, but I feel so sad thinking about this. This incident has caused so much suffering for Maria and Mary.

After the suicide incident, Mary was admitted to a mental health hospital. Mary was viewed as dangerous for Maria. She didn't want to go through this again having suicidal plans involving Maria. The psychiatrists assessed Mary's mental status and suicidal risk. They prescribed anti-psychotic and anxiety medications so Mary could deal with the stress that she experienced. Mary suffered from horrible guilt that she carried around. She didn't feel that she was a good mother to Maria.

From now on, Juliet looked out for Maria in every way. Maria lived with Juliet and felt good about that. Maria thought that Mary didn't understand what love was. Juliet loved her and protected her. Maria didn't trust Mary anymore. Later, Juliet visited Mary in the hospital.

How are you feeling? Juliet asked.

I'm just sad. It won't happen again. Thank you for taking care of Maria, Mary replied.

You're going to be okay, Juliet said.

Juliet said goodbye. When Juliet left, the tears fell

41

from Mary's eyes.

Maria was raised by Juliet when Mary was in the mental health hospitals. Maria told me thousands of times that Juliet was the person that has meant the most to her in life. She was always there for Maria and strengthened her spirit. Maria had a turbulent relationship with Mary, and she often had to be the adult. It was very hard for her. She felt that Mary had abandoned her.

Maria had a lot of questions when she thought about the fact that she could have died that evening with Mary. The planned suicide incident became a secret that nobody talked about in the family until later. When Maria didn't have answers to her questions, she came up with her own. Why did Mary want to kill herself and her? Why?

Maria felt a deep kind of sadness that went on for a lifetime. Mary's suicide plans were scary for Maria. She was thinking about the scenario if only Mary had jumped off the bridge. What would have happened to her being left there on the bridge and in life in case David wouldn't have shown up at the last moment?

Later, Maria understood that Mary was in a lot of emotional pain. Mary felt that living was just too hard. She didn't believe anyone could help her and didn't know how to go on. She felt very sad and couldn't see any other way to make the sadness stop. Suicide is when a person is so sad that she or he ends her life. Maria was in fear about Mary planning to commit suicide again.

When Mary is telling me about the suicide incident she is very anxious. I hug her and tell her:

Never go back, Mary. Just be grateful for being here right now with me. I love you, Mary.

Mary cries for a long time.

I love you, Karl. You're so sweet to me.

When Mary was in psychiatric care, Juliet helped Maria to keep up her normal routines going to preschool and on play dates with other children. At the house, Maria had bronchitis. Juliet was a chain smoker. Maria was feeling awful when Juliet smoked inside the house. She was scared that Juliet could die in case she kept on smoking.

Granny, I want you to stop smoking, Maria said.

Juliet quit smoking that day. After the last time in the mental institution Mary remained with Juliet and got a monthly shot with her psychiatric medication for decades.

7 FLORIDA AND CAJUN COUNTRY

Pensacola, Florida, and Church Point, Louisiana, 1999

Maria is not feeling good.

Let's do something together just you and me. Let's go somewhere. Where do you love to go? I ask.

I remember when I went to Florida with a dear friend. We had so much fun, Maria replies.

Let's go to Florida, I say.

Maria's face is shining up.

YES! she says.

We tell Juliet and Mary about our travel plans for Florida. They promise to take care of Bianca. We get up early the next day. It's still dark. Bianca is sleeping next to Juliet. We say goodbye.

Maria and I drive through Mississippi. In Alabama, it is pouring heavily. We drive on a bridge. The car is sliding on the water. A large truck is just behind us. Another truck is in front of us. We glide on the water. I don't have full control of the car and feel scared. I steer straight. Finally, the tires get a grip, and we don't crash into the bridge wall.

Here we are, Maria says and points to the Pensacola sign.

We stand upon the shore gazing at the beautiful Caribbean Sea. The mild temperature, crystal clear waters and sugar-white beaches of Pensacola are breathtaking. We rent a room close to the sugar-white sand beach and the beach's emerald-green coastline.

We walk down on the soft beach sand together and touch the warm water. There are no other people on the beach. We walk out in the rolling waves. We're playing and kissing. We throw ourselves into the big waves and laugh.

In the sunset we go back to our hotel room. We undress and shower together. We walk to the bed.

Maria hugs me warmly. We slowly touch and passionately kiss each other all over our bodies using our mouths and fingers. We make love.

Afterwards, we smile and listen to the soothing waves. We go into deep sleep. A couple of days later we return to the house in Louisiana. It was nice to relax and have a change of scenery. We're so happy to see Bianca again.

My parents come to visit us in Louisiana a couple of weeks later. We're having a lot of fun. We go on an alligator trip through a bayou. We eat an Alligator Bisque made with Louisiana alligator tail meat, bell pepper, onions, celery, lemon, and sherry. For dessert, we enjoy vanilla ice cream, meringue shell, chocolate fudge sauce and chopped almonds.

The next day, we visit Maria's paternal grandmother Eula in Church Point close to Lafayette in Cajun Country or Acadiana. Her husband Weldon Guillory has passed away. We drive to Eula in the French Louisiana landscapes with rice paddies, bayous, and canebrakes to the west of New Orleans.

We are astonished by the oaks with ragged gray buntings of Spanish moss form canopies over the bottle-green bayous. We drive on the country roads following the contortions of the Teche, Louisiana's longest bayou and meander through communities. We see cypress cabins on stilts and fishing boats in the waters.

When we arrive at Maria's paternal grandmother Eula's house she says that she has prepared lunch for us. Eula has placed fifteen different types of spicy red pepper sausages laced with roux, a mixture of fat and flour. Her food tastes amazing. My forehead is sweating like crazy!

I speak French with Eula. It's very difficult for me to understand when she speaks Cajun French. Cajun French is an oral tradition in which French vocabulary and grammar encounter the American accent. Cajun French is very different from French

45

spoken in France.

We will stay for a few days with Eula and go to some Cajun and zydeco music concerts and dances. The Cajun culture dates from about 1604, when French settlers colonized a region they called *l'Acadie* in the current Canadian provinces of Nova Scotia and New Brunswick. The British took control of the region in the early 18th century and the French were expelled.

That evening we go to a zydeco, a Zydeco music party. Zydeco is the music of the black Creoles of Acadiana. Zydeco is also dancing as a social event and dance styles. At the party community musicians described as zydeco kings, queens, and princes perform. The word zydeco also refers to hard times and to the music that helped black Creoles to endure suffering.

In African American tradition, this music is called the blues. Zydeco's bluesy side is inspired by melodies and rhythms of a delta blues tradition. When the zydeco king performs on stage I can hear rock and rhythm and blues, the piano accordion, saxophones, trumpets, electric guitars, and percussion beats making the crowd go crazy in a jumping rhythm including me.

This is an incredible music and dance performance. It's almost completely dark on the field where the stage is. I can rarely see the other people's faces in the shadows and lights. I listen to the accordion sounding like an African thumb piano. I reach out my hand to Maria.

Would you like to dance? I ask.

Yes, let's dance, Maria replies.

We dance to the Zydeco music. Soon we're muddy. We laugh. By the time we return to Eula's house we walk straight to the shower to wash off the mud. We stand in the shower close together and hug. We put the clothes in a bag and put on fresh bed clothes. What a lovely night. We had so much fun. Bianca has been sleeping through all of this. I will never forget this Zydeco party. They were so nice to us.

We sleep late. Today Eula is driving us to Eunice. We are going a Cajun music concert. My parents look like they are in heaven.

Allons danser, the singer says.

I get up to dance to the happy music with Eula.

J'adore cette musique, I tell her.

Cette chanson est tellement bien! Eula replies and sings.

Zydeco and Cajun music are closely linked comparable music forms. Cajun music is the music of the white Cajuns of south Louisiana. They share common grounds in the repertoire and style of each. The colonial French Creoles were singing the same stock of western French folk songs as the Cajuns. Native Americans contributed with a wailing singing style, and Black Creoles with rhythms, percussion techniques, improvisational singing, and the blues. The Spanish contributed with the guitar and tunes, and Anglo-American immigrants with fiddle tunes and dances. Singers translated the English songs into French.

After cuddling at home with Maria and Bianca for two days, I go back to work at the museum. We have a barbecue in the museum garden for the staff.

How do you like your steak? The security guard asks.

Medium rare, I reply.

I love the food and all the snacks in Louisiana. I love the chocolate custard and pudding filling inside my chocolate eclairs. They are marvelous. Other goodies are cream puffs, sand tarts, boxes of glazed donuts, brownies, breads, and rolls. I gulp coffee. I feel so energized. I'm getting bigger and bigger. I love the lunch breaks when I indulge in the amazing Louisiana dishes. I eat shrimp étouffée and banana pudding for dessert. I used to be skinny weighing 123 lbs when I arrived in Los Angeles in 1995. Four years later, I weigh 211 lbs. I have been putting on 88 lbs.

47

My sister in Sweden doesn't recognize me anymore.

My goodness, my sister says.

I'm panting.

I don't know what you're talking about. Maybe I have gained a little bit weight okay. I am what I eat, I reply.

My sister laughs. I'm feeling good. Some of the side effects of eating too much include me snoring and having to get bigger clothes. I need to unbutton my pants when I sit in the office chair. I don't even think about holding back. I'm not able to control my body anymore. I even bump into things with my stomach. I need to pay attention to my relationship to food for my health. I know that I am overeating which I view as an unhappy consequence of the stress I feel in my family life.

Maria suffers from severe post-partum and mental illness. To my knowledge Maria hasn't been going through episodes of depression at other times in her life. Maria thinks that returning to Sweden would be the best thing for her. Hopefully Maria will find refuge and escape from the daily pressures that caused her condition.

I can't stand Mary anymore. She gets on my nerves. She is so intense and controlling, Maria tells me.

I comfort Maria by hugging her.

A couple of weeks later, I play tennis in a park in Baton Rouge when two men drive up their car behind a bush near the court. They leave the car with their shotguns installing fear in me. They look at me and walk over to a nearby house. I hear a shot. I think that they may put me down. I run back to our house and lock the door. My heart is beating fast. I'm in shock. I don't remember the faces of the men.

Are you good, Karl? Maria asks worried.

I am now, but that was scary, I reply in fear.

This is the first time I experience the fragility of life.

8 SCHIZOPHRENIA

Louisiana, 2000

Maria, Mary, and I drive to New Orleans. We visit the
U.S. Citizen and Immigration Services. I'm applying
for a green card and get my fingerprints taken. We
have planned to go to a restaurant in New Orleans.
Maria says that she is not feeling well and wants to
drive home. Mary says that she has talked to Ruby.
Ruby said that Maria needs to be admitted to a
psychiatric hospital because she is not eating and
drinking properly. Maria thinks she is fine and
doesn't need any psychiatric care.

Suddenly, Maria drives back and forth on the
highway and has a panic attack. We're in La Place
between New Orleans and Baton Rouge. We stop at a
chicken shop to rest. I visit the restroom. When I
return to the parking lot Maria and Mary are gone.
Maria must have panicked and driven off.

I walk to the nearest rental car place. I rent a car
and start driving to Baton Rouge. I turn on the car
stereo. Ry Cooder plays his acoustic blues in *Paris,
Texas*. The music is from Wim Wender's film with
the same name. One of the first things that Maria and
I talked about at the international party in 1995 was
Wender's brilliant film *Der Himmel über Berlin*
about a guardian angel that is tempted to prefer
human experience over the outsider's perspective.
I'm upset with Maria, but I understand that she has
mental health problems. At least I have magnificent
music in the car.

Maria is admitted to a psychiatric ward. She has
post-partum depression after childbirth and has not
been eating and drinking enough. It's very difficult to
connect with her. At the hospital she eats and drinks
under supervision. There is an order of the day in
Maria's psychiatric ward. It looks like this: Maria eats
breakfast. She has quiet time. Maria watches TV with

other patients. After lunch, more of the same activities follow until a break for dinner. This is followed by visitor hours. I see Maria in the evening. Bianca comes with me. Maria has an evening sandwich before the lights are turned off. Maria is expected to go to bed at a reasonable hour. She sleeps for at least 8 hours.

The first time Maria is admitted to the psych ward, she is 23. Depression and anxiety are present in her, leading up to the admission. Maria is very quiet when she meets the psychiatrists. She doesn't see any problems. Maria is admitted to a secured unit, locked in.

Maria is disoriented. She has a psychotic episode. Mary, Ruby, and I visit Maria at the hospital. The psychiatrist says that she is suffering from severe postpartum depression and catatonic schizophrenia. Schizophrenia is a chronic brain disorder. Symptoms include delusions, hallucinations, disorganized speech, trouble with thinking and lack of motivation. Maria is not moving her eyes and isolates herself from other people. Maria is still and mute. It's not possible to connect with her. I remove her contact lenses for her.

I got your glasses, my love, I say.

I put the glasses on her. I kiss and hug her until Maria wakes up.

How are you doing? I ask.

I want to leave this place. I want to go home. Please give me some water, Maria says quietly.

I love you so much, I say and hug her.

You will go home soon. First, you need to stay longer at the hospital to recover before you go home my love, I say.

We need to keep you here for some time, the psychiatrist tells Maria.

Maria's eyes are filled with so much pain. We cry together. The other patients on the ward look at me. I have never thought that mental illness is a shameful thing. My sweet paternal grandmother suffered from depression and attempted to commit suicide one time. I like to talk to others about mental illness. Even if Maria is a diagnosed with schizophrenia, she denies that she has any mental health problems.

Bianca stays with Juliet when Mary and I visit Maria at the hospital. When we return home, Mary says that it is very important that Maria takes the anti-psychotic meds after leaving the hospital as well. Mary speaks her mind. She has had mental health problems and has been taking anti-psychotic medication a large part of her life. By doing that she has prevented going back to the mental health hospitals she used to go to.

After chatting with Juliet and Mary, Bianca and I drive home to our new apartment. I think it's here that the bond between Bianca and I strengthened even more. We will be alright. I need to be strong for Bianca and Maria. I will care for them even in the most difficult times. I'll do the best I can.

Maria's reality is distorted. She is serious. When she has delusions she has no humor. Maria is not interested in what is happening with myself and Bianca or other people. She is only interested in what is happening with her and her needs. She becomes irritable when she doesn't get what she wants. It's not easy to communicate with her.

I talk to Maria on the phone. She is taking it easy. Maria ate and read a book. She sounds happy. I look forward to seeing her this evening. Maria is so happy to see me. I stay with her during the visiting hours. When Maria regains her senses she doesn't realize that she has mental illness. She thinks she is fine.

I do everything I can to strengthen and make Maria feel better when I see her in the psychiatric ward. When Maria is in the hospital I decide to massage people. We need the money. I hang up flyers in stores with the text:

Swedish massage. A source of peace for body and

mind. Call your Swedish masseur Karl Hedman.

I write that I can come to the location of the client's choice. The most popular massages are the foot massage and full-body massage. When I was 18-20 years old I worked in a bookstore and shared an apartment with a masseur. When I went to the apartment during my lunch break I saw him massaging clients hundreds of times. I ate my vegetable soups and observed his massage techniques. I'm so grateful that I can use my massage knowledge and skills in Louisiana.

Maria is home again. We're sitting next to each other playing with Bianca by the swimming pool.

A couple of days later, Maria and I celebrate our third wedding anniversary. We have a romantic evening together at the most exclusive seafood restaurant in Baton Rouge. Maria wears an emerald-green satin gown that takes my breath away. Bianca is with Juliet and Mary. Maria says that she would like to move back to Sweden.

A week later, three of my museum colleagues drive me, Maria, and Bianca to the airport in New Orleans. We fly back to Europe. When we finally arrive in Sweden Bianca has fever and ear pain. A physician diagnoses her with ear inflammation and prescribes antibiotics. Bianca is still sick. We take her to the child clinic at the hospital. She is admitted. The physician says that Bianca is overtired after the flights.

Maria is feeling better and joins the gymnastics group in my childhood community. She is so happy to make friends and be praised by the female gymnastics leader who is a physical therapist. She joins the church choir and goes with a politician to the local parliament to learn more about Swedish politics. Maria loves the community feelings and the generosity from people living in the community. She also encounters situations in which she sees the worst of country people, including ignorance, sexism, and racism.

Maria gets an English teacher job at the high school where I teach Swedish and social science. One day, Maria faints whilst we are eating dinner. We go to the psychiatric clinic at the hospital. Maria is admitted to a psychiatric unit. She is in a catatonic state for a few days and stays in the psychiatric ward for several weeks to recover.

Bianca and I visit Maria at the hospital. When we first walk into Maria's room we're not able to connect with her. Before we leave she opens her warm eyes and is tender and sweet to us. Maria is very fragile. I'm holding her hand gently. She doesn't recollect what has happened.

The psychiatrist says that a woman can become catatonic after giving birth. He says that other issues can also be behind this state. I tell the psychiatrist that Maria's mother Mary has been admitted to psychiatric hospitals throughout Maria's childhood and that her mother brought Maria with her when she was about to commit suicide.

After some time, Maria communicates better. She is leaving the catatonic state. Maria returns home. In the fall of 2000, Maria really wants to have another child. We talk to Maria's psychiatrist who is visiting our house every week on her way home from the hospital. The psychiatrist says that she will lower Maria's anti-psychotic medication. Maria and I stay in bed and make love most days and nights. One day Maria says smilingly:

I'm pregnant!

I hug and lift Maria in the air cheering. We laugh joyfully.

I never thought that I wanted this so much. I want Bianca to have a sibling, Maria says.

Yes, that's wonderful! I reply.

In the spring the following year when we celebrate my birthday in the garden Maria says, I have contractions.

I call my parents to pick up Bianca. They come immediately. I help Maria into the car. We drive to the maternity ward at the hospital.

My water just broke, Maria says.

Maria delivers our second child. Our faces are wet with thousands over tears of joy.

Congratulations, it's a girl, the midwife says.

We name her Claudia Heidi Maria.

Heidi and I have the same birthday. That is the best birthday gift I've ever received. Heidi is sunshine and fun. She has a sense of humor and is very courageous.

The girls grow up. Maria and I love to see Heidi and Bianca playing and laughing in the garden. Heidi goes to gymnastics. She is not scared of anything when she flies in the air. Bianca is dancing ballet. The girls attend the same preschool. The teachers say that Bianca and Heidi are role models to the other children in that they can sit down and look at picture books for a long time. Most of the other kids have ants in their pants.

At least once a week the psychiatrist comes to our house to talk to Maria and the family. Maria talks in an honest way about how she is doing, what disturbs her like my mother, or if her symptoms are bothering her. The psychiatrist is always there to help her.

Four years later. Maria and I have over the years developed a close friendship with my French friend Leo and his wife whom I first met in Stockholm in 1997. They own a castle in France. They are going to work outside Europe for the coming years and ask Maria and me if we would like to live in and take care of their castle until they come back. We say that we are interested in doing this. We tell them we just need to check with Maria's mother in Louisiana on how she is doing.

Juliet passed away in 2003 at the age of 89. Mary has since then been living alone in the house in Louisiana. Mary tells us that she is not able to take care of the house any longer. She wants us to move back to Louisiana to live with her.

9 HURRICANE KATRINA

Baton Rouge, 2005-2006

Maria and I have a decision to make. The two alternatives are if we are going to move to France to take care of our friends' castle or move back to Mary gin Louisiana. We decide to return to Louisiana in 2005. We tell the French couple that Mary needs our support in Baton Rouge. They understand our decision.

Bianca is seven and Heidi four at the time. I have been living in Baton Rouge for three months when I get a job at the Baton Rouge Center for World Affairs. Shortly after this I'm offered a job at the main library in Baton Rouge in the children's room. I wrote my two master's theses in sociology and anthropology about pre-school children gender relations in make-believe play and have worked in Swedish pre-schools for several years. I love this job leading story time with toddlers and their parents, reading with children and doing art, literature, and theatre activities.

Faith is a central part of Maria's family life. Maria, Bianca, Heidi, Mary, and Juliet were all baptized in the Catholic Church. I was baptized and confirmed in the Swedish Lutheran Church. I know some prayers. Maria and Mary know so many. They have taught me to just pray by improvising depending on what happens in life. Mary and Maria want me to become a Catholic as everyone else in the family.

Bianca attends a Catholic school. Heidi goes to a Catholic pre-school. We attend the Catholic masses on Sundays. I decide to go through the Rite of Christian Initiation for Adults to become a Catholic. I will stay as a member of the Lutheran Church. I will be a Catholic in the United States and a Lutheran in Sweden.

I join a group of adults at the church gathering every

week to begin the process of becoming a Catholic. We talk about the Gospel, faith in Jesus and the Catholic Church, and receiving the sacraments of baptism, confirmation, and Holy Eucharist.

I get my own spiritual mentor that I meet for coffee. We talk about things going on in life. I celebrate the Rite of Election including the enrollment of names of all those seeking baptism at the coming Easter Vigil. On the first Sunday of Lent, we gather in the church to publicly request baptism. I meet with the priest for confession. In the Easter Vigil Liturgy on Holy Saturday, I receive the sacraments of baptism, confirmation, and Holy Eucharist becoming a fully initiated member of the Catholic Church.

A hurricane will hit Louisiana in August 2005. Before the storm, we stock up on bottles of water, tins of tuna, salmon, beans, vegetables, and fruits. It storms a lot in Louisiana with thunder and lightning and hard winds shaking the trees. I sit on the porch and look at the moving oak trees in the garden. The sky is turning dark blue. The rain is falling in great sweeping gusts that rattle the rooftop of our house.

Hurricane Katrina makes landfall off the coast of Louisiana on August 29th, 2005. Hurricane Katrina is a violent storm and bears down hard devastating South Louisiana. When the hurricane hits, the oak trees move back and forth outside our house. Branches from the oak trees make a hole in the roof. The rain is pouring down.

Bianca and Heidi sink onto their mattresses and fall asleep. For three days we don't have electricity after the hurricane. We stay home those days and pray that everything is going to be alright. Maria blocks out the hurricane days.

If you don't block it out Karl you will not be able to live here, Maria says.

I didn't block it out. I want to take in as much as possible and learn from my first hurricane. Over the next few days, we are hungry. Our tuna cans are running out. I'm dreaming about smothered chicken, rice, and spinach. Finally, there is a turning point. Maria shouts out:

Oh, the power is on.

We smile and hug each other. When the electricity returns, we can cook hot food again. We're so grateful.

Hurricane Katrina is one of the deadliest hurricanes ever to hit the United States. Many people in South Louisiana and Mississippi suffer catastrophic damage. Over 1800 people lost their lives in the hurricane and the flooding that follows. Millions of others are left homeless along the Gulf Coast and in New Orleans. Trees fall over and crash into power lines. Flooding and high winds result in property damage and loss of power. People relocate to temporary shelters throughout the area. Homes, school buildings and other buildings were destroyed. Children and families are stuck in a recurring nightmare as relief efforts falter.

Although Baton Rouge does not witness physical devastation on the scale of other parts of South Louisiana, it is hugely impacted by the storm. Baton Rouge's population doubled overnight. Displaced people from New Orleans come to Baton Rouge changing the social, demographic, and economic structure of Baton Rouge. It's a city in crisis. People crowd into Baton Rouge's shelters. When I work with the children in the children's room at the library after Hurricane Katrina I see that they search for signs of comfort and hope. We have very emotional story times in smaller groups composed of children and their parents.

In the evenings, Maria and I drive through the sunsets on Highland Road in Baton Rouge. We listen to her favorite music cassettes that she makes herself. I know that this is what Maria loves the most, being together driving in beautiful natural settings. It rains in the early hours of every afternoon. It's an opportunity for love, kissing and passion.

One afternoon, Maria undresses and takes a shower. She leaves the door open to the bathroom. I can see her through the mirror. Maria steps out of the shower and smiles at me. She pulls her hair back. Maria invites me in with a flirting gaze. I kiss her cheek softly. Maria smiles. My fingers slide over her breasts and nipples touching her softly. Maria trembles. We kiss the sweetest kiss with gentle lips. I place one hand lightly around her waist. We take a bath. We stand up dripping water in the bathtub after the bath. I give Maria a towel and kiss her passionately on her lips. I hold her hand and we walk over to the bed and make love.

After Hurricane Katrina, we read in the local newspaper about daily robberies, kidnappings, and traffic accidents in Baton Rouge. More than 200000 people from New Orleans moved to Baton Rouge. They drive faster than the people in Baton Rouge. Because of their different traffic rhythms, I see daily accidents when driving to and from work at the library. This ongoing crisis in Baton Rouge makes Maria and me ponder the idea of returning to Sweden for a quiet life in my childhood community.

Maria tells me about a robbery she experienced with two other students one night when they were first year students in college. The landscape of the trauma was the campus of Louisiana State University. Two men walked up to them and put guns to their heads. This is the traumatic incident that Maria has talked the most about. The memories of fear and the loss of control are kept in her body.

In the spring the following year, Maria is depressed and sleeps a lot. Maria has also worked at the library. She is fired from her library job because of her mental health problems. She says that she wants to move back to Sweden.

The next day, Mary pinches Heidi so hard on her leg that it starts to bleed. I tell Mary to let go of Heidi and to never touch her ever again. Mary grabs a glass of water. She throws it in my face.

I knock you down, Karl! You always take the girls' side! Mary screams.

That's right. That's what I do. I love and protect my girls. Mary, don't you ever touch them again. You're their grandmother. You're supposed to always love and be sweet to the girls. Stay away from them, I say.

Mary looks furious. I have not seen this violent behavior in Mary before. I understand what Maria has told me so many times about Mary's aggressive side when she hit Maria in her girlhood. I hadn't fully realized it until this moment. I start to dislike Mary and see the dangers of living with her. I don't want her to hurt Heidi and Bianca.

We return to Sweden in 2006. Happy to be back in Europe we fly to Marseille to go on vacation in Provence. We enjoy a lovely *bouillabaisse*, a Provencal dish from Marseille with shellfish and other types of fish. It's infused with saffron and served with *rouille* which is garlic and cayenne mayonnaise that is spread on grilled bread or croutons.

The airplane from Marseille to Nice is delayed. When we go to pick up the reserved rental car at the airport in Nice the representative says that they don't have any rental cars available. We take a taxi to our apartment in Èze outside Nice. Èze extends from the French Riviera and the Mediterranean Sea (Èze-sur-Mer) to the hilltop with a medieval village (Èze-Village) where we stay. Maria's idol U2 singer Bono lives with his family in Èze-sur-Mer. That evening, Maria tells me her dreams and fantasies about Bono. I like U2 too but listening to Maria in a psychotic state talking about the gorgeous and amazing Bono, is not my favorite activity.

The next day I go to Nice to find a rental car. It's Easter. All the rental cars are probably gone. The neighbor at the apartment complex where we stay says that I could go with him to the city to get a rental car. He drops me off at a rental car place. They don't have any spare cars. I walk to another rental car company. They don't have any cars either. I continue like that until I realize that no agency has any available cars. I go to the bus station. I get on a bus and go back to Maria and the girls.

In the apartment, Maria feels that she is left alone after I went with a stranger in his van. She thought that anything could happen. Maria becomes anxious. She walks down the mountain road with Bianca and Heidi. The police pass and pick up Maria and the girls.

Maria doesn't want to stay in the apartment when we don't have a car. She wants us to take a taxi to Aix-en-Provence several hours away. I think Maria is getting delusional again. In her delusional state, she stays awake and does not take in another person's perspective. It will be very expensive, but when Maria decides to do something in her delusional reality she argues for that decision for hours until I usually give in which I also do now. The taxi is 300 dollars. We have the money. I'm just going to accept it and enjoy the ride. It's a beautiful drive in the Provence landscapes. We find a cozy hotel in Aix-en-Provence and have a nice holiday. The girls love the carousel in the center of this art city.

We return to Sweden. Maria is fully delusional. When she stops taking the anti-psychotic medication she always becomes psychotic again. She is struggling with her mental health. Her psychotic behaviors wanting to control me and the girls in detail create massive stress for all of us. When Maria is psychotic she has no feelings for us. Maria doesn't think she is sick.

We need to do a family intervention to help Maria. She is involuntarily committed to the psychiatric ward after I talk to Bianca and Heidi and consult the psychiatrist about Maria being psychotic. She stays at the hospital when she gets on the anti-psychotic medication. Maria says that there are times when patients get out of control and the staff members need to intervene. Maria always follows the rules and avoids confrontation with other patients at the psych ward. She keeps her distance physically and emotionally from people whom she thinks may have the potential to be violent. Some caretakers in the psych ward like Maria and they chat.

Maria's psych ward is plain on the inside. The interior design of the meal room is light and pleasant to be in. Her room has no pictures on the walls. The shared TV room has some paintings. Her bed is soft. The sheets and linens are cleaned regularly. She stays there for three weeks. Other times Maria has stayed longer. Psychiatrists and staff regularly review her behaviors. Their input in part dictates the length of treatment at the facility. The staff wants to ensure that Maria is okay before she is discharged. In the ward, she wears casual, comfortable everyday clothing. They confiscate razors, belts, strings, shoestrings, and other things to take away anything that may pose a safety risk. There is a recreation time once per week to dance in the cafeteria. She likes to participate in the physical activities. Maria returns home.

After Maria is discharged from the psych ward she belongs to an open psychiatric unit. Her psychiatrist and nurse of the open psychiatric unit help Maria to make her life as normal as possible while continuing the medication treatment and therapy. After a while, Maria thinks that she is totally fine. She stops taking her anti-psychotic medication. Then the chaos starts all over again, but this time it will be far worse than ever before.

10 THE DISAPPEARING

West Sweden and Louisiana, Fall and Winter, 2007-2008

It is a fall morning. The cold air is fresh. The rain does not stop. The yellow and orange leaves fall from the trees. Maria is off her meds and has a psychotic episode with paranoia. Maria decides herself to not take any anti-psychotic medication even if the psychiatrist instructs her to do so. She thinks she's fine anyway.

After Hurricane Katrina in 2005, Maria's psychotic behaviors become worse. Her fragile mental state deteriorates. Maria's schizophrenia and not taking her meds makes it difficult for her to tell the difference between reality and fantasy.

Her symptoms affect the way she perceives and interacts with us. She has delusions of grandeur believing that she has exceptional abilities, wealth, or importance. Maria says that she has the keys to all properties in the United Kingdom and France. She can go into any property and take over that estate. She says that she can go on any train or bus in those two countries without paying anything. Maria becomes very controlling. Because of her paranoid and psychotic behaviors, the family begins to fracture. We argue a lot which means a very stressful home environment for the girls.

I have offered unconditional respect and support to Maria for nine years no matter what Maria has been going through. Now, I don't know what to do. I could just be quiet and not argue with her. That would make the situation calmer. That would mean that our family practices and principles would be ruled by her psychotic thoughts creating instability and insecurity.

Maria is paranoid day and night which is the main cause of our constant fights. Our family life is so intense and dysfunctional. She wants to control everything I do in detail. Maria says that I have sexual relationships with many mothers at the girls' school and women at my workplace. It's devastating for our intimate relationship. Maria and I don't even hug each other. We drift further away from each other. Everything is so fragile. I don't have the strength to stay with her to deal with this forever.

One evening, I'm in the kitchen cooking supper. Maria accuses me of having a relationship with a colleague at my work. She tells me to throw away all the food that I'm cooking because it has a red stain on it. I don't see any red stain on the food. I feel massive stress. I don't want to be with her anymore. Maria is psychotically screaming at me in my face to throw away the food in the garbage can. These kinds of situations happen as a routine now. This isn't working out. I tell her that I don't want to be with her anymore and that I want to divorce her.

I want us to separate because we argue all the time. It's not good for the girls or for us. We can live next to each other in two apartments and have joint custody of the girls. The priority is the care of our daughters, I say.

It feels like a relief to say this. Her face is filled with fear and anger. Maria attacks me. We have a row screaming, arguing, and holding each other's arms. We're both very upset. I tell her that I will stay the night in my sister's home.

I need to go, I say.

I hate you, Karl! I'm so disappointed in you. You're so mean that you want to leave your own daughters, Maria shouts after me when I leave.

I don't want to leave Bianca and Heidi. I want you to take the anti-psychotic medication again and that you get well because it's not working out anymore. I always want to be with Bianca and Heidi, I reply.

I leave the apartment.

A couple of days later, I visit Maria. I have filled out the divorce papers. I want to have joint custody.

Maria has changed her mind. She wants sole custody of the girls. The judge sets a court date for the hearing. It's in two weeks. We have an appointment to meet in the family court to talk about the divorce and the custody.

Maria doesn't say anything or open the door before the court date November 5, 2007. I look through the newspaper hole in the door. I can't see anyone inside the apartment. Maria and the girls are missing. I leave the apartment building and see a large group of crows flying over the church in front of me. I start to worry about what has happened.

On the date of the court proceedings, I wait at the court. I enter the conference room following the judge. Maria is not showing up. I sit through the meeting with the judge. When I visit the apartment where Maria and the girls live it's totally quiet. They are gone. I walk to the girls' school and talk to the teachers. They say that the girls are not there.

Initially, I'm naïve. I think that Maria has gone somewhere with the girls in the city. I wait and wait. Then I realize that they are really gone. My worst nightmare is coming true. Maria disappears with Bianca and Heidi in November 2007. My world collapses.

Two weeks later I find out that Maria has made a phone call from London to one of her friends in the United States. I am so scared and panic. I feel despair. I try to calm myself. My whole body goes into shock. I know that Maria is not feeling good. I'm terrified about what could happen to Heidi and Bianca. When Maria is psychotic, she's not able to see the needs of the girls. It's a volatile situation.

After my daughters were taken abroad by Maria without my consent, I become very cautious. I contact the Catholic priest that Maria used to call on a regular basis. He says that Maria has gone to France with the girls. I think that I need to go to the police and ask for help. At the police station, I make a report about the disappearance of our daughters and arbitrary conduct. I tell the police what has happened.

Arbitrary conduct means the crime when one parent takes children without the other parent's consent. The police make a report of international notifications of missing persons to Interpol and the Schengen Information System which gets information and photos of the girls. Sweden demands that countries in the Interpol network look for the girls in their records. The police put up photos of the girls on the international website *Our missing children*. Nordic countries cooperate with Sweden in the search for the girls. In case the police get tips about the whereabouts of the girls and Maria, the Swedish police contact the local police in the other country and is urged to arrest Maria and send her and the girls back to Sweden.

Time passes. Nothing happens. Everything is unpredictable. I miss Bianca and Heidi. It's very hard. I long for the girls so much that my heart feels like its exploding in thousands of pieces. I feel really hurt. I call Maria and it goes straight to her voicemail.

They have been missing for forty-eight hours now. I'm concerned about their welfare. I feel worried out of my mind. I can't stop thinking about the girls. I need to know where they are. What has happened to them? For weeks, I hear nothing. They disappear out of my life. With every day that passes, I become more worried. I return to the police and ask:

Where are they?

The police can't find their location. My eyes fill up with tears. I cry and cry. My tears explain what I'm experiencing. The tears help me to relax a little bit. I can't sleep. My tears carry me with hope of seeing them again in the future. I can't stop thinking about Bianca and Heidi. I stay hopeful but I'm scared that they are dead.

What am I going to do? I decide to get our daughters home as soon as possible. I contact the Swedish Foreign Ministry in Stockholm. I tell the staff members of the child abduction unit what has happened. The Foreign Ministry investigator gives me the name and contact information to a parental abduction lawyer in Stockholm. The lawyer helps me to file a Hague Application.

The Hague Abduction Convention is a treaty that many countries have joined including the United States. The purposes of the Convention are to protect children from the harmful effects of international abduction by a parent by encouraging the rapid return of abducted children to their country of habitual residence, and to organize or secure the effective rights of access to a child. The idea is that custody should generally be decided by the appropriate court in the country of the child's habitual residence.

Over the next few weeks after filing the Hague Application, I wait for a response from the police about what has happened. I cry and hardly sleep. Finally, I close my eyes. If I go to sleep, I dream strange dreams. The first light of morning is breaking. I wake up after a short sleep. I'm very tired in the mornings. I haven't slept properly for weeks.

It's terrible. Doubts are beginning to close in on me. I don't even know if my children are alive. I think they are alive, but I don't know for sure. I feel a constant sadness and darkness. A picture of the girls hangs next to my bed. I spend most of my awake time alone at home looking at pictures of my daughters. The worst that could happen, has happened. I think about the girls non-stop. I can't sleep. I was unable to go to sleep last night and stayed awake all night. It exhausts me in the end. The weather has grown bitterly cold. Snowflakes fall heavily from the night sky. I put on my wool coat. I go for a walk in the snow. My face is pale. My soul feels drained.

In the beginning of December, I receive the first sign of life on the whereabouts of the girls and Maria from the United States. A friend of Maria has seen the girls on the street in Maria's hometown Baton Rouge.

I feel a short moment of happiness and reassurance and then powerlessness. I find out that Maria moves the girls between different locations, that they are not going to school and don't get enough nutritious food.

First, they stay with Mary in the old people apartment complex. They received rice and beans, snacks, and energy drinks. The receptionist gave the girls used clothes. Bianca liked these clothes. One of the clothing items was a red skirt with a teddy bear on it.

Then they lived in a shelter organized by Catholic nuns. It was possible to take a shower, but they never did. Bianca remembers that they served fried chicken. Bianca recalls a black mother making braids on her daughter's hair.

After some time, they moved to an apartment with Mary. They used Mary's pension to pay for the rent. Maria is not showering the girls or herself. Maria has gotten a haircut her friend says. Bianca and Heidi did not get any haircuts, or their hair brushed. Bianca plays a rabbit game when she sees Maria returning to Mary's apartment from the hair stylist at the exclusive apartment store.

I think that Maria is doing everything she can to look after the girls, but when she is delusional she can't see the girls' needs. Maria is thinking and talking fast. It's difficult to follow her reasoning because it's psychotic talk. Maria home school the girls by letting them play games on the computer. Bianca does math problems on her own.

I realize that I can't wait for the American authorities to handle the Hague Application. I must do more. My daughters are depending on me. I fly to the United States to find Bianca and Heidi. I'm hopeful and scared to death when I fly over the Atlantic Ocean. I feel isolated. Why is this happening to the girls and our family? Will they be returned to me by the police? There is not a single minute that goes by when I'm not thinking about the girls. My thoughts are that I may never find them and what if the American authorities don't agree to return the girls to me. It brings me to tears and worry. My biggest worry is if they are safe.

My lawyer and the Swedish Foreign Ministry put pressure from Sweden on the American authorities. The Swedish General Consulate in New York City has prepared the trip home for me and the girls. They issue temporary passports for the girls and are prepared if anything wrong should take place.

I decide to just go. We're going to get through this. When I arrive in Baton Rouge, I go to the detective division of the sheriff's office. They say that they can help me to find Maria and the girls as soon as I get sole custody.

Over there, I stay with friends and spend my days and nights looking for the girls. First, I stay with a work colleague from the political history museum where I used to work. He lives outside Baton Rouge in the countryside and takes me to the city on weekdays when he goes to work.

Later, I stay with another colleague from my old library work and her husband. When I worked in the children's room of the main library in Baton Rouge I got to know a Swedish woman with two children and her husband, a university professor in music. To give back, I baby sit their children and translate an important music theory thesis from Swedish to English. After I have been looking for the girls during the days I sit in his university office. I enjoy when the music department students perform their musical instruments to him.

Finally, I stay with another friend and his wife with a small baby. They live in between New Orleans and

Baton Rouge. I help them with their baby and cook. He works in Baton Rouge. I look for the girls when he is at work during the days. I go to relatives and friends of Maria and walk and drive around the streets, spend hours in the city libraries in Baton Rouge, at Louisiana State University, and other places where I think Maria may show up with the girls.

One day when I walk around the campus of Louisiana State University, Maria appears in a parking lot. She notices me. I walk towards her. Maria stands by her car far away. I have no chance to get to her before she drives off. I still feel happy about this encounter knowing that Maria is alive. This is giving me hope that the girls are okay.

I go to different places in Baton Rouge where Maria and the girls may be. I show pictures of Bianca and Heidi to people and ask:

Have you seen these girls?

No one has seen my daughters.

In the fading evening light, I drive around with my friend in the neighborhood where Ruby lives. I know that Ruby would never open her door to me. She never liked me because she thinks that I took Maria away from her all the way to Sweden. I hire a private investigator. He enters the gated community and knocks on Ruby's door. Ruby opens the door. She is agitated. He doesn't see any signs of Maria and the girls and leaves.

I use every means I can. I look broadly. To never give up is the only thing that works. I regularly visit the social services, the police, and other authorities to find out something about where the girls may be. I make an appointment with the FBI for 3.00 p.m. Before that I'm led into a conference room. There I'm being aggressively interrogated by three FBI investigators. They ask why I want to find the girls and why I want to get sole custody of them. The questioning is very invasive. I feel very uncomfortable. I don't feel any understanding or support from the FBI agents, so I leave the office.

After the visit to the FBI, I feel that nothing works. I'm losing hope of ever finding the girls. I'm filled with sadness. Maria hides with the girls. She doesn't respond to letters from the authorities and the Family Court in Baton Rouge. Because Maria is gone the family court can't decide to return the girls to me. Since the court hasn't decided, the police are not able to look for the girls. It's a catch 22 moment.

The next day, I drive to the Coroner's Office handling murders and suicide in Baton Rouge. I meet with the coroner. There's a long silence when she's checking her records. I fear the worst.

I'm looking for my daughters and ex-wife, I say.

I'm sorry. I don't have any information about your ex-wife and daughters, she replies.

I freeze. It's very emotional for me. Pain heaves underneath my breath, grabbing my throat – I can't speak. I lose hope for a moment. Thoughts that the girls are dead come to my mind. When I drive back out on the highway I break down. I drive to the side of the road. I'm sobbing uncontrollably. The tears are coming hard in a huge wave of hopelessness and dejection. The tears don't stop. I cry like I never cried before in my life. Several months of built-up fear, anxiety and stress are coming out through these tears. I am motivated to keep looking for Bianca and Heidi, I won't give up.

I can't believe that my daughters have been abducted for more than four months now. I tell the police about what happened at the coroner's office and ask them if they have any updates. They can't help me unless I have sole custody of my daughters in Louisiana. I think about that the fact that Bianca is nine years old and Heidi six. Maria abducted the girls and hid them from the world. I have no proof that they are alive.

Finally, the Swedish judge decides to give me sole custody of the girls. This decision is only valid in Sweden. I need sole custody of my daughters in the United States. I present the proof of parenthood and the sole custody documents to the Family Court in Baton Rouge to prove that my custodial rights are violated.

The turning point comes. When the Swedish court gave me sole custody of the girls the Family Court in Baton Rouge was able to give me sole custody of the girls in Louisiana. The police can now enforce the decision. I have the U.S. laws on my side, and I will now be able to bring the girls back to Sweden. I feel hope, strength, and a will in me to find the girls. First we just need to find them.

From this point on everything happens fast. It's like pushing a button. It's very emotional and healing at the same time. The police begin to look for the girls. They discover where Maria and the girls are located. They connect Maria to an apartment after a tip from an utility company.

Five police vehicles drive to the address. I sit in one of them. Armed police knock on the apartment door. From the inside, Heidi and Bianca hear the banging. They start to cry and hug each other. The police enter the apartment and arrest Maria. They bring her out to one of the police vehicles. I notice that she is breaking down. I don't want her to break down, but she abducted our daughters. I haven't known where they have been for months. It's a massive relief to be here with the girls. Bianca and Heidi hug each other when they walk out of the apartment with a police officer. I begin to shiver. I feel that my legs can't hold me. Mary screams from the balcony.

Maria doesn't have a chance to say goodbye to the girls she loves most. Maria and I were not prepared to handle this arrest situation. Everything will change. Her world falls apart as my world fell apart when she abducted the girls.

It's not easy for me to be in a relationship with her having schizophrenia viewing life through delusional glasses. We both feel sadness and sorrow in this situation. We've been responsible for the girls together since they were little. We've taught them almost everything we could about life. We've been there to help and support them when they've needed it. The girls have experienced many stressful situations in their short lives.

The police officer takes the girls to me. I tremble. I hug Bianca and Heidi for love, warmth, and protection. We say hi in these dramatic moments. It is incredibly wonderful to see the girls and hold them. I relax.

I'm not going to cause or participate in a serious conflict with Maria. I will do what I can to understand and support her. I can't see Maria accepting this reality in her inner world. It will be incredibly painful and an enormous loss for her. Hopefully she can come back to us when the situation has calmed down and she takes anti-psychotic medication again.

The police escort us to the airport. I sit next to Bianca and Heidi in the police car.

Are you alright? I ask the girls.

They nod.

Don't worry. It's over. I have missed you endlessly, I say.

Bianca and Heidi smile. The girls have greasy and tangled hair and holes in their dirty clothes. The first thing Bianca says in the car when I say that we will fly back to Sweden is:

Daddy can we get some glitter shoes?

I ask the police officer if we can stop at a shoe store. After a few minutes we see a shoe store. The police officer stops. The girls come with me into the store. They pick out glitter shoes that I buy for them. We're back in the police car after a few minutes.

Thank you, I tell the police officer.

73

You're welcome, he says and smiles.

I don't know if Maria is going to stay arrested or if she will try to take the girls again or appeal in the family court. In Sweden, my lawyer and the Swedish Foreign Ministry are on standby to act if anything goes wrong. The Swedish Foreign Ministry, the Swedish Consulate in New York City and my lawyer in Stockholm have all been working intensely for months to find the girls. I call my Swedish lawyer. She answers and gives me the advice to leave the United States as soon as possible. At the airport we get on the first plane we can.

When the airplane door closes, and we are about to take off I break down in massive tears. I'm sobbing and shaking all over my body. I'm euphoric and massively relieved. My happiness is complete. The girls are here with me. It's over. We are returning to Sweden after four months. I feel overwhelmed.

After an hour into the flight, I get up to go to the toilet. I don't want to leave the girls after all the things that have happened. I look at the girls.

See you soon, I say and smile at the girls.

The girls smile back. In the aircraft toilet, I tremble when I look at myself in the mirror. I look very happy and at the same time totally drained after walking and running several marathons on hundreds of streets in Baton Rouge the last weeks. My lips are chapped, and my hands are shaking. Bianca and Heidi look up at me when I walk back. I sit down in my seat and enjoy this unforgettable moment going back home with the girls. The trembling begins to fade away. I laugh with Bianca and Heidi.

After we return to Sweden, we all sleep late the next day. I walk into the shower and enjoy the hot water relaxing my tense muscles. I wash my hair and body. Bianca and Heidi go back to their old Montessori school in Sweden with the other children. I'm so relieved that the girls are with me and play with their friends at school. One of the girls in the school asks

Bianca if she and Heidi had been abducted and were in the newspaper. Bianca confirms this. I feel so much hope. Abducted children can be returned home. It's important to never give up. Hope is what kept me going in finding my beloved daughters.

I think about Maria and how devastating these events must be for her. I still care about her and love her. She has been psychotic and made decisions in that condition. She did what she believed was right.

When the police release Maria she goes to the airport in New Orleans. Maria doesn't have the money to pay for the tickets. She attempts to buy an airplane ticket with a fraud check. The New Orleans police arrest Maria. They take her to a correctional institute for women outside New Orleans. Maria is in incarceration for check fraud. The police take her fingerprints and DNA.

It's time to lock you up, the guard says.

Maria walks back to her cell. She is locked up in a small box. Maria is doing whatever she needs to not break down. She lies down on the mattress and closes her eyes to rest.

When I later talk to Maria on the phone, she says that being there too long will be detrimental for her. There is no privacy. Maria has her period and is using the bathroom where the other women can also see her. Hopefully she will be free soon.

Another day, Maria calls me in Sweden. She's not feeling good from the strong anti-psychotic medication.

Are you alright? I ask Maria.

No. I'm not feeling good. I'm gonna lose it. I'm scared. It just hurts. I will not last. Help me Karl! Please, Maria replies.

I'm worried about her.

You'll get through this Maria. I will help you, I say reassuringly.

Ruby tells Maria that she will probably be released because of her schizophrenia. That evening, two other female prisoners pray with Maria before she may be able to leave the women's correctional center:

Dear God. Guide and protect Maria and send your angels to cover her. In the name of the Father, the Son, and the Holy Spirit. Amen.

Ruby helps Maria in court. They show evidence that Maria is psychotic. After that, Maria is released from the correctional institute for women. I talk to a relieved Maria.

I'm so happy to walk out of the court as a free woman. I'm going to stay with Ruby. I miss you and the girls, Maria tells me.

Everything is going to be alright, okay. I wish you were here. I still love you even if you took the girls, I say.

I wish I was there with you, Maria says and cries.

Maria stays with Ruby. She wants to return to us in Sweden. I still love her. She asks for money for the airplane tickets to Sweden. I pay for her tickets.

Thank you so much for helping me. I really appreciate it, Maria says.

How did you know where we were? Maria asks.

The sheriff's office found your address from your utility company after I got sole custody of the girls in Louisiana, I respond.

Oh, Maria says.

I call Maria's Swedish psychiatrist and update her about what has happened. She says that she will give Maria a milder anti-psychotic medication with less side effects as soon as she returns. Maria flies back to Sweden and reunites with us. The first night home I hold out my arms to Maria. Maria looks into my eyes, takes a step forward, and gently comes to rest against me.

I'm so glad that you are here, I say and close my arms around Maria.

Me too. I love you Karl. Thank you for everything you did for me so I could return, Maria replies.

We begin a consolation journey. Maria visits her psychiatrist. The psychiatrist changes her anti-psychotic medication. She feels so much clearer in her head. I forgive Maria.

We need to be strong together for us and for the girls. We're family, I say.

I want Bianca and Heidi to have stability in the family so they can build strong self-esteem and self-confidence. Maria and I love our daughters. We support each other after she returns to Sweden and do our best to take care of the girls.

We'll work it out, I reassure Maria.

Maria smiles. We have a life to live together.

I want to start all over. I just want to be a good mother for Bianca and Heidi and be there for you, Karl, Maria says.

West Sweden, 2011

I'm happy with my appearance. I stay fit by going swimming most days. I only have one problem. There is a patch the size of a tennis ball growing next to my left collarbone. Maria wants me to contact the primary healthcare center. I talk to a nurse practitioner. She wants me to come in immediately. The nurse practitioner observes a skin change and the fat ball on the collar-bone close to my throat. I get a referral to the skin clinic to have it removed.

Two weeks later, two physicians assess that the fat ball is placed in a sensitive position. They decide that a surgeon needs to remove it at the hospital. The same day we have a fun bowling party for Heidi and her friends on her 10th birthday. A few days later, Maria and I attend Bianca and Heidi's Montessori school musical. Bianca is papa bear and Heidi another animal.

I fly to Paris and Lisbon. I attend an international conference about care relations at the beautiful Portuguese Red Cross Palace in Lisbon. In the evening, I go to a breathtaking Fado music dinner. Fado songs tell stories about love and longing to be with the family.

When I return home from Portugal, the surgeon removes tissue on the area around my collarbone. I see the surgery in a mirror. The surgeon sends the removed tissue to the laboratory.

The following week, I'm leading the international week of the School of Health and Welfare working a full-time job as the director of international relations. I'm finishing deadlines on my doctoral thesis which I write at another university in southern Sweden. I'm the coach for the girls' soccer team. I'm volunteering as a church host reading from the bible in the Lutheran Church on Sundays. Looking at it in retrospective it sounds insane. I'm doing too many things. I need to start setting up limits. I decide to leave being a church host and cut down on the other activities. I'm having family time with Maria, Bianca, and Heidi. We're planning our summer trip to Denmark. The surgery wound has turned into a scar.

Vancouver, Canada, May-June 2011

I fly to Vancouver to attend an international conference. I'm staying at a hotel in downtown Vancouver. I visit friends on their sailing boat in the harbor. I attend a reception at the Vancouver Art Gallery. The next day, I get up early to be picked up by a nursing lecturer friend. We take the ferry from Vancouver to Victoria on Vancouver Island. We see killer whales.

When I return to Vancouver, I listen to a lecture by the Chinese Canadian author Wayson Choy. His books are about the lives of immigrants growing up in Vancouver's Chinatown during the second World War and being between cultures. After his lecture, I go up to talk to him. We talk about human connectedness. He makes me a paper butterfly and signs two of his books. In one of the books, he writes, For Karl in flight with joy. Best wishes Wayson Choy. In the other book he writes, For Karl. Family is who loves you. Wayson Choy. I'm so happy having met and talked to him in person. He is such an inspiring writer.

West Sweden, Summer 2011

I get a call from my surgeon when I return home from Vancouver. He says that I need to visit him the next day. When I enter his office the surgeon has tears in his eyes. He says that I have cancer. My cancer diagnosis is Dermatofibrosarcoma Protuberans which is a very rare type of cancer tumor. It happens to one in a million.

The surgeon explains that Dermatofibrosarcoma Protuberans is a soft tissue neoplasm with intermediate to low-grade malignancy. It's a locally aggressive tumor with a high recurrence rate. Dermatofibrosarcoma Protuberans manifests as an irregular red-to-violaceous plaque on the skin. It invades deeper subcutaneous tissue, as fat, fascia, muscle, and bone. After having received the cancer diagnosis, I drive home to my family.

I need to tell you something sad. I have cancer, I explain with a hopeful face.

I may die, but I don't say that to my family.

What kind of cancer is it? Maria asks.

It's called Dermatofibrosarcoma Protuberans. It's sometimes described as having tentacles that can grow into surrounding fat, muscle and even bone. It's usually on the torso. This type of cancer can be seen on the arms, legs, head, and neck. It often recurs in the same location after it's removed, I say.

I have a racing heart and I'm filled with anxiety. I need help. I want to tell my family and others that I had been diagnosed with cancer. I want to stay open about having cancer. My maternal grandmother died from uterus cancer when my mom was only eight. I don't want to hide the cancer diagnosis from our daughters. Talking to others helps me to understand what I am going through and stay strong for the ongoing treatment and follow ups. I want to show our daughters that talking about difficult things in life helps.

I think that cancer doesn't need to mean death. Cancer treatments have been improved in the last decade. At the same time, it's extremely difficult to take in the cancer diagnosis. In shock, I ask myself Why me? I have moments of helplessness and hopelessness. I think about how I should live the last days of my life. I have anxiety about the well-being of Maria, Bianca and Heidi who depend on me and how they will live life without me especially if Maria becomes psychotic again. I experience some moments of fear when I think that this is the end for me. I can pass away when I'm only forty-four years old.

On the first day with cancer, I'm in distress. Maria cries that night. Bianca and Heidi stay with us in our bed. I'm awake until 3 a.m. I think that death awaits me. I'm thinking why me. Was it because I pushed myself massively to work full-time at one university and at the same time sit up awake until 1 a.m. in the morning every night writing on the doctoral thesis? I'm addicted to black tea. I drink it massively to stay awake. I know that the tea has large amounts of chemicals in it. Could that have affected me? If the worst would happen, I'm not scared of dying. I'm ready to die, but I promise myself that I will do everything I can to survive this cancer. I just need to be strong. I'm not afraid of dying. I pray to God that I will get well. I write my will in case I die.

Bianca writes a poem in my diary:
The summer is pleasant, and the grass is green
The butterflies, the flowers and the bees are beautiful
The sun shines and I see happy faces
The sun is yellow, and everyone is having fun
I'm going to swim this summer and I think everyone is happy.

The following week, I have my magnetic resonance imaging. I meet with my tumor surgeon. I ask what caused my skin cancer. He doesn't know for sure. The cellular origin of Dermatofibrosarcoma Protuberans is not clear. He thinks that it may be connected to me living in Louisiana being outside in the sun cutting grass and working in the garden having very pale skin, not wearing a shirt and not using sunscreen in the cancer alley area between Baton Rouge and New Orleans. Cancer Alley is an area along the Mississippi River between Baton Rouge and New Orleans which contains toxic petrochemical plants. A person that I met at a hospital in Baton Rouge told me that in this area out of every 10 houses, there's a ratio of one or two people who have died of cancer.

The surgeon talks about the results from the magnetic resonance imaging, his examination and cell tests. I want to maintain a sense of hopefulness. He says that the tumor has not spread to other parts of my body. I will be scheduled for surgery during the summer. This surgery should be enough and take both radiation and chemotherapy out of the equation I feel such a feeling of relief and hope hearing this.

We go on vacation to Legoland and the beautiful art community of Skagen in northern Denmark. We are standing on a white, sandy beach when the sun sets. An orange glow fills the sky. It lights up Maria's and the girls' faces. These moments with my family are so valuable and will help me in the upcoming surgery.

Once we are back home, I start preparing for the surgery and rehabilitation that will take place after. It's time for the surgery. I clean my skin taking three showers. I stay in the hospital. Sadly, my cancer surgery is cancelled. I feel a little bit disappointed. I go home in a taxi. I call Maria who is happy that I'm coming home. She needs me to do something. Maria asks me if I can get up into a crane to bring down our cat. I answer that I'm on my way and will be there shortly.

See you then. Goodbye dear, Maria says.

When the taxi stops outside our home a huge crane vehicle is standing next to our apartment building. Our cat sits five meters up in the air. I step out of the taxi and walk straight into the crane box. The crane operator lifts me up in the air. Our cat looks terrified in the tree. She takes quick steps backwards when I come closer. I'm almost losing her. I grab her swiftly and hold her softly in the crane box when we go down. We thank the crane operator and go inside with the cat.

A few days later, I'm back at the hospital to go

through with the cancer surgery. In my drugged condition, I soon fall asleep. The surgeon removes the cancer tumor. The first days after the surgery, I'm given morphine which makes me sleepy. I take pain medication for six months. My thigh heals fast. I go to the nursing practitioner several times per week before work. She cleans my surgery wound. The hole in my shoulder stays open for half a year and finally heals.

At the hospital, I empathize with the cancer patients in my ward. Two of the cancer patients in my room died that summer. I saw a teenage girl with cancer in a wheelchair. Looking back at the cancer period, it made me feel stronger because I was faced with an end-of-life situation. A part of me still believed I could get through it. My concern for my own life made me more compassionate. I stayed hopeful that I would live and that all would be good in the end. Faith helped me to not go under. As my cancer observation period came to an end, I could look back through each phase of my journey. I could now say that I have survived cancer. I have over the years built a close friendship with my surgeon.

12 NEW ORLEANS

New Orleans, 2014

Mary and I drive to New Orleans. Maria has instructed us to get Mary's birth card in the Vital Records Central Office at the Department of Health. The closer we get to the French Quarter the thicker the traffic becomes. I get off the highway and park. We walk into the office and sit down to wait for Mary's turn. Mary explains her errand to the officer. After Mary get her birth certificate, Mary and I drive to a Creole cookery. We listen to the jazz pianist playing in the restaurant. Mary and I sit in holy silence deeply enjoying the music and the delicious pan seared red fish. The red fish is served with succotash, lump crab meat and creole sauce. I have Praline Bread Pudding and Mary has Peach Cobbler for dessert.

Mary always brings her rosary wherever she goes. We pray to God for the unbelievable meal. Thank you Jesus. We make the sign of the cross taking our time, thinking of what we're doing. We let it take in our whole beings, our bodies, souls, minds, wills, thoughts, and feelings.

The heart of Louisiana Creole culture is food. Mary and I love creole food. This is a style of cooking originating in Louisiana. Like the people, Louisiana Creole cuisine is a blend of the various cultures of New Orleans including West African, French, Spanish, Caribbean, and Native American. Creole cooking use seafood found in and around the Mississippi River including crawfish, oysters, flounder, and redfish. Creole gumbo is based on the French roux which is mixed with okra, celery, onion, and bell pepper. Gumbo can have French Andouille sausage, seafood and meat like shrimp, crab, and chicken. Andouille is the name for Cajun Sausage made with coarse-grained smoked meat using pork, pepper, onions, and seasonings. Spanish and Native American spices such as paprika and cayenne pepper are used. The last part of cooking gumbo is to add filé powder or gumbo filé made of ground, Native American sassafras leaves.

Mary and I leave the restaurant. We cruise the French Quarter and love it. The houses are so beautiful. The Creole architecture has lace iron balconies, sweeping fan-light windows and traces of French and Spanish influences. We listen to jazz on the radio. We sing improvised songs together. That's something that Mary and I have in common. We love to play and laugh. We pass the historic destination for traditional New Orleans jazz lovers Preservation Hall.

New Orleans can be an evil and messed up city. Destruction, shootings, mental illness and drugging crack cocaine, heroin and meth can mess people up. We see homeless people on the streets. Everyone doesn't have a chance in New Orleans.

Mary and I stop at a café to have cafe au lait with chicory. The woody and nutty tasting chicory café au lait and the warm beignets, deep-fried dough confections, topped with powdered sugar taste wonderful.

Mary and I listen to street artists and musicians performing jazz, zydeco, and rhythm and blues. When we walk back to the car we see people walking into streetcars. We keep on cruising and pass Labranche House. It's one of my favorite buildings in the Big Easy. This house has multi-level patterned balconies with oak leaves and acorns woven into the ironwork. The curved balcony is made of the wrought iron lace, typical of New Orleans in the 1830's. We pass the St. Louise Cathedral, a 1724 church overlooking Jackson Square in the French Quarter.

We pass the Lafayette Cemetery No. 1 in the garden district. We go for a short walk under the magnificent oaks of New Orleans' historic City Park to visit New

Orleans Museum of Art and the Besthoff Sculpture Garden.

When it's time for supper, Mary and I stop at another Creole restaurant having a warming seafood filé gumbo with crabmeat, shrimp, and oysters. We both look so happy eating. We sit together in complete silence again. The waiter comes with our desserts. I have chocolate dipped Cannolis topped with pistachios. Mary has Bananas Foster with butter, cinnamon, brown sugar, and bananas made in a pan adding dark rum and banana liqueur. The flames flared. I see the excitement building up in Mary before the caramelized mixture is plated along with a scoop of vanilla ice cream. Mary and I drool. We're both in love with Bananas Foster, but I wanted to try something new this evening. We drink cappuccinos with the desserts. I love New Orleans.

In the car, we listen to Juliet's favorite song Stardust. It's a jazz song composed by the American singer, songwriter, and musician Hoagy Carmichael. Mary closes her eyes. I can see that she's exhausted after this busy day. Mary says that she and Juliet used to sing the song Goodbye, My Lover, Goodbye sung by Bing Crosby and the Jesters. I see that Mary is getting sleepier and sleepier. The blues guitar impresario Robert Johnson plays on the radio. He is brilliant. His spirit is with me and Mary when she is going to sleep in the darkness. We're driving over the wetlands and the swamplands in the heart of the Deep South.

13 TWENTY DOLLARS

West Sweden and Louisiana, 2014-2016

Mary keeps on falling in Louisiana. She falls in the elevator and on the sidewalk on the way to church. Mary is admitted to the hospital.

Maria wakes me up at 4 a.m. She tells me that she used my debit card to buy airplane tickets to New Orleans. I ask her to talk to me before she orders airline tickets for more than 2000 US dollars. This was half of our money. Now we can't pay for all the bills in Sweden this month. That means that the utility company will turn off the electricity in the house.

Three days later I land in New Orleans. I get a rental car and drive to the hospital. Mary and I are happy to see each other. I talk to her physician. He has diagnosed her with dementia and ataxia which is another word for unsteady walk. Mary gets a stroller that we bring when checking out and walking over to the rental car. I help Mary into the car.

I feel sick, Karl, Mary says.

Mary vomits all over her clothes, the passenger seat, and the floor. I help Mary to clean herself and the car. I give Mary 200 dollars. When we arrive at the senior housing complex Mary gives away several twenty dollar bills I gave her to other seniors in the apartment complex. I forgot that she always gives away money that I give her. I tell her to say that she doesn't have any money to give when someone ask her for money. If the person keeps on asking her for money, she can tell him or her that she needs the money to pay for her high healthcare bills.

The next day, I help Mary to get home care with a social worker, a nurse, physical therapist, an occupational therapist and apply for Medicaid. We celebrate July 4th together.

When I return to Sweden Maria is psychotic with

delusions. She closes doors between myself and the girls when I talk to them. Maria talks over me if I talk to Bianca and Heidi. She stands in front of me to block any contact between us. If Maria doesn't start to take her anti-psychotic medication I'm thinking about divorcing her.

What will it take to make this work? I haven't had a good night's sleep for weeks. After caring for Mary in Louisiana I was flying home without staying in hotels. Instead, I slept and rested on airport floors. Maria has removed over 700 of my Facebook contacts. I am so exhausted because of her delusional behaviors.

Two days later, I tell Maria that I want a divorce. This is when Maria loses it. Suddenly she jumps on me without any notice. Maria physically assaults me and scratches my face all over. I bleed. She does not stop. My skin is raw and peeled in several places. I am scared to death, looking at her behavior. I have eleven large areas on my face where the skin has been ripped off. Bianca wants me to report the abuse to the police. I wait and take photos of my face. I never report the abuse. Maria doesn't realize what she has done. She never says she's sorry for what she has done to me. I feel emotionally and physically drained.

After going to Louisiana, we can't afford to pay our electric bills. We have no electricity in the main house. Bills in my name go to the repro office and I get penalty charges.

Bianca receives a summer job offer at the local pre-school. Maria is upset.

My daughter is not going to change any baby diapers, she says.

This makes Bianca very sad. I argue for Bianca to take the job at the pre-school, but Maria psychotically wears us all down. Bianca decides to not take the pre-school job because of the fear she feels of being controlled by Maria. I'm feeling so bad inside that Maria's psychosis is affecting both Bianca and Heidi in extremely negative ways.

The following week, I find a bag with a thick pile with bills in my name. Maria has used my debit card and applied for many credit cards in my name, without telling me. She has bought clothes and shoes for herself for over one hundred thousand dollars!!!. We have a family meeting to talk about the financial situation which is rapidly getting worse.

After that, I start a house painting company. I paint five houses in the area where we live. We still can't pay all the bills. I apply for a payment plan with the Swedish government. I need to pay for this plan for many years until I become debt free. Maria's exclusive shoes and clothes are everywhere. She doesn't even wear them.

Mary is doing bad again. I need to fly to Louisiana again to care for her. After buying the airfare the money situation is worse than before. I have only twenty dollars left in my wallet to travel back and forth to Mary in Louisiana. Having this little money will have many dangerous consequences for me. I will not have any extra money for anything on the trip. Everything needs to flow. Otherwise, I will be stuck in London, New York City or Atlanta without having any money. My 27-hour travel day from Sweden to Baton Rouge, Louisiana, will be one of the trickiest of the year. I plan it out to the minute.

I will fly to London early in the morning the next day. I can't afford a hotel, so I leave immediately that evening. I get on the bus. I use my bus card for work that I have already paid for. I don't have money to take the airport bus. Instead, I need to get off on the highway as close as possible to the airport outside Gothenburg. After getting off the bus, I need to walk nine miles on the highway in total darkness and pouring rain.

Trucks and cars drive very close to me on the highway. I risk getting hit and killed over and over.

I'm soaking wet when I make it to the airport. I sit down inside the arrival hall where the air conditioning is on. I'm still wet and it's freezing. It's only me and some refugees from Syria in the arrival hall. I sit down in a chair and close my eyes.

Early in the morning, I fly from Gothenburg to London, and later to New York City. I rest on a hard and cold bench inside the cold airport in Newark. A woman with mental health problems walks next to me back and forth and screams most of the night. I get up at 4 a.m. to get ready to fly to Atlanta and Baton Rouge.

Mary and I are happy to see each other again. We participate in the Thanksgiving Dinner of the Council on Aging. I sit opposite to a lawyer that contributed to ending school segregation between black and white pupils in Baton Rouge in the 1960s. It's fascinating to listen to his experiences. I give Mary my 20 dollars which is the only money I have. When we return to her apartment complex she gives away the 20 dollars to one of her friends. My memory is short. I totally forgot that she gives away her money all the time. That is one of the reasons she often doesn't have any money. It's good to be generous, but Mary doesn't need to create constant precarious life situations for herself by giving away her money. We walk back to her apartment. I cook red beans and rice.

The next day, Mary and I get on a bus to go to a senior center. I use my last coins on the bus. A few minutes later, Mary is paranoid and accuses me in front of all the bus passengers. She says that I have taken 20 dollars from her. I have not taken 20 dollars from her. I remind Mary that I gave her 20 dollars that she gave away to another lady at the apartment complex. I feel insulted. I know that Mary has mental health problems, but still. Mary goes from being polite to delusional the next moment. I'm so fed up with having a delusional mother-in-law and wife. I want to leave them both alone and move on with my life. When we arrive at the senior center we talk to Mary's best friend who is the senior center coordinator. She is my dear friend too and we're so happy to see each other again. Mary and I stay there during the day and walk around to chat with all the seniors.

After chatting with the coordinator and the seniors I rethink my relationships with Mary and Maria from a positive viewpoint. Thanks to Maria and Mary I've grown as a person to for example standing up for myself and the family and praying to face fears and worries in life.

The next day, Mary and I are hanging out in the lobby of the apartment complex. Ruby walks up to Mary. This is the first time I see Ruby since 2006. I walk up to her to give her a hug. Ruby walks backwards. A large group of seniors stand around us and look forward to seeing Ruby and me hugging. Ruby refuses to hug me. She smirks.

Ruby! Don't be so ugly to Mary's son-in-law. Mr. Karl is always nice to Mary and us. Why are you acting like this? An older man says.

Ruby makes a cold smeared face. I walk up to Ruby again and give her a hug.

It was nice seeing you, Ruby, I say.

Ruby is quiet. I can see a tiny smile in her face. Theoretically, Ruby could have replied, you too, Karl, but she doesn't. I respond to myself in my head, you, too, Karl. I don't need to be desperate with Ruby.

Ruby, that wasn't too bad. Karl is nice, huh? the man says.

Ruby smiles at the man. Mary is so happy to see that Ruby and I hugged. A moment of reconciliation is possible.

When I'm about to fly back to Sweden I find some American coins in my suitcase from previous visits to Louisiana. My flight to Atlanta at daybreak is leaving at 4:30 a.m. I need to take the last bus to the airport in the evening. Hopefully I can stay at the airport before I fly. I get on the bus and chat with the female bus driver. She tells me that this last bus from downtown Baton Rouge is not going to the airport. It goes to Southern University. The distance between Southern University and the airport is 5 miles. The bus driver says that it's not safe for me to walk on that road in the middle of the night because the neighborhood is very crime-ridden. She says that she doesn't want to read in the newspaper the next day that a Swedish man was killed near the airport. The bus driver offers me to stay on her bus the entire evening. She promises to drive me to the airport after her shift in her car. I stay on the bus chatting with her. After her shift three hours later, she drives me to the airport. I thank her so much for her kindness. The security guard doesn't want to let me in the airport until the morning.

There is no one inside the airport building, he says.

I'm pleading to be able to stay inside the building.

Okay, you can stay here on the bench just inside the door during the night. Don't go anywhere. Do you understand? There is a bathroom, he says and points to a door.

Yes Sir. Thank you very much. I'm so grateful, I reply.

I sit down on the metal bench. It's very cold under the air conditioning, but I'm very happy to be inside the airport. When the airport opens early in the morning I move to a leather sofa in the baggage reclaim area. I go to sleep for thirty minutes. I wake up drooling with passengers all around me. My hair looks wild. I wash off and walk to the Atlanta gate. I land in Sweden the next day.

14 EVICTION NOTICE

West Sweden and Louisiana 2017

Maria is taking her anti-psychotic medication. She is feeling better. Maria writes a letter to Mary:

Dear Mary. How are you? I am fine. I am writing to you because I thought that you might want a letter. I'm writing from a coffee shop. Later today, I'll print out pictures of Bianca and Heidi to mail to you. There is a lot of snow outside which I'll be walking in after I leave the coffee shop. It has been an unusually cold day today for this winter, but overall, it has been quite warm compared to previous winters. I'm going to the library after the coffee shop. It's a nice library in a rather small town. I'll write more later.

Love, Maria

Later in the spring, Mary receives a notice to vacate from her apartment building from the director of the building:

Dear Mrs. Guillory:

On March 3rd, 2017, you received a letter regarding the deplorable condition of your apartment. A recheck inspection date was given to you and after two weeks from your initial apartment check, I returned to the unit. Listed below are the items that were still not cleaned: Kitchen stove, Refrigerator, Kitchen Floor, Countertops, Dirty dishes in sink, Cabinets still have dead roaches and fecal matter, cabinet drawers were still dirty, carpet needs professionally cleaned, toilet needs cleaned and disinfected, bathtub, lavatory, bathroom floor, organize closet, and remove dead roaches from the unit. This letter serves as a notice that your lease is being terminated and that you have 30 days to notify me of your intention to formally vacate and not return to the apartment.

Mary explains to me and Maria that if she doesn't notify the director about this a rule to evict will be filed with the Baton Rouge Court. Mary is worried. Even if I'm on the phone I can hear Mary's hands shaking. I've been with Mary in the apartment when she is anxious and seen her hands shaking whilst talking on the telephone. Mary knows a lady who has a cleaning company. I say that I can pay the lady to help Mary clean so she can stay in the apartment.

Mary talks about her residential insecurity with her doctor and asks for help. The doctor talks to the director of the apartment complex. She convinces the director to let Mary stay in the building. We're so grateful. I start transferring money every month to Mary so she can pay for cleaning costs to prevent a future eviction notice. One month later when I talk to Mary on the phone she tells me that she passed the inspection of the apartment.

I fly to New Orleans. I'm having dinner at the creole cooking heaven Dooky Chase's Restaurant in Tremé. I'm having Creole Gumbo and Chicken a la Dooky with boneless breast of chicken stuffed with oyster dressing, baked slowly in marchand de vin sauce, served with sweet potatoes. I visit Preservation Hall in the French Quarter to enjoy jazz. I continue to the lively crowds at Tipitina's to listen and dance to blues, jazz, soul, and funk. I go to sleep smilingly.

I visit Mary the next day. We are invited to my friend and her family for supper. Mary feels so happy to be included. We have so much fun. Mary has been feeling lonely recently. After staying with Mary, I fly to San Francisco.

I stay with my friends in Oakland and call Mary every day. My friends and I visit the San Francisco Museum of Modern Art. I especially enjoy looking at artwork by my favorite artist Mark Rothko. I return home to Maria and the girls.

Mary receives a new eviction letter. Maria and I talk about how we can contribute to residential security for Mary. She lives in a retirement facility designed to provide an independent living environment for seniors of low income in downtown Baton Rouge. Her neighborhood is quiet. She walks to every mass at the Catholic church nearby.

Mary tells us that she will be evicted from her apartment in one week from now. She has received the final disposure action letter. Mary explains that that she will have to leave because of roaches in the apartment. She says that she didn't bring the roaches to the building or her apartment. The roaches came from other apartments.

Mary's hospital doctor visits her. She spots few roaches in the apartment. The doctor says that Mary's apartment looks good. She says that only those few roaches are not enough to put Mary out of her apartment as a senior citizen. The doctor says that they should keep Mary in the apartment because they are supposed to protect low-income seniors in this facility.

A few days later, I travel with Maria to Louisiana. I have travelled to Mary in Louisiana for a decade to look after her. When we arrive in Louisiana I visit the director of apartment complex. She tells me that Mary forgot to turn off the stove when frying eggs causing smoke. After that, the director gave Mary the final eviction notice. I understand the director. Maria and I clean out Mary's apartment and move her furniture to an apartment that Maria and I lease close to the campus of Louisiana State University.

After living in Sweden for a decade, Maria decides to move back to the United States to care for Mary. Maria wants me to get a green card and move to her in Louisiana at a later point. I need the green card to obtain employment in the United States. Our nice apartment is in a quaint area called College Town. Maria thinks about and misses Bianca and Heidi, but she feels that she needs to be in Baton Rouge for Mary's sake. Bianca is already an adult and Heidi will be an adult in three months. Maria says that they can come to visit her and Mary for Easter and during the summers. I tell Maria that I don't want to move to Baton Rouge right now. I want to live in Sweden with Bianca and Heidi. I have a wonderful job as a university professor. I tell Maria that I love the people, the culture, and the nature of South Louisiana. Louisiana will always be my second home in the world. Maria smiles and understands my decision.

I love you and I'm gonna miss you, Maria, I say when I hug her.

I always love you, Karl. I'm gonna miss you too. I just need to do this for Mary. I want her to feel safe, Maria says.

I understand, I reply. I'm thinking about Maria and Mary when I fly back to Europe. I hope they will be okay.

15 MOVING TO SWEDEN

Louisiana and West Sweden, 2018

Maria stays with Mary for five months in the apartment. Maria was first working in a sandwich shop close to the apartment. After a while Maria doesn't feel good. She doesn't know what it is. Maria can't work as fast as the manager wants her to work so she can't stay at the job. Her intention was to stay in the United States and not to move back to Sweden.

Maria informs me that she is not strong enough to care for Mary and work at the same time. She says that she wants to return to Sweden with Mary. This means that Mary will soon live in a rural Swedish community with us. Her life will be very different. I'm thinking about what will happen when she comes here.

A couple of days later, I'm talking on the phone with Maria and Mary in Louisiana. I hear a hard knock on the door after 10 p.m. a Friday night. My sister and her tall muscular body and extraordinary tall bouncer looking boyfriend with minimal impulse control knock on the door. Their visit is unexpected. They walk into the house with frustration and anger. They push themselves into the house and follow me to the kitchen. I sit in a chair beside the window. My sister and her boyfriend sit down at the table. The air is heavy and tense. Maria is still on the speaker of the phone with me.

First there is silence. Then they threaten to evict us. My sister sits down at the window side of the table. Her boyfriend stands up and radiates aggression towards me. His eyes widen. He shouts that they have sent an application to the Enforcement Authority to evict us. His expression is impatient and irritated. I sit in a corner in the kitchen. He stands in front of me. Maria talks from the speaker of the phone saying that we intend to stay. I confirm what

Maria says. This makes my sister's boyfriend even more angry. He has extremely low self-control. Any spark can ignite his rage to hit me. He takes a step forward and looks down at me. His face is filled with rage and his huge body presses against the kitchen table. He tilts the table with the heavy weight of his body and grunts. I'm feeling uneasy, cramped, and threatened.

Bianca and Heidi are hiding in their bedrooms. They are scared. I think about why I let these two into the house. The situation becomes more and more tense. How long is this going to last? Finally, my sister tells her boyfriend, Come on. Let's go.

He grunts again and looks at me one more time with fury all over his face. He points aggressively at me before he walks out of the kitchen. After they leave the house, I lock the entrance door immediately and go to talk to the girls. They are scared about what just happened. I feel very uncomfortable and guilty that I was so naïve to let them in. I failed to protect my daughters. I call Maria and update her about what happened.

I send Maria the remainder of my wages for them to take the train from New Orleans to Chicago. Maria brings Mary onto the train all the way to Chicago. In Chicago they renew their US passports. I contact two dear friends in Chicago. They let Maria and Mary stay with them. They stay for a week to recuperate before the trip to Sweden. I don't have enough money to pay for their airline tickets. I ask one of the hosts if he can lend me the airfare. He buys the tickets. I promise to pay him back when I get my next university salary.

Maria and Mary get on the airplane to London. Mary sits next to an Englishman. She chats and flirts with him. In London, Mary refuses to get on the aircraft to Sweden. Mary is chatting with another polite and good-looking Englishman. Maria is exhausted and gives up her attempts to convince

Mary to get on the plane. Maria calls me and says, I don't know if I can do this. I give up.

All the passengers get on the plane. At the airfield, Mary refuses to get on the plane. Maria leaves Mary and get on the plane. The airline hostesses convince Mary to get onto the plane at the last minute. She sits down and the plane takes off. Mary goes to sleep immediately. So does Maria a few minutes later.

Maria and Mary arrive in Sweden. It's a warm evening just before the Midsummer celebration. Maria says that the immigration officer gave Mary a visa valid for one year. I believe Maria and never check Mary's passport. We are all happy and excited to see each other. They are exhausted after the long journey. Mary sits in a wheelchair. I get the car.

How was your flight from London? I ask.

Awful. It wasn't easy to get Mary onto the plane. She didn't want to get on, Maria says.

I didn't have a car to pick up Maria and Mary in. I asked my mother if I could use her car. She said that she didn't want to lend me her car because everything is so difficult in her life. I called a friend family. They let me use one of their cars.

On the way home to the country house, we talk without stopping. The only thing Mary can see along the highway are thousands of pine trees.

I have seen moose, roedeer, fox, lynx, and wolf in the forest, I tell Mary.

Jesus! Jesus! Jesus! Jesus will protect us from those wild animals, Mary exclaims.

We also have three sweet cats at the house, I say.

Mary is so happy about that. Maria smiles.

We arrive at the house. My childhood house was built in 1936. It is a yellow wooden house close to a river. Mary thinks the house is beautiful. She likes the garden with the apple trees and berry bushes.

Mary has only two teeth left after a life of drinking soda. I make pancakes. Mary puts more than a cup of sugar on every pancake and then licks the sugar from her teeth. She smiles at me.

Oh, these are good pancakes, Karl. Can I have another one? Mary says.

I serve Mary pancakes until she looks sleepy. I help her to her new bed in Sweden.

Are Swedes Christians? Mary asks.

Some of them are Christians. Others are Muslims, Buddhists or have other faiths. Some are unaffiliated. Some don't believe in God, I say.

WHAT? Mary asks and goes to sleep.

The next day, we celebrate their homecoming. I cook a gratin-style creamy potato-and-sprats casserole, called *Jansson's temptation* which Maria and Mary love. The dish is named after Pelle Janzon, a Swedish opera singer and celebrated foodie in the 1800s.

Mary is journeying off the English-speaking path. I give her the first words in Swedish for understanding the family members better and to grow her Swedish language confidence chatting with locals in the community.

Let's get talking Swedish, Mary, I say.

How to say pants in Swedish? Mary asks.

Byxor is the word for pants in Swedish. *BYXOR*, I say.

Byssor, Mary says and smiles.

Good. You almost had the correct pronunciation. *BYXOR*, I say.

Byssor, Mary says and laughs.

Mary reads the Bible all day long every day. She has dementia or decemia as she calls it. Mary remembers details of what happened in her life from the 1940s to the 1970s. She can't recollect what is going on right now. Mary adapts to a new life in Sweden without knowing the language and the customs. But does Mary care? No, she doesn't care because she is fine Louisiana beauty queen and has a sweet loving family that loves her very much. It's going to be alright. I think.

The housing arrangement is many times challenging and entertaining. Mary rushes around all over the house, in the garden and on the streets and roads in the community when she impatiently looks for dead family members and principals in the schools where she taught. Most of them died a long time ago. She screams and hollers because we don't give her answers right away. Mary talks about all the sexy boyfriends she loves and who love her. As summer days wane, a fragile bond between Mary and us develop.

Mary loves to pray to God. She loves to say the rosary and she has gone to holy communion every day for seventy years. Being in a new environment is making Mary manic and filled with high anxiety.

Oh God! Oh God! Oh God! Mary says pantingly.

Mary screams and squeaks in a falsetto flush roaring up into our ears. I think about how I can remain calm in this situation. I speak calmly with a caring voice. I don't react to Mary's insults. Mary usually reacts with strong resistance to everything I say. It's impossible to reason with her. If I criticize her she turns violent screaming or attacking me physically. Mary doesn't understand that she is ill. She shares this with Maria. Maria has had schizophrenia now for 18 years with psychotic episodes. She has never acknowledged that she has any mental health problems. At least I'm happy that Mary takes her anti-psychotic medication with her explanation that she is missing a chemical.

At times I feel that I'm breaking down. I do things to feel better. I walk out into nature close to where we live to reduce the stress. I love the fresh air in the forest. I can move the focus away from Mary to my own needs. I want to help myself before I totally break down. Walking in the woods help me to look at tense events with a fresh mind.

Mary was cute and charming when she first came to Sweden, but things take another turn. First Mary let people have a honeymoon when she praised the family members.

Mary commented on Bianca's green hair, Bianca, you could be a movie star.

She also praised Bianca's pancakes.

Mary's honeymoon phase always turns into chaos. Her frustrations about different things have bottled up. She has a rage problem. Mary's rage attacks affect the entire family. Mary takes over in every way. She follows us around the house. She torments us with endless talk about herself, squeaking and preaching her arguments in a charismatic TV pastor way. The attention needs to be on Mary. I need to think about how I react to her. I'm not going to let Mary stress me out. She's getting under my skin. I tense up and start to do nervous gestures. I put my right palm on my forehead as a routine gesture. I decide to be cool, calm, and collected, but I don't know if it is going to work.

Maria cooks a delicious gumbo that we enjoy. Mary needs a shower. I help her to the shower room. Mary takes off her clothes. She sits down on a plastic chair. I wash her hair and body. So far it has been working out well at home with Mary with her hygiene and toilet visits. She needs support to put on clothes and climb the stairs. Mary brushes her own hair. She dips her finger in a plastic box of Vaseline and applies it to her hair every morning. After that she applies a thick layer of lotion on her face, hands, and arms.

Shortly after that Maria returned to Sweden, she shows signs of entering a new psychotic episode. I wash sheets and towels. Because it's the summer and the sun shines, I hang them in the garden. Maria goes outside immediately after I have done that and takes them down. She puts everything in the dryer inside the house. I'm starting to worry about the electricity bill. I want to take the load out of the dryer, but I know that this will make Maria angry. We start to argue. I say that we can save money to air dry the bed clothes outside. Maria doesn't want to show the neighbors the sheets and towels. They are in her view private accessories. I say that the neighbors can't see them because of all the apple trees and bushes. And the argument continues.

Bianca wants to talk to me alone. Maria follows us and sits next to us controlling everything we do. Bianca wants Maria to start taking her anti-psychotic medication again. Maria has never in our relationship acknowledged that she has ever been having a psychotic episode and refuses to take any meds.

I don't need any medication. I'm fine, Maria says.

Maria and Mary left the furniture in our apartment in Baton Rouge when they left for Chicago. I call Mary's dearest friend to ask if she can help us to move the furniture out of the apartment. I pay her. She hires two men to move the furniture. We all feel relieved about having moved out of the Louisiana apartment. Mary's closest friend has been there for us the last decades.

Maria becomes more and more controlling at home. She doesn't let the girls talk to me. If we don't do exactly what Maria wants, she argues for hours. We all feel a lot of stress from this. Bianca views Maria as a dictator in a prison.

I take deep breaths to accept and adapt to the intense home situation with humor and strength. When they arrived, Maria told me that the Swedish immigration service issued a one-year visa upon arrival. Today, I look in Mary's passport and see that she only has a tourist visa valid for three months. After those three months she must go to another country before she can return to Sweden. If Mary is not leaving Sweden she will be an illegal immigrant. Maria plans for her and Mary to go to a convent in Ireland to stay there. When Maria is not psychotic she is very gifted in legal reasoning having gone to the UCLA School of Law. When she has a psychotic episode she argues from a delusional viewpoint. I suggest to Maria that she can get back on her medication. She refuses. Mary wants to be a good role model to Maria. I go with Mary to the nursing practitioner to get her monthly anti-psychotic shot.

16 HOMELESS

West Sweden, 2018

I call my mother to ask her if I can use her car to pick up Heidi from work. Heidi works in a nursing home nine miles away. Early this morning, Heidi biked to the nursing home. When she returns to her bike after her shift in the evening she sees that she has a flat tire. My mother doesn't want to loan us her car. She even tells me that she will never loan it to us. Fortunately, Heidi gets help from a friend to get home.

My biological family does not protect its own at any cost. My mother, sister, my sister's boyfriend and one of her daughters want to make us homeless. My mother asks me if we have received the letter from the Swedish Enforcement Authority yet. I say no. Since 2014, I have used a large portion of my university salary to pay for the electricity, water and sewer, garbage, chimney sweeper and all other costs for my mother's house that we live in. I have also paid the monthly rent for the house. I recently painted my mother's three-story house, investing hundreds of hours. I paid for the house paint and the painting equipment. At the same time, I paid for Maria and Mary's rent in Louisiana. When Maria stopped working in Baton Rouge I couldn't afford to pay the rent in full in Sweden for a short period. I now owe my mother some money that I will pay back to her as soon as possible. But she wants the money now.

I tell my mother that the Swedish Enforcement Authority pulls 1000 dollars every month from my salary to pay the debt from Maria's shopping spree in 2015. When Maria had a psychotic episode she used my debit card and ordered credit cards in my name. She maxed out the credit cards without informing me about any of the things she had done. Maria used the credit cards to buy shoes, clothes, interior design items and all kinds of things. Later I found a bag with bills from fifteen credit card companies. Maria always got the mail when I was at the university during the days and put the bills in a secret bag without telling me about it. I also explain that when Maria and Mary lived in the United States in 2018, I sent 1200 dollars per month to Maria so she could pay their rent in Louisiana for six months.

I explain to my mother that we have a rental contract and that we intend to stay in the house. I can pay the debt to her just in a few weeks. Everything will then go back to normal. My mother is not convinced. With the support of my sister, her boyfriend and one of my sister's daughters she wants us to leave the house immediately. My mother reminds me that they sent the application to the Swedish Enforcement Authority to evict us and that they want us out now.

The Swedish Enforcement Authority advises us in a letter that their officers will evict our family in a few days. My mother continues to threat to sell the house to make us homeless. Heidi and I walk over to my mother. We talk to her about the eviction notice and that I need a payment plan. I pay more than half the debt up front. I suggest that I can pay the rest (1300 dollars) in a payment plan. She says no. We walk back to the house. I write an invoice of 20000 dollars to my mother for the 350 hours that I spent painting her house and also add the 2500 dollars that I paid for the paint and equipment. I walk back to my mother and give her the invoice. She looks scared when she looks at the invoice.

My mother continues her threat to evict us. We all become very worried and vulnerable. What will happen? Where will we live? I'm usually able to maintain my cool when difficult things happen. This time I feel very stressed. I don't sleep. Heidi, Bianca, Maria, Mary, and I get different physical and psychological stress symptoms. Becoming homeless will be traumatic for us.

On the last day before the planned eviction my mother, Maria and I reach an agreement that is beneficial for all of us. We will be able to stay in the house. The deal is that I pay the most of my debt to my mother and have a short-term payment plan to pay back the rest of the money within two months. We also increase the monthly rent for the house. She calls the Swedish Enforcement Authority and says that she agrees to a payment plan with us so we can stay in the house.

This experience of residential insecurity has affected all of us in the family. In my case, my own biological family members have not been my allies. Instead, they have been my enemies and actively worked against us. I will never fully trust my mother, sister, her boyfriend and one of her daughters again after this incident. Bianca, Heidi, Maria, and Mary are the only people in the family I trust. I will not forget how massively stressful this was for us. I worry about possible negative health outcomes. Negative health consequences already include a lack of well-being in all of us in different ways including negative stress, anxiety, panic attacks and stomach aches.

My mother visits us to inform us that she met with my sister and her boyfriend and has changed her mind. She will continue with the eviction with the help of the Swedish Enforcement Authority. She wants to sell the house immediately. She tells us that we need to move out right away.

I walk back to my mother. I tell her that I will send the invoice for painting the house to the Swedish Enforcement Authority and that she needs to pay the invoice to me within 10 days. Finally, my mother agrees to the payment plan. I call the Swedish Enforcement Authority again to inform them that we have solved the problem. They cancel the eviction.

Maria, are you alright? I ask.

I don't feel good, Maria says.

You'll be fine. You'll be okay, I say.

I go outside in the garden and pick flowers for her.

For you, my love, I say when I give her the flowers.

Thank you, Maria replies and smiles.

I put the flowers in a vase.

Good night, I say and smile.

Good night, Maria says and smiles.

Maria doesn't want to hug or kiss or have any physical contact with me. She gets irritated by most of the things that I say. When I talk to Bianca and Heidi she tries to change the topic. This behavior affects all the conversations that I try to have with my daughters. It gets worse. Maria aggressively threatens Bianca.

I will destroy you little girl, Maria says.

It is so destructive of Maria to say these kinds of things to Bianca. I'm afraid of the effects of this ongoing phycological abuse by Maria together with the eviction stress that my mother, my sister, her boyfriend and one of my sister's daughters caused.

I have money worries. Maria argues with me to transfer my salary to her account. She stays awake all night until I do whatever she tells me. I need to go to the university in the mornings. I don't have the energy to stay awake having lengthy arguments about money. I feel exhausted. I have sent all the money to Maria. When I go to the grocery store to get food she wants me to call her just before I go to the cashier so she can transfer the amount to my bank card. Sometimes she doesn't answer. Other times she says that she has transferred the money for the food, but when I try to pay, the card gets declined. Every time I go to the store I worry about not being able to pay. I already have enough stress in my life.

After consulting with Bianca and Heidi I call the psychiatric ward at the hospital. I tell them about Maria's psychotic behaviors. The psychiatrist comes to visit Maria at the house. Maria thinks that there is nothing wrong with her.

Karl, why did you call the psychiatrist? Maria says.

The psychiatrist is diagnosing Maria as psychotic after spending time with Maria in the afternoon. Maria is repeatedly insulting the psychiatrist:

Are you really a psychiatrist? Where do you come from? You can hardly speak Swedish.

The psychiatrist calls the police to plan an involuntary psychiatric hold of Maria. One hour later, two police officers drive up to the house. I open the door for them. Maria walks out with the police officers to the police car. Before that happens Mary jumps up and pushes one of the police officers and screams:

YOU'RE NOT TAKING MY DAUGHTER.

Mary pushes the police officer many times. After the police and Maria leave for the hospital I sit down with Mary and talk to her about the dramatic events. She tells me about all the times she was taken by the police in Louisiana to go to the mental health hospitals.

It's the fall break. Bianca is on her way home from the university she is attending. The bus stops outside the house. Bianca knocks on the house door. Mary opens the door. Bianca arrived just in time to save Mary's life.

I'm choking on a cough drop, Mary says.

Bianca helps the choking Mary having trouble breathing. Bianca positions herself behind Mary. Bianca wraps her arms around her waist. She bends Mary slightly forward at her waist. Bianca makes a fist with one of her hands. She places the thumb side of her fist between Mary's belly button and the lowest part of her ribs. Bianca puts her other hand over her fist. Bianca performs abdominal thrusts on Mary. She presses her fist into Mary's abdomen with quick inward and upward thrusts. Bianca's Heimlich maneuver on Mary pushes air out of her lungs and makes her cough. The force of the cough moves the cough drop out of her airway. Bianca saves Mary's life. Bianca learnt how to do the Heimlich maneuver in 4th grade. She feels surprised and gratitude that her grandmother is alive. Mary thanks Bianca for saving her life. When I return home I go to the living room to thank Bianca. I call her a heroine.

Heidi makes chocolate oatmeal balls. She puts them in the refrigerator to cool. Later, Mary looks in the refrigerator to pick out some food to cook. She thinks that the chocolate oatmeal balls are rolled meatballs. Mary puts them into the tomato sauce that she is cooking together with the spaghetti on the stove. We sit down to eat her food. Mary is proud of her cooking. We taste the sweetness in the balls. Silently we understand what has happened. It makes us break out into a joint laughter. Mary doesn't understand what is going on. She has just invented the perfect supper and dessert all into one dish: Chocolate oatmeal balls in tomato sauce with spaghetti.

Maria is doing fine taking the anti-psychotic medication. Maria and I are going bowling with the girls. We're having so much fun.

17 TERMINAL BRAIN CANCER

West Sweden, 2019-2020

Maria is weak in the beginning of January 2019. She has been sick with the flu. Maria is incontinent and pees in the bed at 4 a.m. in the morning. I help Maria to a chair when I change her night clothes and the sheets in the bed.

Mary gets up at the same time after 4 a.m. She starts doing dishes very loudly in the kitchen. I walk upstairs and ask Mary to go back to bed and do the dishes during the day. I tell her that Maria is sick, and we all need to rest.

SHUT UP, KARL. I WANT TO DO THE DISHES NOW, Mary screams.

Mary keeps on doing the dishes for another twenty minutes. Tears run from my eyes, but I keep it together.

Maria collapses in the bathroom. I help her to get up. Her legs begin to falter. She leans back at me. I love her and I want her to be okay. I take Maria to the emergency room at the hospital. I sit next to Maria and pray to God that she will get well. Maria meets with a physician. The physician sends Maria to the psychiatric ward. Maria meets a Polish psychiatrist who is also trained as a physician in medicine. He admits Maria to the psychiatric clinic and arrange for Maria to get a magnetic resonance imaging to diagnose Maria's medical condition.

Maria gets the magnetic resonance imaging. It shows that Maria has a large tumor in her brain. She is sent instantly in an ambulance to an oncology hospital in Gothenburg.

Maria is having her brain tumor surgery. The surgeon removes most of the tumor. The surgery went okay, but the situation looks bad and challenging. Things quickly take an even darker turn. When Maria wakes up, we're seeing her oncologist.

It's not the best news, the surgeon says.

Maria is diagnosed with a malignant brain tumor. She has glioblastoma multiforme grade 4. The surgeon says that Maria will receive treatments to delay its progression.

The surgeon tells us that the brain tumor could have caused the psychotic episodes that Maria has suffered the last decades. When Maria and I are alone I say, If we had known that you had brain cancer and you were treated much earlier maybe you would have never had the psychotic episodes. I'm so very sorry, Maria.

Surprisingly, Maria's face is shining up. When the surgeon gives the explanation that the brain tumor is a possible cause of her mental illness Maria has the liberating realization that is helping her to overcome the mental health stigma that she has been struggling with the last decades. We don't say anything. She has experienced internal pain, loneliness, depression, anxiety, and isolation. I'm amazed that Maria always remains hopeful. She has a strong faith in Jesus.

My biological family and so many others have judged her for decades due to her mental illness. Maria's psychotic episodes caused a lack of understanding by many people of what Maria was going through including me over the years. Both Maria and Mary have experienced negative attitudes and beliefs toward their mental health struggles. They have received supportive love from Bianca, Heidi, and me. Judgments from others about Maria and Mary stem from a lack of knowledge and understanding of mental illness. They are so much more than their mental illnesses. I also realize my own role in not understanding Maria. At the same time, I needed to protect the girls and have time for self-care to be able to cope in life.

Mary has wanted to seek help and treatment for her mental illness. Maria has never acknowledged that she has had any mental health problems. She always thought that she was completely healthy. Maria never understood why I called the psychiatric clinic to ask for help when she was psychotic. She never thought she needed psychiatric care. All these times when she was admitted to the psychiatric clinics we had do it by force, when the police came to our home to pick her up.

When Maria took her anti-psychotic medication she was acting normal, loving, and caring. Often she stopped with the anti-psychotic medication after staying at the hospital and then had new psychotic episodes. Maria's psychosis stopped her from having deeper relationships and trusting me and others. The psychosis made it difficult for her to find work and keep a job. Mary usually took her anti-psychotic medication. She learned to accept her condition and recognized the steps she needed to take to treat it.

Maria is admitted to the oncology hospital in Gothenburg. She begins her thirty radiation treatments. She will get five radiation treatments per week.

Later, Maria becomes weaker and weaker. She comes home to us in the weekends. I visit her in the oncology ward during the weeks.

Maria gets the last radiation treatment and is totally exhausted. She returns home. We are all so happy that she is with us again.

Mary refuses to believe that Maria has cancer. In anger, Mary throws her wet incontinence pad in Maria's face in the kitchen. Maria reacts by starting to turn around fast in a circle. Maria's eyes blink. Her entire body is cramping in spasms. She is falling. I catch Maria before she hits her head on the refrigerator. She has her first epileptic attack. I call the emergency number. The nurse instructs me what to do until the ambulance arrives to pick up Maria.

Maria is breathing heavily for more than 20 minutes when we wait for the ambulance. Saliva is running out of her mouth. Maria can't speak at all for over thirty minutes. The ambulance arrives. At the hospital Maria is getting a CAT scan.

I talk to Maria on the phone.

You're coming home soon, baby. I love you so much, I say and cry.

I'm coming home soon. I love you, Karl, Maria replies.

I can hear that Maria is crying hard.

Maria is coming home to us. Maria and I go to the wig maker. He makes a beautiful wig for Maria. She smiles and shines. Maria will receive home care with doctors, nurses, and nursing assistants from now on.

Maria begins her first chemotherapy which will be one of many for the coming year. She is also doing regular magnetic resonance imaging scans.

Bianca is in the living room and Mary enters. She looks hostile towards Bianca. Mary continues to follow Bianca several times around the table. Bianca is scared that Mary is going to hit her.

Mary is playful sometimes which is charming, but usually she screams disturbing the family. Bianca puts on the speaker to drown out Mary's squeaking. Another strategy that Bianca uses is to put on math problems on YouTube videos to distract Mary. Mary laughs dark and gloomy.

Mary stands at the break of day and waits for Bianca. She traumatizes Bianca by pulling her hair, following her around the house and trying to control what kind of food Bianca makes and eats.

Stop it, Mary! Bianca says.

Mary bangs on Bianca's door when she is busy and screams, Bianca! Bianca! Open! Open!

In the days that follow, Mary becomes more abusive to all of us. She bangs on Bianca's door every day. Bianca feels like a captive at home with Mary. Mary abuses Bianca verbally.

When I'm at work Mary screams at Bianca, You're nasty. You're stupid.

Another time Mary follows Bianca around the house and threatens to kill her. I feel helpless when I need to go to work and know that Mary will probably harass Bianca. Mary doesn't care when Bianca says no.

Mary damage other people. She hits a terminally ill Maria. What I can do protect Maria and the rest of us? The uncertainty is ever-present. We know that Mary has dementia and mental health problems, but it's draining us to care for her having no or minimal impulse control.

In December 2019, Maria receives the fantastic news from her oncologist that she is cancer free. We are cheering together. Hopefully Maria will stay cancer free. Because Maria is cancer free we feel a burst of hope. We celebrate and have a lovely Christmas holiday.

There's always hope, Maria, I say.

Maria and Bianca sit in the kitchen and drink coffee. Mary is doing the dishes and says:

Maria, have you seen your mother? She's got a nice ass. Maria and Bianca look at Mary and at each other and smile.

Maria wants me and Bianca to fly to London for a few days. This is Bianca and Maria's dream. Maria is happy to experience London through Bianca's eyes even if she has cancer. Bianca and I stay at a hotel on Earl's Court. At National Gallery by Trafalgar Square, we admire paintings by Goya, Renoir, Rembrandt, Turner, van Gogh, and da Vinci. We visit Chinatown. The next day we go to Victorian afternoon tea at Victoria and Albert Museum. We end the evening at The Jazz Café in Camden listening to a band playing music by David Bowie. The next day we go to British Museum and Tate Britain. With new experiences we fly back home to Maria, Heidi, and Mary. Maria is so excited to see us again and to listen to Bianca's stories from the trip.

In the winter evening we find a letter in the mailbox.

Mary's dearest friend in Louisiana Alice has sent a letter to Mary. Mary is so happy to read that her friend misses her and that she views her as close as a sister. They love each other. I'm so grateful for Alice who is also my friend. When Maria and I have been in Sweden Alice cared for Mary in Louisiana. Maria suffered multiple psychotic episodes over the last decades and hasn't been able to visit Mary. I've been visiting Mary and looking after her, but Alice has done the most for Mary over the years. She invited Mary, Maria, and I to celebrate New Year's 2018 with her.

Maria and I celebrate our 23rd wedding day. Will this be our last wedding anniversary together? Will Maria survive another year?

Mary has been manic for a week. She usually stays manic for a week at a time. She lays down in Bianca's bed. I ask Mary to use her own bed. Mary is provoked by me asking her to move. She gets a large wooden hairbrush and hits it hard in a table. When I ask her again to get up from Bianca's bed she hits me and I get bruised.

We celebrate Mardi Gras Day with a family dinner. We cook a seafood gumbo and barbecued shrimp in New Orleans-style with lemon and pepper sauce. For dessert we eat Fat Tuesday rolls called *semla*. It's a wheat flour bun flavored with cardamom and filled with almond paste and whipped cream. Maria loves *semla*. She smiles.

Maria, Bianca, and I drive to a mountain and look at the beautiful view. I go with Maria to her magnetic resonance imaging scan of her brain.

We celebrate Maria's 47th birthday. We kiss passionately. We talk about the chemotherapy and her pain of losing the hair.

Heidi gets her driving license. Maria, Bianca, and I are so happy with Heidi. The Covid-19 pandemic continues. Maria's planned checkups, and MRIs are delayed with disastrous consequences for her.

Maria and I go to see her oncologist. She diagnoses Maria with brain cancer again. The CT scan shows new cancer tumors. The oncologist points to the image and says that the brain tumors are growing. Maria has pain in her ribs. We are all feeling so sad. We're all breaking in different ways. Maria begins a new chemotherapy treatment.

Chafing winds with snowflakes whirl around the house. Mary sits in her kitchen chair and eats her morning oatmeal.

Karl, give me more oatmeal, she says.

I serve her more oatmeal.

I need to go now. Otherwise, I'll miss the bus. Have a good day, Mary. I love you, I say.

Mary stands at the sink rinsing dishes.

My lover is coming soon. We're gonna have sex, Mary says.

Okay, good luck with that. Bye, Mary, I reply.

I run out and catch the bus.

Maria starts her second chemotherapy treatment.

In the beginning of June 2020, Maria receives a terminal brain tumor diagnosis from her oncologist. The oncologist recommends her to end the chemotherapy treatment as it is not working anymore. The doctor says that at this point it only gives detrimental side effects. She informs us that Maria will stop with all treatments.

Maria is going deeper into the cancer darkness. The cancer is spreading to her brain. She stops taking her chemotherapy medication. The brain cancer makes her weaker and weaker. This causes Maria and all of us in the family to think about what decisions we need to make in the end of her life, and what support we need to help us throughout this difficult time.

Maria lays on the bed. We have just bought the softest mattress in the bed store. I put my hand in her hand. Maria asks me to rub her body with the massage oil. I massage her all over her body for over two hours. Maria smiles. She loves the massage.

Maria goes to sleep. When I go upstairs to the kitchen which is next to Mary's bedroom and the bathroom, Mary asks:

How's Maria?

I reply with a low and calm voice, Maria is not doing well. The oncologists decided to stop her cancer treatments because they are not working anymore. The cancer is spreading in her brain. I hope that Maria will not suffer too much. She will become more and more sick. The oncologist said that the best thing for Maria now is that she is in a stable environment with low stress.

There is a long silence.

SHUT UP, KARL! Mary screams.

I feel like crying but can't.

I'm going downstairs to the basement to take a shower. When showering I can hear Maria crying. I get out of the shower and run upstairs. When I come into the bedroom I can see Mary hitting Maria while screaming:

MARIA, GET UP! GET UP! GET UP!

I lead Mary out of the bedroom and lock the bedroom door. Maria is crying hard. I'm lying down close to her and comfort her the rest of the day.

Maria becomes frailer day by day. It's difficult for me to understand what she is saying. Mary follows me around all over the house to convince me that Maria is getting better. Mary tells me that she doesn't believe in the cancer diagnosis by the oncologist.

Maria sits in the bathroom.

Are you alright? I ask.

Yes, Maria responds.

The second time I ask how she is doing she doesn't respond. When I enter the bathroom Maria is leaning against the wall. I call the home care nurse. She comes immediately to our home to assess Maria. She calls the ambulance. The ambulance drives up to the house. Maria suffers from a stroke. I kiss Maria and say that I love her. Maria and I smile. Maria goes

119

away in the ambulance to the palliative ward at the hospital.

Maria's oncologist calls me. She says that Maria's X-ray pictures show that the cancer tumors in her brain are bleeding. Bianca, Heidi, and I visit Maria in the palliative ward. She is asleep when we come to her room. I hold Maria's hands and kiss her cheeks. Bianca and Heidi kiss Maria and hold her hands. Maria is half awake. Heidi gives her a compliment for having white teeth.

Thanks, Maria says.

Maria loves Madonna and Cindy Lauper. The girls sing *Like a Prayer* and *Time after Time*. Maria smiles. Bianca dances to *Vogue*.

Wow Bianca, Maria says.

Heidi gives more compliments to Maria. Maria says a complete sentence, but I can't really hear what she is saying. Maria is awake when we say goodbye.

Maria is brain tired. She slips in and out of consciousness. Her arms and legs are weak. She can answer questions, and needs help 24/7 to eat, visit the toilet and shower. Maria is viewed as a terminal brain cancer patient by the physician.

Even if there is ongoing Covid-19-pandemic we can visit Maria anytime in the palliative ward. She has her own peaceful room. Maria rests awake and can see the ambulance helicopter land on the hospital roof. She sleeps a lot during the days and has problems to sleep at night.

Bianca, Heidi, and I visit Maria. She sleeps the first hour. The physician says that Maria has been leaning on the side. Maria opens her eyes and listens to the cookie conversation that we have.

Chocolate covered marshmallow puffs, Maria adds.

After a long silence, Maria asks me to help her to go to Bianca and Heidi's room.

We're at the hospital, I say.

Maria looks confused. We sit with her and hold her hands. Later, when we leave we tell Maria that we love her and wave goodbye. Maria smiles.

Maria moves to a short-term care facility in the municipality where we live. Maria has problems to stand up. The cancer takes away her mobility. I hold her to prevent her from falling.

She is now paralyzed. I'm holding Maria's hands. The cancer is destroying her organs. I lift and hold Maria close when we hug. I slowly help her back into wheelchair. I break down and weep. Maria is calm. I do all that I can to support her. Maria's brain cancer takes her memory, speech, and strength in her arms and legs. I become Maria's memory. People that know Maria ask me, Is Maria all right? Is Maria sick? Even if they ask these caring questions, I don't want to answer them. I reply, No. Maria is not all right. She has terminal brain cancer and is paralyzed.

Bianca and I visit Maria in the short-term unit. Maria is happy to see us. We kiss and hug her until she goes to sleep. After visiting Maria, Bianca and I go to the lake to swim. The lake is shimmering ahead of us. The waves are streaming against the shoreline. It's so relaxing. We look at each other and think about Maria.

Due to the pandemic, the municipality have a visitor ban at the short-term care home. They make an exception for Bianca, Heidi, and I because Maria will die soon. The physician will have a care planning meeting the following week with Maria, me, and the municipality to talk about Maria's needs in the upcoming weeks. Our main goal in the planning meeting is to be able to visit Maria at any time.

When I enter Maria's room she is sitting up and smiles at me. We hold each other's hands and say, I love you. We sit in silence and look at each other. I tell Maria that I'm so grateful that we met and for the shared life experiences including having Bianca and Heidi. I hold her hands until she goes to sleep. When I drive home to the house I'm sobbing thinking about the tragedy of Maria having terminal brain cancer being so young.

I experience massive demands and pressures caring for Maria and Mary and start to feel very low.

Ever since Maria and I met in Los Angeles in 1995, we love to listen to music together. I sit with Maria and listen to jazz music. Maria's eyes are more energized than they have been this summer. We are so happy about this. We're sharing some jazz music that very gifted students at Maria's former high school, Baton Rouge Magnet High School, perform. I kiss her. I start crying. My face is wet with tears of sadness and happiness that we share this moment. Our eyes are vulnerable and naked. Slowly happiness begins to fill my heart again after feeling low for a week. I'm grateful for Maria's consciousness and warmth. I'm responding with pleasure to each kiss and touch with Maria as if they were happening for the first time.

Bianca, Mary, and I visit Maria.

I love you, Maria, I say.

I love you, Karl, Maria responds.

Mary goes to the toilet.

I'm happy to have a consciousness, Maria says.

I nod and cry. The tears keep coming. I think about Maria having a bleeding cancer tumor in her brain. It has bled for some time now. I'm so grateful that she is conscious and recognizes me.

A strong crushing loneliness lances through me and stays with me for days. I talk to my psychotherapist. I tell him that I have been feeling down lately because of Maria's terminal brain cancer. I also feel the constant pressure caring for Mary with dementia and mental health problems. She is constantly screaming and insulting me even when I care for her. She is manic and intense again. I feel totally worn out.

When Bianca and I visit Maria in the evening the nursing assistants have helped her to sit up. She just had dinner.

I love you Maria, I say.

I love you Karl, Maria responds.

We bring beautiful flowers from Maria's close friend Laura who lives in Louisiana. Maria is so happy about the flowers. Her face is glowing. I massage Maria's hands, shoulders, and feet. I rub her neck. I kiss her feet tenderly. I cut her finger and toenails. I lift Maria up so we can hug. Maria's legs are not holding her up anymore. I hold her up so Bianca can hug her too. I help Maria back into bed. We're all so happy. Maria and I kiss. We wave goodbye.

When I return home to Mary in the house I tell her about Maria's deteriorating condition.

My daughter isn't dying! Mary screams.

Mary prays the Hail Mary, the traditional Christian prayer of praise for the Blessed Virgin Mary. In Catholic Church, this prayer forms the basis of the Rosary prayer which Mary recites daily. Mary screams insults and abuses me when she is not praying or reading the bible.

Mary can be kind and civil sometimes. I serve the supper. I ask if she would like some milk.

Yeah, she says with a cute baby voice.

Usually, she squeaks all the time. I give her the evening medicine and a salmon oil capsule. She swallows the pills.

What was that orange capsule? Mary asks.

I explain that it's fish oil. According to the package it's good for the heart. I add that it could prevent a heart attack. In response, Mary sings:

Karl, you prevent a heart attack. Salmon fish oil. It prevents a heart attack.

Mary burps in the middle of the song.

Excuse me, she says and continues to sing about the health benefits of eating fish oil capsules.

Mary always sings American TV commercial jingles from her childhood when she used to memorize them. Today she did something new in creating her own jingle about fish oil capsules. Before I leave the kitchen I remind Mary to not use the stove.

But can I use the oven? Mary asks.

No, you can't use the stove or the oven because if you fall asleep there could be a fire, I explain.

Then you should add oven on the do not use sign, Mary says.

Okay. I'll do that, I reply.

Maria sleeps when I visit her. I kiss her forehead and cheeks. She wakes up for a few minutes, smiles at me and goes back to sleep.

Bianca and I visit Maria. She is awake and sits up in the bed. I have brought bananas that she loves.

Usually, Maria only says a few sentences when we visit her. When eating the banana Maria participates in the conversation with many sentences and responses. Bianca and I are so happy about this. I massage her hands and arms with lotion. I see that the massage relaxes her face and body.

Is there anything else that would make you feel better? I ask.

Maria shakes her head no. Bianca and I say goodbye. Maria smiles.

Bianca and I go swimming in the sunset waves in the nearby lake. There are only a few people on the beach. The silence is very soothing. I drop off Bianca at her apartment and go to a cold bath house in the middle of the lake. I sit down on a chair and enjoy the last moments of the sunset.

A nursing assistant is helping Maria with her lunch when Bianca and I enter the room. Maria is happy to see us. The nursing assistant leaves. I massage Maria's face, arms, legs and back.

Do you like it? I ask Maria.

She nods smilingly. Bianca does manicure on Maria's fingernails. Maria wants to move towards me. Last time I helped her stand up so we could hug. This time I feel that her legs are not strong enough to keep her standing so we hug for several minutes close to each other. I kiss her cheeks and forehead. Maria looks sleepy. The nursing assistants enter the room

124

and use a lift to help Maria from the wheelchair to her bed. Maria is sleeping already. Bianca and I leave, watch a comedy, and go to the beach for an evening swim. The waves are powerful and calming.

It's still warm outside. Heidi, Mary, my mom, and I will have a summer burger barbecue party. Two days later Heidi will move to Gothenburg to pursue her college studies. I tell Mary that the party starts now in the garden. Mary stays at the kitchen table praying. Fifteen minutes later, Mary has still not come so we start eating. Twenty minutes later, Mary arrives at the table and screams in falsetto:

WHERE'S MY MAMA?

Juliet passed away in 2003, I say.

How is my child, Maria? How is my child? How is my child? What did the doctor say, Karl? Mary asks.

The doctor said that Maria has a bleeding cancer tumor in the brain. It fills the brain with liquid and can enter the spine. The bleeding tumor affects Maria's ability to talk, remember and move around. Part of her body is paralyzed, I respond.

Mary doesn't scream back in the way she usually does. Instead, she makes up a song about our party. We hear thunder. The rain touches our faces. We end the party.

Maria is awake when Bianca and I enter her room in the evening. Maria sits in the wheelchair and leans to the right.

I love you, Maria, I say.

I love you, Karl, Maria replies.

I massage Maria's face, arms, shoulders, back, legs and feet with lotion. Maria thanks me by waving with her right hand. She touches my hand with one of her fingers and moved it back and forth as a sign of love and gratitude. It brings me to tears.

See you tomorrow, Maria. I love you, I say.

Mary screams in my right ear when she wakes me up early in the morning, FIRE! FIRE! FIRE! C'mon, Karl, c'mon. Get up! Get up! Go! Go! Go! It rings from the icebox.

She puts on her coat and shoes. Mary runs out from the house down the street to three carpenters working on the neighbor's house. Mary shouts to the carpenters, FIRE! FIRE! FIRE!

Does she speak English? one carpenter says in Swedish to the other carpenters.

The carpenters keep on working and ignore Mary. She runs back to me in the house and does a three-step squeaking scream. The last scream is in falsetto: FIRE! FIRE! FIRE!

I have already checked the kitchen and the refrigerator. Everything looks normal. There is no fire. I closed the refrigerator door. I explain to Mary that everything is fine. There is nothing to worry about. I always unplug the fuse in the basement to prevent Mary from starting a fire on the stove. Before I realized that I could do this Mary started a fire on the stove when she made fudge. Thank God nothing happened.

I drive to the forest to pick sweet blueberries and chanterelles. It's silent and soothing. Mary and I have barbecued chantarelle sandwiches for lunch. After lunch, we drive to Maria. Mary promises me in the car to stay calm with Maria. I call the nursing assistant to open the closed entrance door. They keep the doors closed because of the pandemic.

I need to pee. I'm peeing, Mary says.

I asked you to put on a pad. You should always have a pad on day and night. Remember how many times we have talked about this? I tell her.

The nursing assistant opens the door. I tell her in a rushed way, Hi. Mary needs to pee.

Use this toilet, she says and points to a toilet door.

Mary runs into the toilet and sits down. I assist her.

Ah, she says and really enjoys peeing.

Mary flushes and puts a paper towel in her underwear.

Karl, I put on a pad now. Look, she tells me happily.

That's not a pad. That's a paper towel. Do you promise me to put on a real pad when we get home and always to wear a pad? I ask.

Yes, you're right Karl. This is not a pad. This is a paper towel. I will wear a real pad, Mary replies.

When Mary enters Maria's room she breaks out into the loudest and wildest laughter followed by celebratory squeaks and sounds.

Remember what you promised me in the car Mary? I tell her.

Mary continues to talk about an old lover in Louisiana.

Do you think we can bring Paul here? Mary asks me.

I think Paul must be over 110 years old if he is still alive and he probably wouldn't be here in Sweden, but in Louisiana or somewhere else in the United States. Can't you just support Maria by being here without talking constantly? I tell her.

Okay, Mary replies.

Maria looks at me.

Hi Maria, I love you, I say.

I love you, Karl, Maria replies.

I touch Maria's hair and face. She relaxes and closes her eyes. She looks content. I feel Maria's hand around mine. I smile at Maria. I ask her if I can do something.

Please raise your hand if you want me to feed you chocolate, I ask Maria.

Maria raises her hand a little bit and smiles. I give her small pieces of chocolate.

Maria has just had coffee when Bianca and I visit her. I massage Maria all over her body this evening. She loves it. Maria points to new places where she wants me to massage her.

Bianca and I visit Maria. She is in the wheelchair. She sits up straighter. Maria is happy to see us. We all smile and are happy to be together again. I have brought a lot of bananas for Maria. Maria eats two bananas on her own. The last weeks I've been breaking the bananas into smaller pieces and putting them in her mouth. I show the latest family pictures to Maria. I tell her that I was feeling low and sad one day because she has terminal brain cancer. To comfort myself I made a chocolate cake with almonds.

You're going to be alright, Karl, Maria replies and smiles.

I love you, Maria!

I love you, Karl!

Maria stretches out one of her legs on my knee. I take off her socks and fold up her pants. I put skin lotion on my hands, warm them and massage Maria all over her body. She looks so happy.

Maria is lying down in the bed when Bianca and I enter the room with dark red roses with white lines, chocolate, and bananas.

That's kind of you, Maria says quietly.

Maria smiles and enjoys the chocolate with Bianca.

I massage Maria and she enjoys it.

You're the love of my life, I tell Maria.

She smiles.

Mary is confused today. I hear her walking around in the house opening doors.

Karl, where's the bathroom? Mary asks.

I walk with her to the bathroom.

Bianca is 22 years old today. I call and sing a birthday song. Bianca is so happy.

Happy birthday sweetheart, I say.

Mary falls in the bathroom. I help her back to her bed. Bianca and I go to Maria with a Belgian chocolate cake. Heidi is in Gothenburg. We call her on Messenger. We are all together. After talking to Heidi, Maria wants me to massage her feet. I massage her feet. She smiles.

Maria sits in her bed when Bianca and I visit her. I help Maria to eat and drink water with a straw. Maria removes the blanket that she has over her legs. She points to her legs. I massage her legs with lotion. She smiles with her eyes. During the massage Bianca creates three new songs about her life. It's so painful to think that Maria only has a few more weeks to live. When I return home, I tell Mary that I visited Mary.

Which Maria are you talking about? There are two Marias, Mary says.

There is only one Maria, my wife, and your daughter, I reply.

Maria died in a car accident, Mary says.

That's not true, I reply.

I wake up by hearing loud laughter. The laughter goes on for over fifteen minutes. I enter the kitchen to make oatmeal for myself and Mary.

Why are you laughing? I ask.

Because I have a laughing spell. I'm thinking about a washing powder that is making people's clothes black and green and all kinds of colors, she replies and continues to laugh.

I love to laugh. God and the Holy Spirit got me laughing. They like me with laughter and happiness. HA HA HA HA HA. God I love you. Thank you for making me laugh, God, Mary says.

Bianca and I drive to Gothenburg on the Swedish west coast. Heidi lives here and studies at the university. Gothenburg is a beautiful seaport known for its Dutch-style 17th century canals, leafy boulevards, and lovely cobbled streets. It is a vibrant city with Neoclassical architecture and tram-rattled streets. The waterfront abounds with fresh fish, ships, aquariums, and sea-related museums. Gothenburg has a gorgeous archipelago. Bianca and I visit a textile museum and the Gothenburg Museum of Art. We meet Heidi outside at the Gothic Place outside the art museum and eat sushi together. We talk about Maria.

When I return home late in the evening Mary tells me the good news:

I'm gonna have a baby boy with Jesus and he's gonna have all of Jesus' ways.

Okay, would you like to have some supper? I have something from Japan called sushi, I say.

What is that? Mary asks.

It's fish and rice, I say.

Mary eats her sushi. I help her to change her pad and tuck her in. She goes to sleep immediately.

The next day, Maria is drowsy when Bianca and I visit her. I help her to eat a banana and drink water from a glass using a straw. I massage her legs, arms, and face. She smiles and shows with her warm face that she deeply enjoys the massage.

I love you, Maria, I say.

I love you, Karl, Maria responds.

Tears fill my eyes. We stay until the sunset when Maria looks sleepy. We kiss and wave goodbye.

Mary tells me just before midnight, My sister Ruby and the guy that she is dating are coming to pick me up.

Mary has put on her winter jacket, hat and gloves and waits for her ride.

Ruby is dead, I respond.

She ain't dead. That's my sister. Why do you think Ruby is dead? Yes. She sure died but God put her in heaven. Is that confusing. Oh God, Mary responds.

No, I say.

When are you coming, Ruby? Mary asks.

They're not coming. Please go to bed. I want to sleep, I reply.

I'm going to bed. Ruby, are you still living in heaven? Ruby says I'm still coming. Karl, I'll tell you when they are coming, Mary responds.

I don't want to you to wake me up. Goodnight. I love you, I say.

I love you. Goodnight. God bless you, Mary says.

God bless you, Mary, I say.

I'll sit down on the chair in the hallway to wait for my ride, Mary says when leaves the room.

Okay, I reply.

Mary stays awake the entire night sitting on the

chair outside my bedroom talking to the cats. She is ready in her winter clothes to go with Ruby. Around four o'clock in the morning Mary talks so loud to the cats that I wake up again.

Please go to bed because I really need to sleep, I tell her.

I'm God. I don't need to go to bed, Karl, Mary explains.

I don't understand why Mary is talking like this because she is taking very strong anti-psychotic medication. By the time I go to sleep it is nearly four in the morning.

Where's Ruby? is the first thing Mary says when I make oatmeal for breakfast.

Ruby has passed away, I reply.

I've felt low back and forth the last two months because of Maria's palliative situation and the parallel supporting and strengthening efforts to make Maria, our daughters, Mary, and my mom feel better. I have my focus on love and hope. I feel good being in nature. I find chantarelles and blueberries. Even working at the university teaching and researching is relaxing to me.

Mary waits for two men to bathe her. She walks around in a purple top and her pink underwear. I give her new clothes.

Don't you want to put on a skirt or pants, Mary? I ask.

That's not necessary, Karl, because two men are coming to bathe me today, Mary explains.

The next day, Mary is still walking around in her underwear waiting for the two men from God to bathe her. She smells of urine. I make her oatmeal and put out new clothes.

Karl, I'm not going to change clothes, she replies.

She lays down on my bed with the pee clothes. After she goes to the bathroom she returns to my bedroom. I remind Mary about how important it is to stay fresh and to wash daily. I help her to the wooden chair outside my bedroom. I lock the door and tell her that she can't come into my bedroom again until she has washed changed her clothes. I say that I have put new fresh clothes and a towel for her on the kitchen table. I hear Mary going back upstairs to the bathroom to change her clothes. I put her urine clothes in the washing machine and change my bed clothes.

I love you, Karl. You're like Jesus. You help me so much. Thank you. Thank you. Thank you, Mary says when she returns to my bedroom in fresh clothes.

Suddenly she screams:

Maria ain't my daughter. She's some strange girl. Who is Maria? Who is Maria? Who is Maria?

Mary says everything three times with high anxiety and with a falsetto squeaky voice which is very stressful to listen to.

Why do say everything three times? I ask.

Because God told me that people understand better if you say it three times, Mary explains.

For me it's very stressful when you say everything three times because it leaves no room for a break or a silence in our conversation. You fill up all the spaces, I say.

I do what I want. I don't care, Karl. Shut up, fool! Mary replies.

Today we're reaching back to Maria's past. Maria has made efforts to talk to her dad and half-brother in California since our wedding in 1997. She has been thinking about her dad half-brother so much. A couple of weeks ago I wrote a letter to Maria's dad and half-brother explaining that Maria has terminal brain cancer. I was happy to receive a message on Messenger from Maria's half-brother.

We decide to set up a conversation on FaceTime. Bianca and I come to Maria and tell her about it. Maria is shining up. We call the number and see Maria's dad and brother. They look happy to see us. Maria's brother praises her for inspiring him in what kind of music he likes. Even if Maria can't talk much I can see that she is shining and being so grateful for these unforgettable moments. She has been waiting for 23 years to talk to her dad again. She is also able to see her half-brother and his family. Maria looks so content. Bianca enjoys talking to her grandfather and uncle. During the conversation, Maria's brother's wife and daughter enter the room. We are also so happy to talk to them. I start crying when Maria's dad is praising me for being caring and strong for the family. We have a lovely conversation for an hour.

After the call I help Maria to eat cheesecake at the care home. The nursing assistants bring plates with cheesecake for all of us. I fall asleep overjoyed when I return home.

Today Maria looks stiffer in her face when Bianca and I walk into her room. Maria doesn't talk at all.

Are you happy about having talked to your dad, brother, his wife, and daughter? I ask.

Maria perks up and nods. Today our entire encounter is non-verbal. I've brought cheddar and sour cream chips for Maria. I break the chips in small pieces. She opens her mouth and chews the chips. I give her orange juice from a straw. She drinks the entire glass. We call Heidi and talk to her. Maria's lips are chapped. I put on Vaseline and kiss her face.

She looks so stiff. I give her a long and sensitive full body massage. I massage her hands and arms. When I'm done with the neck and shoulders, I move onto the arms. When massaging her hands, I take her hands in mine and massage the palm with my thumbs, using small circular motions. Then, I take each finger in turn. I massage the fingers slowly. I dedicate time to each individual body part, giving it my full care and attention, and keep my strokes long, smooth, and slow. Maria smiles with her eyes and says several sentences after the massage. Bianca and I say goodbye to Maria. I drop off Bianca and drive home.

I walk out into the garden and look at the starry sky. Thousands of stars light up the sky. I feel stronger than ever before in my life. Recently I've had to fight feeling too low because of Maria's cancer. I'm the crisis leader of our family organizing care on several fronts. I'm strong for Maria, Bianca, Heidi, Mary, and my mother. Before I've sometimes felt sorry for myself. Now I accept any type of situation and adapt to it and organize whatever I need for our family to cope. I'm not scared of embarrassing myself or setting up limits.

My sleep has come and gone in little spurts living with Mary. It's 1 a.m. when Mary enters my bedroom and screams, I want my oatmeal!

I'll make the oatmeal in the morning. It's 1 a.m., I reply.

Oh, Mary says and walks out of my bedroom.

Early in the morning I'm sleeping when Mary enters my bedroom again and screams, Oh God! Oh god! Oh god! I want this man. I want this man. I want this man.

Before I open my eyes she pushes her lips on my right cheek and drools saliva all over my face.

When I open my eyes I feel uncomfortable when Mary is kissing my face.

Stop! Please, go to your bedroom, Mary. I want to sleep, I reply.

Mary and I approach life differently. She is awake all night long and sleeps during the day. I go to work at the university during the days. I need my sleep at night. Mary is impatient in getting what she wants. If I don't do what she wants immediately she is yelling, banging, and howling. Her behavior is fraying my nerves and generating dislike. I experience stressful stuff at home.

Maria's nurse calls me from the care home and says:

We have now started giving Maria morphine because her pain has increased. The morphine helps Maria to relax. She receives 16 Cortisone pills per day to reduce the swelling in her brain. Can you go to the pharmacy to get more Cortisone? When are you coming to see Maria again? the nurse asks.

I'm coming to Maria this afternoon. I'll get the Cortisone from the pharmacy, I reply.

I tell Mary that the nurse called from the care home. The nurse said that they are now giving Maria morphine because of her pain. My stomach hurts when Mary replies:

That's not our Maria. Maria is just a little girl who has been in the hospital and who has had a heart transplant. She's fine, Karl. Maria belongs to other people now. She goes to my principal every day at the elementary school. Maria is in good health. She doesn't have cancer. Maria has nothing bad. The principal at the elementary school will straighten you out Karl and say that Maria doesn't have cancer.

I know that Mary's words are her delusions and dementia talking. The reality is that Maria will die. All we can do is to love Maria as much as we can in her last moments. I walk out into the garden and feel the strong winds. The wind gusts move my body. Many apples have fallen on the grass. I pick some and make an apple pie for Maria and Bianca.

I bring the apple pie and drive to the pharmacy to get Maria's medicine. Bianca joins me and we drive to Maria in the care home. Maria's eyes are open when we walk into her room. When we sit down next to her she closes her eyes. Five minutes later Maria opens her eyes.

I love you, Maria, I say.

I love you, Karl, Maria responds quietly.

Do you want some apple pie? I ask.

Maria nods. I help her to eat. The soft pie crust melts in Maria's mouth. She stares at Bianca every now and then.

Do you feel pain? I ask.

I can barely hear her whispering word.

Yes, Maria says.

Maria is in such physical pain. She is not as comfortable as before. Maria experiences cognitive decline, headaches, and fatigue. Her pain is in the brain because of the swelling that the cancer tumors are causing. Maria takes Paracetamol and gets Morphine as needed. She has an IV in the throat that she got installed in the palliative ward at the hospital in case she needs a continuous Morphine infusion. She has moments of wakefulness. She is awake for a few minutes and then goes back to sleep for a few minutes or longer and then opens her eyes again. Maria has been taking anti-psychotic medication since the end of the 1990s and the 16 tablets of Cortisone every day increase the risk of psychosis. Maria opens her eyes. I have sad, watery eyes. We kiss each other passionately. This may be our last kiss.

Now we're taking it a day at a time. Maria experiences a progressive loss of consciousness. She is drowsy. Maria sleeps most of the time. Right now, she is conscious when Bianca and I visit her. She has motor deficits, aphasia, and coordination problems. When she is about to eat some food and wants to move her hand toward her mouth the hand sometimes ends up on her shoulder. We help her to move the food toward her mouth. I see peace when I look into Maria's eyes.

Maria has a soft cozy bed in the care home. I will buy a neck pillow to support her head and upper body leaning to the right. Maria's unit is calm with very caring nursing assistants. Maria has a strong spiritual faith and hasn't expressed any fear of dying. Moments later, Maria goes back to sleep.

I drop off Bianca and I go to a counseling meeting with a social worker for support. After the counseling I drive home. In the evening Mary and I eat together. We sit across the table and look at each other.

Where did you go? Mary asks.

Bianca and I went to see Maria. Maria feels more

pain now. She takes morphine, I reply.

SHE'S NOT MY GIRL. I DON'T KNOW HER! Mary screams.

Mary shouts the same thing several times. I leave the supper table and walk downstairs. I lock the door to my bedroom to relax. Mary races down the stairs and grabs the handle. When she recognizes that the door is looked she starts to hit it hard with one of her fists. She takes the broom handle and hits the door even harder. I turn up the volume on the electronic dance music that I'm listening to and finish my dinner. I think back on the last two years. I haven't had one calm day since Mary came to us in Sweden. I'm looking forward to the decision by the Swedish Migration Agency. Hopefully, Mary will get a residence permit. I can then apply for an apartment for her in the local care home. Mary has been acting abusive to me day and night for more than two years. I've been feeling low the last few weeks because of Maria's condition and the abuse inflicted upon me by Mary. I want to be able to be with and love Maria during her last days and at the same time grieve in peace.

Mary keeps on banging on my door with the broom handle. I think about having supported Mary in a major way not only the last two years in Sweden, but also the last years in the United States. I need a break to recover. I don't want to be Mary's punching bag forever. Finally, Mary gets tired of hitting on the door and goes back up the stairs. From now on I'll always look my bedroom door. I don't want to wake up when Mary is pushing my sleepy body and slobbering her saliva all over my face. It's disgusting and I've had enough.

The situation is most distressing to Mary. She is screaming at me and wants to aggressively convince me that Maria doesn't have cancer and that she died in a traffic accident. Mary tries to convince me that Maria is not her daughter. She says that Maria lives

137

in Baton Rouge with a principal from the elementary school where Mary worked. I know that she suffers from dementia and mental health problems so I'm trying to act as understanding and caring as possible.

Maria sleeps when I arrive. I have brought her Cortisone medication and a neck support pillow. I sit next to her in my Covid protection gear and stroke her forehead and hair gently. I touch her skin just behind one of her ears and she opens her eyes and goes back to sleep.

Heidi visits Maria. Maria's eyes are looking up into the ceiling. Her breathing is strained.

Bianca and I visit Maria. I'm holding Maria close. I see that Maria is not doing well. She can't have eye contact. The pupils of eyes are almost under her eye lids. Her breathing is strained. I caress and massage Maria's face and right arm. Bianca massage Maria's left arm. My tears bulk up inside. I can see that Maria's organ are not working anymore. I feel that our lifelong love story is coming to an end. I'm filled with tears and sadness. Maria's silent gentleness makes my tears flow faster. Her eyes reveal that her life energy is disappearing.

Maria goes to sleep. Bianca and I return home. Later in the evening, the world turns darker when the nurse at Maria's care home calls. I have a feeling that something is wrong. The nurse gives me the terribly sad news that Maria has passed away. In grief after the call, I'm sobbing and talking loud to myself, I want you back, Maria.

I'm preparing the unbearable task to tell Bianca and Heidi about what has happened to their mother.

We're all in deep pain and sadness. We will always miss Maria. She will be a part of our lives forever. Heidi is in Gothenburg. Bianca and I have broken hearts and trembling bodies when we go to see Maria in the care home. Candles are lit all around her bed. She wears her most beautiful clothes. We hold Maria's hands and say goodbye to her. Maria is cold and yellow. I kiss Maria's soft forehead. We pray for her. The pain of the last goodbye is relentless.

Maria was dying of an aggressive brain cancer when she was only 47 years old. Grief-stricken in my soul I need to find my own way back after Maria's passing. I talk to the family therapist, the priest, the deacon, and the counsellor. We receive condolences and I hear many, I'm sorry for your loss.

The grief fluctuates, some moments I feel ok, other moments I am shattered. It is like a rollercoaster of emotions going up and down. I sit down on my bed and break down in tears and cry and cry. I call and talk to a grief counsellor. I feel better afterwards.

In the evening, I go upstairs to make supper.

What did you do today? Mary asks me.

Bianca and I went to see Maria. Maria died yesterday, I say.

I look very forlorn and sad.

Mary explains:

Maria got a whipping today. It was the principal that she stays with that gave her the whipping. He gave her five lashes with his belt because she was outside mama's house and didn't want to go inside. Both me and my brother were cheering the principal for whipping Maria.

I serve her supper and say goodnight. I take a shower and get under the blanket. I think about Maria. I love her. Maria was loving, kind and genuine. Maria's death starts to sink in. I go to sleep.

In the morning, I sleep late and stay in bed all day long. My spirit will not give up. I think about the fact that Maria's soul has finally found peace. I love you, Maria. Maria will always be with me. Her beauty and love will stay with me. Maria was the essence of love. She had a natural stoic elegance. She has been bravely fighting against her brain cancer. We are together in spirit. I have so many questions in my head. Was Maria scared? I don't think so. Did she have pain? Yes. She had pain. The Morphine relieved some of her physical pain. Her passing leaves my heart broken in darkness. I miss her.

Maria and I were together for 25 years. I could be myself with her except for when she was delusional. Now she is gone. I'm so happy that Maria and I met and that we created beautiful memories. Maria left me with two sweet daughters in Bianca and Heidi. I'll be here for the girls. It will be alright. The life of Maria was full of ideas and courage to do what she dreamt about doing. Maria was humble. She had high morals always thinking about what we can always do better. Maria liberated me from being bound by my parents. She encouraged me to stand up to them and form a strong family with Maria, Bianca, and Heidi. Maria taught me to believe in my own power and she also believed in me.

Mary denies that her daughter has passed away. She can't believe it. Mary shares her solution to the situation, You can bring Maria back to life. You go to the people at the courthouse in downtown Baton Rouge and tell them that you want to revive her. They will tell you what to do. She'll see us again. I know that she'll appreciate that so much. Maria used to tell me I'm not dead. I'm living with you.

A few minutes later, Mary screams:
WHERE'S MARIA? WHERE'S MARIA? WHERE'S MARIA?

I take a breath and reply, Maria is dead.

Mary's voice keeps squeaking and shouting:
JESUS CHRIST, KARL. HOW MANY TIMES DO I NEED TO TELL YOU THAT MARIA AIN'T DEAD. MARIA AIN'T DEAD. STOP SAYING THAT SHE'S DEAD. YOU'RE STUPID AND USELESS!

I am who I am, Mary. I do my best to help you in life, I say.

YOU'RE A STUPID FOOL. THAT'S WHAT YOU ARE, KARL! Mary replies.

Mary, you should speak to me with respect. You're so abusive towards me, I say.

I don't care. Shut up, Karl! Mary replies.

Mary drools all over my shirt. Her hands are shaking. When she talks to me or someone else even if I'm just in front of her she talks as she would be in large auditorium with hundreds of people. To not get ear damages, I routinely put my fingers in my ears. Mary loves to scream just for the fun of hearing the nuances of her loud scream. I used to work in pre-schools. The young children used to scream when they played. The main difference is that Mary has a very high pitch voice that is much more powerful. The usual reaction in other people is massive stress and anxiety hearing Mary's screams.

Maria is really gone from us. Grief comes in waves breaking my heart. Massive tiredness takes over my whole body. I stay in bed. I've lived a high paced life the last decades. I take a deep breath and drink some water. I climb back into bed and go to sleep. I sleep for days. Some moments Maria is very close to me. Other moments I realize that Maria is gone. It feels like living two realities at once. In one reality I'm here with Maria. In another reality I'm all alone. When I'm doing certain things I think about experiences that I shared with Maria.

I loved Maria so much. I'm totally devastated. I have been crying for several days now. I have spent most of the time in bed with a cover over me. I need to get through this and move forward.

I'm sleeping. Mary enters the bedroom and wakes me up by screaming with squeaking high pitch:

CROCODILE! CROCODILE! CROCODILE! Where's the crocodile?

Who's the crocodile? I ask.

Heavenly father says you're his little boy crocodile. You don't know anything about it, Mary replies.

No, I say.

Maybe it wasn't you. What is that little boy's name? The priest said when he was a little boy he said that you were a little boy crocodile. It was just a little pretty boy that was called the crocodile, Mary explains.

Okay, I respond.

I will try to view Mary positively. I think that the coolest thing about Mary is that she knows hundreds of songs from her younger years. She was a member of brass bands performing African-influenced jazz in the streets of Baton Rouge and New Orleans, featuring all manners of brass instruments and drums often played with marching musicians. She played the trumpet and improvised in jazz, soul, blues and rock'n'roll. Mary can still activate her music memory anytime she hears a melody and flourish. That is beautiful to see.

Maria is gone. I meet with the priest to plan Maria's funeral.

I'm deeply sorry, the priest says sensitively.

The priest makes eye contact. She is kind. I feel comfortable with her. We sit in the kitchen of the congregation home and have coffee and delicious cinnamon rolls. She asks me questions about the funeral service. After that we have talked through what is going to happen at the funeral we walk upstairs to the organist to talk about the hymns in the service. I say hello to the deacon. I have met the deacon many times in this building in weekly counseling sessions after Maria passed.

I go back home to have lunch and will then go to the university.

Bye, Mary. I'm going to the university to teach, I tell Mary.

Mary runs out and sits down in the car.

I didn't realize that we were in a rush, she says.

We're not going together. I'm going to work alone. It's not possible for you to come with me. I need to teach at the university. It's the Corona pandemic. Only teachers are allowed into the school, I say.

I'll sit in the car in the parking lot, Mary says.

It will be too cold for you. I need to drive now.

Otherwise, I'm going to be late for my class, I say.

I'm going with you, Mary says.

She grabs one of my arms to stop me from leaving alone. I get out of the car and walk around the car. I open the passenger door.

Please go inside the house, Mary, I plead.

Stay at home with me, Mary pleads.

I would like to stay home, but I need to go to work, I reply.

NO, I'M GOING WITH YOU! Mary screams.

I lift Mary out of the car and inside the house. I put her on my bed.

I'M GONNA KILL YOU, KARL! Mary screams and gets up.

She barricades the door to keep me in the bedroom. After standing up for a few minutes Mary gets tired and sits down on a chair.

You'll be okay, Mary. See you later this afternoon, I say.

I run back to the car and drive off. My heart beats fast. I sweat and feel nervous. I take the forest road to the university which is a shortcut. I think about the older women and men on my mom's street. Most of them receive daily home care services and many of them have less needs than Mary. Mary is not entitled to any home care services because she is not a Swedish resident. This fact is putting massive pressures on me to care for Mary 24/7 and at the same time be a full-time university professor. When I return home in the evening, I make a tuna salad for us.

I want to go down to the courthouse to tell them to revive Maria, Mary says.

Mary, we're in Sweden. If you want to, we can go for a drive to the church after supper, I say.

We can tell father to revive Maria. We want her living because she has a wholesome family that cares for her. Tell him how many we are and tell him our names. Ask him what time he revives people. I'm

143

sure you can do that Karl. You're this big college professor, Mary says.

I eat from my tuna salad.

When is the priest going to revive Maria? You need to tell the priest to do it. You're a stupid old man, Karl, Mary says.

Mary is worried as usual. A plethora of words flow fast from her mouth with a denial that Maria was her daughter and not even kin to her. She denies that Maria was my wife.

Why are you even here then if we're not related and Maria is not my wife? I ask.

I'm here because Maria brought me here. You, stupid man, Mary responds.

After supper I drive Mary to the church. We sit down on a bench outside the church. Mary has brought her bible and is talking to Jesus. Maria is not revived.

Karl, where's Maria? Mary asks me.

She's in the morgue, I respond.

You're brilliant Karl. She will come here on the funeral day. You, sweet little man can do so many things. Karl is helping me, Jesus. Let's ask our father to revive Maria, Mary says.

I want to a have a peaceful funeral. I don't want Mary screaming over everyone in the church.

At nightfall, the frost covers the grass outside my bedroom window. It's the first cold night. I've increased the heat in the house. I'm sleeping deep.

3 a.m. Mary enters the bedroom and screams in my ear:

HURRY! HURRY! HURRY! KARL!!! GET UP! GET UP! GET UP!

I open my sleepy eyes.

C'mon. C'mon. We need to find Maria. She's on a trip. Where is she? Mary says.

Tomorrow it's Maria's funeral day. We can prepare our clothes today and dress up. We're going to look great. We can bring the bible to Maria's coffin tomorrow and say prayers, I reply.

Before the funeral we're going to the courthouse, right? We can fill out the form so the holy men can give Maria the shot to bring her back to us. You're going to organize that Karl? I'm just going to church with you and be with Maria in her coffin with all the beautiful red roses, Mary says.

Are you going to brush off the cat hair from your clothes, Mary? I ask.

Yes, I love you, Karl, Mary replies.

I love you Mary, I say.

IT WILL BE ALRIGHT, KARL, Mary says.

Through the windows of grief, I speak hopefully to Bianca and Heidi that we will stick together in these hard times and forever in life. I meet Bianca to go to a restaurant to have lunch and talk about the funeral. We go swimming to wind down. I have supper with Heidi who is back from Gothenburg. Heidi goes to the gym. I go to a yin yoga and meditation session which is so relaxing. I feel at peace when I return home to Mary. I make a sandwich for her and say good night.

Maria's funeral day has come. The funerals in my life have been milestones wherein huge changes happened each time. When I wake up I go down to the river and look at the streams. It's a wonderful way to start the day.

Bianca, Heidi, and I give Maria a funeral service based on her wishes. Maria wanted a burial and didn't want to be cremated. I want to give Maria the full works: a beautiful, warm, and sensitive funeral ceremony, an intimate dinner with the closest family members, friends and the priest, deacon, and an organ player.

Mary has cried, screamed, and said delusional things so it would be highly stressful to bring her to the funeral after lunch, so I bring Mary to Maria before lunch. I have talked to the funeral home representative about bringing Maria's coffin in earlier.

When we sit down close to the altar, Mary asks God to revive Maria. It doesn't work. Maria is still in the coffin. We say the 23rd song "The Lord is my shepherd." We say other prayers to the saints so they can pray for Maria.

Holy people from God will come and use a needle to put a solution into my daughter to revive her, Mary says.

We stay in the church for an hour. Outside the church, Mary tries to forcefully convince me that Maria isn't dead. I help Mary into the car. I return home with Mary. When we return to the house Bianca and Heidi are waiting for me. I take a deep breath. I smile at Bianca and Heidi. We drive back to the church. The organist has started playing.

In the funeral service we grieve together and cherish our beloved Maria. Singing *Hallelujah* gives consolation. Heidi's friend from the Netherlands sings the spellbinding song *Roller Coaster* by Danny Vera in the Americana music genre with the sound of weeping from all of us in the family. It's so beautiful. I think about Maria and break down in tears.

We sing the hymn *When a child returns home*. The priest talks about God carrying everything and spreads the soil on Maria's coffin. We sing *You embrace me*. I read the prayer *The Lord is my shepherd* from Psalm of David in English. We sing the hymn *Spread your broad wings*. Heidi's friend sings another song on the theme without your breath. I cry endlessly. The funeral service inside the church ends with *Amazing Grace*. I lean down towards Maria's coffin.

I walk in the front of the funeral procession through the church and the graveyard carrying Maria's coffin with five other people. We walk to Maria's grave outside the church with a rural Swedish river landscape view. I take the rope with the other people and lower Maria in the coffin into the grave.

At the graveside, I imagine Maria's life and let go off the flower bouquet from my hand. The flowers land on Maria's coffin. Bianca and Heidi throw their flowers. The grass feels soft under my shoes. Maria's memory will never be forgotten. Her coffin is now out of sight. Maria's beautiful loving spirit is on my mind. I send the love that's deep within me to Maria.

Being at the funeral gives me no anxiety, but deep peace. I can see Maria smiling. Her life ends happily with her closest family next to her. The priest prays to God to give Maria peace. We say farewell.

I close my eyes and say my last words to Maria in silence.

Maria, I will always love you with love that is deep inside of me. Our love will heal the wounds and scares inside of us. I'm full of the love that we shared.

Our spiritual hearts will be close to comfort and support each other. We have shared joy, anguish, smiles and tears.

You live in the hearts of our daughters. You died too young. I wanted us to share milestones in Bianca and Heidi's lives. Our daughters can always share their lives with you in burning candles, flowers that bloom, birds that sing and falling snowflakes. We will always miss you and keep you in our hearts my dearest.

I open my eyes and talk about how I remember Maria at the funeral dinner. We sit in the candle filled room where I had my confirmation training with the priest when I was thirteen years old. We sit in a ring. We are a small group of guests including Bianca, Heidi, Heidi's friend who performed at the funeral service, my mother, my sister, the priest, the deacon, and the organist. We talk about Maria's life. I'm full of the love that we shared. With Maria's passing I burrow even deeper into the heart and darkness of the family tragedy.

18 EXPELLED

I thought that Mary had reasonable reasons to be able to stay in Sweden. Even if Maria passed away Mary still has her granddaughters and I living with her in Sweden. The Swedish Migration Agency officer explains that when Maria passed away Mary has no rights to stay. She must leave Sweden in a few weeks. I write a letter to the Embassy of the United States of America in Sweden to ask for support in Mary staying:

To Whom It May Concern:

Hello. I'm writing regarding my American mother-in-law, Mary J. Guillory. Mary received a rejection decision from the Swedish Migration Agency after my American wife Maria Guillory Hedman passed away on September 28, 2020, after having had brain cancer.

Mary lived in an apartment complex in Baton Rouge, Louisiana, for low-income seniors, until December 2017. According to the housing director she was not independent enough. She needed to move out from her apartment. My wife and I flew immediately to Baton Rouge and rented an apartment where my wife and my mother-in-law stayed from January to June 2018. My wife was not feeling well. She was later diagnosed with brain cancer. She brought her mother back to Sweden on June 12, 2018. We applied for a Swedish residence permit for Mary. When my wife died the Swedish Migration Agency decided that Mary is not able to stay in Sweden because the connection between mother and daughter was lost. According to the rejection decision from the Swedish Migration Agency Mary needs to leave Sweden before December 9th, 2020.

My wife had a miscarriage in 1997 which was the

beginning of a series of psychotic episodes from 1997 to the autumn of 2018 and has not been able to care for her mother. Over the last two decades I have traveled alone to Louisiana to care for my mother-in-law. My wife's brain cancer and my mother-in-law's dementia, psychosis and anxiety disorder have put a lot of strain on our daughters and myself. They need support from me here in Sweden.

I am writing to ask the American Citizen Services for help in returning Mary to Louisiana. I have asked the Swedish Migration Agency and the local municipality in Sweden if they can purchase the tickets for Mary. Both services said no because she is not a resident.

Mary is a retired teacher and has a medical insurance plan in Louisiana. She does not have Social Security. I helped Mary to register to receive support through the Affordable Care Act a couple of years ago. Mary receives a monthly pension from the Louisiana Teacher Retirement System which she has used to pay her medication and healthcare costs in Sweden. Mary needs elderly care in Louisiana. My friend has agreed to help Mary to look for a care home in Baton Rouge and pick up Mary from the airport in New Orleans or Baton Rouge and drive her to the care home. The American Citizens Services of the Embassy of the United States of America replies that they can't help Mary.

19 WALKING ON THE HIGHWAY

West Sweden, November 2020

Mary lets herself silently out of the house when I'm supervising my social work students via Zoom. One of the national roads is located outside the house. Mary walks in the middle of the road in the dark Swedish winter. She's getting cold as she walks. Mary is not looking out for her own safety. She keeps her face turned to the ground looking for Maria. Mary passes the bridge over the black river. She reaches the sign which marks the end of the community. Cars and trucks almost kill her. I remember my dad walking out to the grocery store in a snowstorm when I was a kid. He passed this same road in the heavy snowfall and saw a body lying on the road. It was an older lady that had been crushed by a truck when she crossed the road. My dad often talked about this traumatic incident. Mary could have died in the same way.

A local woman driving past notices Mary in the middle of the road. She slows down and stops her car. The woman chases after Mary. She smiles at Mary and helps Mary back to the car.

Where're we goin'? Mary asks.

I'll take you to my home, the woman replies.

The woman takes Mary in the car to her home. She calls the police. The police officers arrive and take a report. Mary who has attacked police officers before thinks they look good and are charming.

I finish teaching and realize that Mary is missing. I run outside to look for her. My phone rings. I answer. It's a police officer.

Do know someone named Mary? he asks.

Yes, that's my mother-in-law, I reply.

She is with a lady here. Can you come? the police officer asks.

I'll be there as soon as I can, I say and get into the

car.

I arrive at the woman's apartment. Mary smiles when she sees me.

Here's Karl! My beautiful, Karl. Karl is a very charming man. Look at him, Mary tells the lady and the police officers.

Mary is trying to convince the lady and the two police officers that Maria is still alive. She explains to the police officers that her sister Ruby told her to look for Maria on the road.

The lady smiles and nods. Mary is drinking hot tea. The lady has put a warm blanket around Mary's shoulders.

Are you alright?, I ask Mary.

Where were you? I've been so worried, I say.

I feel stressed out inside after this incident, but I'm keeping my calm for Mary's sake. Mary doesn't seem to worry about what just happened. I open my arms to Mary. She hugs me.

Do you want to go back home? I ask.

Mary nods.

I help Mary back to the car. When she has her seat belt on I start to shiver out of fear and shock. I just sit in the seat for a while shaking before I start driving.

Do you want me to sing that song? Mary asks me.

Yes, please, I reply.

Mary sings her cruising song loud and clear in the dark Swedish winter evening.

The next day I write to the social services to ask for help with Mary. Mary has been manic and psychotic for the last years. The new thing now is that Mary walks on the main road and can get killed.

Life gets heavier and heavier. I suffer daily humiliations and abuse caring for Mary. Today when I write to the social services Mary talks about an old boyfriend. She says that he used to fight other men. Suddenly Mary is punching me in the face.

This is the way he used to hit the men, she says.

Please sit down and take it easy. You can tell me the

story without showing it physically on me. It hurts in my face now. Come here Mary. I can hold you, I say.

I give Mary a warm hug.

I love you sweetheart, I say.

I love you, Karl, Mary replies.

Mary grabs my shirt and starts to pull it hard back and forth.

This is the way he used to shake other men, Mary says.

Mary, you're doing it again. Please stop. Sit down on the chair. You can tell me stories without harming me physically, I say.

It's early in the morning when Mary opens my bedroom door and wakes me up with the loudest voice:

KARL, YOU NEED TO GET THAT STRAIGHT. MARIA IS ALIVE. I'm going to the governor of Louisiana and tell him that you're spreading lies about Maria. You're telling people that she died. That's not true. You're a liar Karl.

A few seconds later Mary says:

You are amazing. You did a lot for me Karl. You helped me to stay in Sweden.

In the afternoon we enjoy a delicious apple pie with vanilla sauce.

Can I give you a kiss for that pie? Mary asks.

Without waiting for my reply Mary kisses me on the cheek.

Karl, when did Maria say that she's coming? Mary asks.

Maria is dead, I reply.

Mary explains:

I don't mean the one that is dead. I mean the one that is alive. She is your wife. When did they say they are coming?

They are not coming because they are all dead, I reply.

They are not dead. Karl, how can you get that into your foolish head? Okay. You think they are dead. I

152

think they are living. I'm so sorry. Is Ruby dead too? Ruby is not dead because Ruby talks to me. You should know that. You are a researcher, Karl, Mary says.

Mary talks loud to Ruby:

Ruby, where are you all? Are you in Baton Rouge? Why? Are you going to the snow? Where? In your yard? Karl, you know they are not dead.

They are all dead, I reply.

Karl, why did you meet them the other night, Mary asks.

I didn't, I reply.

Yes, you let them in. You lie. You lie. You lie. You mean that principal Wilson is dead? He is married to me. He died a long time ago. How is he married to me? He married me a month ago. I love him. How can I fall in love with him if he's not alive? Why don't you believe me, Karl?

What? I don't understand anything you're saying Mary. I'm getting dizzy, I say.

In the afternoon I'm having coffee with Mary in the kitchen. I ask myself who I want to be after Mary leaves. Mary sips from her coffee and adds several spoons of sugar.

Let's not talk about those people if they are dead or alive. If they are dead they are dead. If they are alive they are alive. Isn't that right, Karl, Mary says.

Yes, I reply.

Bye. Bye. Bye, Mary says and leaves my bedroom.

Later, I'm pealing a pineapple for dessert. Where are you putting that stuff? In your pants? Mary asks.

Mary can't see the garbage can under the kitchen table where I put pineapple peel.

Karl, you're a sweet, sweet man. You always think and care about me. I always want to be with you. You might become my husband in the future. Did your mama teach you to be a saint? Mary asks.

No, I reply.

Karl! Let's practice that you are my husband, Mary

153

says. I feel uncomfortable hearing that. The thought makes me feel sick to my stomach. I change the topic.

Let's listen to some music, I say.

When we're listening to Sam Cooke singing Mary says:

Dance for me Karl. You're very good-looking.

I stand up and silly dance for Mary.

Oh, that's so beautiful, Karl. Can you cut my toenails? Mary asks.

No. You can cut your own toenails, I reply.

Cut my toenails! she cries.

Would you like me to make you a warm footbath? It's very soothing, I say.

Yes, Mary replies and bursts into a loud laughter.

That was terrible that the people were not able to go home, Mary says.

What people? I ask.

I don't know. They had guns and thought the people were going to shoot them. I wasn't in that. That was Ruby and them, Mary says.

Do you mean the civil rights demonstrations? I ask.

You were there too Karl. Don't you remember? Mary says.

I remember that you told me about civil rights demonstrations at Southern University the other day. I was not there when it happened, but I visited the university library at Southern University a couple of years ago. I told you about my visit to Southern University, I reply.

Oh, Mary says.

Happy Thanksgiving, Mary. We're gonna have fun, I say when I make breakfast.

Mary smiles. I help her out of her bed. Mary and I will celebrate Thanksgiving together. Bianca and Heidi think Mary is too wild. They are not coming to the dinner. Early on Thanksgiving morning we preheat the new oven before putting the turkey in. We slow roast the turkey all day long. We make cornbread dressing.

Yes. Let's party. I want to make eggnog, Mary exclaims.

Mary accidentally pours eggnog in my lap. She has used so much nutmeg, so I start smelling like a nutmeg man. I put on the full body plastic protection suit that my mother used when caring for my dad when he became sick. Now I will be ready for anything today.

Yummy, Mary exclaims.

Yes. The turkey is delicious, I say.

We have mashed potatoes, gravy, dressing, cranberry sauce, and a green bean casserole. We make a pumpkin pie with cinnamon crust for dessert.

Mary enters my bedroom and says, Karl. One night Ruby wanted to have sex at my place. She brought him in to have sex. I told them to go. I married as a virgin. I didn't go around having sex. She loved having sex. I wanted sex but I didn't have it. Ruby had sex because it feels good. Up and down. Up and down and all around. Sex feels good. Ruby told a woman at her school that she had sex with a man. Ruby had sex with a man in front of a woman. She taught the woman how to have sex. She told a woman that she was going to have sex with a young man in front of a girl to show her how he does and how she should have sex. Ruby taught other female students how to have sex. It caught up with her. The woman told the school that Ruby had sex having other female students watching her to have sex. Mama suspected that Ruby had sex with those men. Ruby told Juliet what she did. Then a man came to the house and had sex with Ruby after that.

It's six days before Mary's 80th birthday on December 17th. Mary has just received a rejection decision on her residence permit application from the Swedish migration services. She was supposed to leave Sweden on December 9th. We haven't found a place for her to stay in Louisiana. A friend of ours in New Orleans has called around to nursing homes. So

155

far there is nowhere for Mary to stay in Louisiana. I've decided just to accept the situation and live to the fullest.

I go to the church service and listen to Lucia songs. I return home and asks Mary if she wants some pea soup.

No, that's nasty. I don't want any pea soup, she replies.

This is pea soup made of yellow peas, I say.

That's disgusting. I don't want it. I want to have oatmeal, Karl, Mary replies.

Okay. I'll make you oatmeal, I say.

Mary slurps up her oatmeal. She has a large wet oatmeal stain on the front of her yellow sweater.

Karl, come here. I want to give you a hug, she says.

When Mary hugs me, the warm oatmeal clings on to my sweater.

Karl, you are such an amazing and handsome man. You're sexy and you can cook too, Mary says.

It's a new morning. The bleak sun warms nothing in the December darkness. I go for a walk along the river. I return home.

Are you coming to my wedding with Jesus? Mary asks.

Yes, I reply.

Do you think Jesus thinks I'm pretty? Mary asks.

You look beautiful, Mary, I reply.

Thank you. Have you seen Ruby and the others? Mary asks.

You don't want to hear my answer, I reply quietly.

What? Mary asks.

Ruby and the others are dead. If you want to meet real people that are alive I'm here and my mother will come here on Thursday at your birthday party, I reply.

Mary strolls around the kitchen in an erratic way. She goes downstairs and opens the door to garden. Cold winter air fills the house.

Ruby, where are you? Karl, bring me my stick! Mary

says and hurries outside with the stick.

Mary is upset.

KARL, FIND HER, she cries out impatiently.

Mary is restless. Suddenly Mary has stroke symptoms. I help her into the car. I put on her seatbelt and drive her to the emergency room at the hospital an hour away. At the hospital, Mary is taken into one of the rooms. We talk to a nurse. She says that the doctor will arrive soon.

An hour later, the doctor has still not come. The hours go by. I go to find one of the nurses. She says that the physician will be with Mary soon. I ask one of the nurses several times. Mary waits in the bed for the physician the entire night.

In the beginning, I stand at the side of Mary's bed. When the hours go by, I sit down on the hard chair in her room. Hours spent on a plastic hospital chair gives me numb legs.

Mary feels a little bit better. She is awake all night long singing and preaching loud at the hospital. Mary is laughing at her own jokes. Mary feels a little bit better. She insults all the nurses in the ward.

I think it's a scandal that she hasn't been able to see a physician the whole night. The physician comes to Mary at 7 a.m. after almost eight hours of waiting. He examines Mary and says that she is fine. Mary falls asleep immediately in the car when I drive her home. We're back at home for breakfast. When Mary is sleeping I look at myself in the mirror. I see a worn-out man with a little bit blood under each eye after all my scratching to stay awake that night.

It's 4 a.m. I'm sleeping. Mary opens my bedroom door. She is a wild powerhouse and totally awake.

I'm gonna marry Jesus today. Are you coming, Karl? Mary shouts.

Yes, after I teach. Mary it's 4 a.m. in the morning. I need to sleep some more to have energy to teach, I reply.

No, the clock must be wrong. I want to bathe my

feet. Where's the pan to soak my feet? Get it now, Karl, Mary says.

The bowl is behind the door there. Can you take it yourself? I reply, half-sleeping.

Where? Mary says.

I get up and show Mary where the pan is. I pour foot salt into the pan and fill it with warm water. Mary smiles at me when she soaks her feet. She sits next to me when I go back to sleep. After Mary bathe her feet she wakes me up again. I dry her feet and put on new warm socks. Mary gets up and screams when she opens the front door to the garden:

Ruby, where are you?

I'm very sleepy. It's silent for a while. I hear an intense and anxiety filled high pitch scream from the street:

RUBY, WHERE ARE YOU?

The neighbor dog barks. Mary has taken off her pants. She wears only underwear and a warm sweater when she is standing on the snowy street in her bare legs. The falling snowflakes kiss her forehead. She has her shoes on. I can only see her behind the wall. To me it looks like she has no clothes on.

I can't see, she says in the darkness.

It's cold, Mary says.

Come on in, Mary, I say.

Mary turns around and walks down the street.

Let's have some hot chocolate, I say.

Mary smiles. It's dark. She walks back toward the house. I start walking towards Mary. Suddenly, she loses her balance. Mary falls straight down on the snowy road. I run to Mary and lift her up. I help her inside. She didn't scratch her knees.

My heart is beating fast! Mary screams.

I make hot chocolate for both of us. I help Mary to her bed and sit down next to her.

Sweetheart, I will sing you a Swedish goodnight song, I say.

I hold one of Mary's hands and sing who can sail

without the wind, who can row without oars, who can part from their friend without shedding tears. Mary can sail without the wind. Mary can row without oars, but you can't part from your dearest friend without shedding tears. I keep on whistling until Mary goes to sleep.

Shadows play in the hallway. We're celebrating Mary's eightieth birthday with a party for her, me and the three cats. Mary and I are singing and dancing to the Rhythm and Blues pioneer Fats Domino. I cook the thick Cajun stew crawfish étouffée. I peel crawfish tails and cut celery, onions, garlic, bell peppers, green onions, and parsley. I make a roux. I use a skillet to heat the vegetable oil and the flour to make the roux until it is light brown. I fry the vegetables and smother the crawfish tails. The pot with the crawfish étouffée is boiling on the stove. It smells heavenly. Mary shakes her head and shouts, Rock'n'roll!

From the speakers on high volume Fats Domino sings, I'm walking to New Orleans. I serve the étouffée on rice. In the early afternoon, I've made a lemon meringue pie that we're enjoying.

Thank you, Mary says.

Mary thinks that I'm married to two women. She explains, Maria had a new heart. My little girl Maria that had the heart transplant. She is fine. She visits Louisiana. She is different from the other Maria that died.

Mary is coming down the stairs to me in the bedroom. She is confused.

Are you okay, Mary? I ask.

She looks puzzled. After a few moments Mary asks:

What is this place? Where am I?

You're in Sweden, I explain.

I'm hungry, Mary says.

What do you want to eat for supper? The choices are salmon or chicken.

I want salmon, Mary says.

159

I bake the salmon in the oven and boil asparagus and artichoke. I fry French bread in garlic and parsley butter. I set the table and fill a glass of milk for Mary. She loves to drink milk with all her food.

As Mary and I enjoy the supper, she says that we got to talk some with Maria.

Let's call Maria now. Okay, I'm ringing Maria, Mary says.

Mary gives me the toilet paper roll that is supposed to be a phone in her mind.

Maria passed away in September after having had brain cancer, I reply.

That wasn't Maria, Mary replies.

You're a crazy man, Karl. I'm gonna call the police on you for saying that Maria is dead. I just talked to her. Where is she? Mary asks.

My heart thumps hard.

I don't know, I reply and look out of the window at the dark sky.

Mary says nothing. She goes to sleep sitting up in her chair at the kitchen table. I go downstairs. I let her sleep until she calls me. I help her to the bathroom and to bed.

Leave the dishes. I'll do them tomorrow morning, Mary says.

Snow begins falling heavily, over the house and the yard. The Korean pine tree in the garden is covered with snow. Mary receives another letter from her best friend Alice in Louisiana. Mary smiles broadly and asks me to read it. Her friend writes that she misses Mary and is praying for her. Mary loves her friend so much. Letters like this one from her friend means the world to Mary - that someone in Louisiana thinks and cares about her. Mary is so happy.

This morning I make oatmeal for Heidi, Mary, and myself.

I miss my little girl so much. Do you miss her? Mary asks.

Yes, I reply.

Please bring her home, Karl. Can you bring her home? Please bring her home, Karl. PLEASE. PLEASE. PLEASE. Where is Maria? Mary says.

She's in heaven, Heidi replies.

Karl, you can go and get Maria, Mary says.

Maria passed away and she will not come back, I say.

Mary looks at me puzzled and grieves for a second.

The last day of 2020 starts with Mary looking instantly worried and storming into my bedroom whilst I'm sleeping screaming at 4 a.m., Karl, where is my daughter?

I open my eyes slowly and explain, Maria died in September after having had brain cancer.

Maria didn't die! Maria got a new heart, Mary says.

Who told you that Maria has a new heart? That's not true. It's only you who believes that. I went with Maria to her oncologist for two years and saw the pictures of the cancer tumors in her brain, I tell Mary.

That's not true, Karl, Mary replies.

Karl, talk to Maria. Maria is alive. Why don't you talk to your wife? WHERE IS MY DAUGHTER? KARL, FIND MARIA. Karl, Get up! Get up! Get up! Mary screams.

Mary looks dizzy and says, I feel that I'm fainting.

I look at Mary shaking out of anxiety. She needs me.

Mary, sweetheart, please sit down and rest on the chair and calm down, I plead.

Mary sits down on the bedroom chair watching me. Her arms are still shaking.

Karl, what kind of strange and big arm is that? Mary asks.

That's not an arm. That's my CPAP machine that I use to breathe more easily during sleep. CPAP stands for continuous positive airway pressure, I explain.

Oh. I thought it was your arm. I'm gonna make oatmeal for you, Karl, Mary replies.

Mary, I don't want any oatmeal. I just want to sleep.

161

It's 4 a.m. I want to make my own oatmeal in the morning.

Mary goes back upstairs. After a few minutes, she returns to my bedroom with a huge bowl of mainly milk, margarine, sugar, and some oats floating around in the liquid. I feel that I'm about to throw up. I usually make oatmeal every morning for Mary and myself in the kitchen. I've asked Mary to not bring food down the stairs because she spills most of it. I usually have a banana, almonds, raisins, cinnamon, and pumpkin and sunflower seeds on my oatmeal. Mary's oatmeal with a big clump of margarine and one full cup of sugar looks disgusting. My heart is beating fast. I get up to check my blood pressure. The blood pressure machines shows that I need to seek immediate medical attention.

I'm under massive stress in life. It's a pandemic, but that's the easiest part of my life. Help me! What can I do to go through this phase? How can I escape my mother-in-law? My wife is dead. I'm now here all alone with my wild mother-in-law. It's a never-ending nightmare. It won't stop. Mary is not going to change. I'm just accepting this fact. Bianca's beautiful artwork on the wall and the snowy landscape outside the window calm me a little bit. I whistle and dance and do characters for Mary to make her laugh.

In the morning, Bianca calls me and says happy new year. I wish her a happy new year too. I'm happy that Heidi is here today. I taste Mary's oatmeal and decide to throw it out. It tastes disgusting with all the margarine and sugar. I can't eat it. When I'm going upstairs to return the plate, I see the milk and oatmeal all over the staircase. I dry it up.

I can't relax. I still feel hyper. I put on my running clothes and go for a run in the forest. When I breath in the forest air and run as fast I can I get out of my mind and enter my body and the nature. I'm working through the feelings I have had after Maria's passing and the stress related to caring for Mary. When running and walking in the forest, I gain control of them and feel stronger. My feelings will not rule me. I feel calmer.

In the morning, I talk to Heidi who had a fun evening with her friends last night. I leave the house and go for a long forest walk to relax. I feel the winds in my face and enjoy the beauty of the nature. All is still in the forest. Only birds are singing. I keep on walking. I find silence and solitude at the edge of the clear river water.

I return home. It gets wild at home with Mary all the time. Sometimes I know when it's going to be one of those wild days with Mary. We have our good days and our bad days. It's a battle. I hug Mary in the kitchen after breakfast.

Karl, your heart is beating fast. Can you help me to bed? Mary says.

I lead Mary to the bed and tuck her in.

You're so fine, Karl. You're all mine, Mary says and smiles.

Mary is increasingly worried. She looks up. Her eyes are full of chaos and pain. She says:

Karl, where is Maria? Shame on you! You don't want to answer about your own wife? It's a shame. I'm gonna call her. Maria, I'm sitting here with Karl and eating a banana. Karl, Maria says that she wants to be with her husband. She says she's coming here. When are you coming, Maria? Tomorrow. That's so nice. I'll be happy to see my beautiful daughter. Karl will buy some clothes for you when you come here. You're gonna get ready and pack? You're flying on an airplane? That's gonna be nice. You're gonna call me before you leave? Okay. Bye. Karl, Maria is coming here tomorrow. Do you want her to come? You should. I set the date for her. I'm so happy. My little baby girl I've been grieving for her. Your wife is in New Orleans, Karl.

Maria passed away in September, I reply.

Mary shouts with a high pitch voice:

SHUT UP, KARL! YOU'RE TROUBLE. I DON'T LIKE YOU. I'M TIRED OF YOU LYING. DON'T YOU GET IT. YOU'RE STUPID, KARL. MARIA HAS GOT A NEW HEART. WHY CAN'T YOU UNDERSTAND THAT? WHY DON'T YOU CALL HER? YOU THINK SHE'S DEAD.

I don't have the energy to stand up to Mary. Instead, I shut and lock my bedroom door to block out Mary's screams. She takes her stick and starts hitting hard on the door.

Please leave me alone! Leave me alone! I plead.

Mary keeps on banging her stick on the door. I put on my headphones and listen to music at the highest volume to drown out Mary's insults.

Mary reads the children's bible next to me in the bedroom. She goes away to the living room and comes back with the bible. She lays it open on the desk in front of me. Mary gets excited.

Karl, look at Jesus' hips. They're so good-looking, huh? Don't you think? Mary tells me.

Yes, I reply.

Are you going to call my little girl, your wife? Mary asks.

No, I reply.

My mom and grandma taught me to be a teacher. My dad came to us every Sunday. He taught us to be sweet, Mary says.

I nod in agreement.

Mary takes her medicine. She always swallows all her medication without water. Mary starts to cry.

The day starts with Mary falling out of the bed at 5 a.m. Mary enters my bedroom, touches the switch and light floods the room. She shakes me hard and says:

Wake up! Karl, are you awake? I fell out of the bed. You need to come and help me. I talked to Maria today. She lives with principal Wilson in Afghanistan. Maria is scared in Afghanistan. They are bombing and shooting and all. She wants to come to you, Karl.

164

You need to talk to Maria before she comes to Sweden. Principal Wilson said that Maria should come back here. He had good advice. I would get my wife. She is scared that you don't want her no more, she thinks. Karl, you need to go to Afghanistan and get Maria. Don't you love your wife?

Mary looks at me desperately for me to help Maria.

Can we go to the kitchen and have some breakfast? I ask.

Yes, Mary replies.

I walk upstairs with Mary. I make oatmeal and boil eggs. Mary puts on red lipstick and combs her hair over the food. Mary has a lot of thick and long hair. I ask Mary if she can comb her hair in the bathroom because her hair is flying around the kitchen into the food. Mary continues to comb her hair over the food. I tell her that I don't want her hair in my food. Mary bursts into a broad smile and laughs. She continues to comb her hair over the food. I finish eating my breakfast with Mary's hair in my oatmeal.

Mary squeaks constantly while closing her eyes. She tells her endless stories in a manic way. I ask Mary to lower her voice because it's very annoying to listen to. She keeps on squeaking. I squeak to imitate her for ten seconds. Mary explodes. She is furious banging her fist on the kitchen table and screaming:

YOU SHUT UP KARL! YOU'RE SO STUPID! STUPID! STUPID!

I'm a very patient person but listening to her ongoing rants and yells is getting on my nerves. My head hurts. Too many things have happened. Mary has been manic the entire day. She is on fire and won't shut up.

Mary says, I'm smart. I'm no dumb, dumb. Can I give Mr. Wilson one of your books, Karl?

Okay, I reply. Mr. Wilson is a very smart person like me. He reads books, okay, Mary explains.

I make the most of what I have in life. I feel constant stress caring for Mary. I feel that the stress is sapping

165

my energy. If I continue living like this it will shorten my life. I go to the shower giving the hot water time to work wonders on my tired limbs. I feel a little better after the shower.

Good night, Mary, I say and tuck her in under several blankets.

Your little girl is coming tomorrow because there is too much shooting over there in Afghanistan, Mary says.

Why do you refer to Maria as my little girl? Maria was my wife. She was an adult woman with two children, and she died in September, I say.

Maria is my daughter. She didn't die. She is in Afghanistan. You're going to pick her up now! Karl, you need to go today to Afghanistan and get Maria. I had it with you. Do something, Mary says.

Maria has passed, I reply.

I'm going to give your wife to principal Wilson. I'll give a house key to him too. He's going to beat your butt, Karl. He's strong. He's going to make you act right and pick up your wife, Mary says.

Mary is talking loud to Mr. Wilson:

Mr. Wilson, what time will Karl go to Afghanistan? 9 o'clock. Okay Karl? You're picking up Maria in Afghanistan at 9 o'clock, okay. If you don't go Karl I'm gonna go with Mr. Wilson. Mr. Wilson, Karl says that he's going to Afghanistan to pick up Maria. I'm gonna go with you Mr. Wilson to pick up Maria. Okay bye bye Mr. Wilson. We're going to have a lovely trip to Afghanistan. We might have sex on the trip. Mr. Wilson is going to plan the sex. He makes me feel sexy.

Karl, do I have any things on my lips from the anti-acid pills? Mary asks.

No, I reply.

Love is waiting for Mr. Wilson. I love him. Do you know when I fell in love with him? Mary asks.

No, I reply.

I fell in love with him at the school. My darling Mr.

Wilson, Mary says.

I open the door. Snow whirls in the hallway.

I'M STAYING HERE IN THE HOUSE. Karl, you can go with Mr. Wilson to Afghanistan! Mary screams.

Karl, you look so handsome. What is your wife going to do? She's gonna be happy. She's gonna grab you and kiss you, Mary says.

Mary jumps up, grabs me, and kisses my cheek.

I love this man. What am I gonna do with this man? Mary says.

It's 5 a.m. It's chilly. The snow falls in frosty white bits outside the kitchen window. Mary enters my bedroom saying, Karl, what am I doing today?

You said you were going to Afghanistan, I reply.

We have a big, big guy called Al. He's gonna help us to take Maria. He's strong. He's the head God and he's above Jesus. Karl, get my shoes. I'm going with Al now, Mary says.

Maria has passed away and Al does not exist, I explain.

Al, Karl says that you don't exist. Aren't you coming, Al. Yes, he's coming. I don't make up things. I never make up things. I'm gonna be with Al. He knows what to do, Mary says.

Mary stands on the cold front steps of the stairs. Snowflakes land on her shoes.

Al, talk to me please. Karl says that I'm making you up, she says.

Mary closes her eyes and concentrates on the conversation with Al.

Karl, do you want to go with me and Al to Afghanistan? she asks.

No, I'm staying here, I reply.

Mary leaves the house. The house door is open. I get up fast to close the door to shut out the chilly draughts. I look out the window at the garden. Mary is in the garden in her winter clothes sitting on a snow-filled chair.

I'm in the kitchen making breakfast. Mary and I sit

at the kitchen table. We have a mealtime ritual. We always do the sign when we say, In the name of the Father, and the Son, and of the Holy Spirit.

We always say grace before meals, Bless us O Lord, and these thy gifts, which we are about to receive through thy bounty, through Christ, our Lord, Amen.

Sometimes Mary and I sing, *Amazing grace*. After breakfast we continue to pray and say Our Father and Hail Mary. We pray that God will protect our family.

Later that day, Mary and I go to church. The mass is held in Swedish. The priest changes one of the Swedish hymns to *Amazing grace* after talking to Mary. She is so happy. Mary tells me that she feels included even though she doesn't understand Swedish. Mary smiles and sings out loudly almost drowning the other attendants.

Later, Mary and I talk about that we value gratitude. Grateful for being alive and healthy. It's snowing outside the kitchen window. Mary eats oatmeal, eggs, and drinks water.

I love the water and the air here. When I lived in Louisiana it used to stink from the plant. We had so much pollution, Mary says.

I'm happy that you like the fresh air. Our municipality has some of the best water in Sweden, I say.

I tell Mary that I'm going on my daily forest walk.

How do you walk downstairs? Mary asks.

Mary opens the door to Heidi's room and to a closet.

You take the stairs here, I reply.

Mary brings an office chair.

It could be dangerous if you bring that heavy office chair down the stairs. You might fall, I say.

I go downstairs. Mary opens the balcony door and walks on the snowy balcony in her socks. She sinks down in the snow and pulls the office chair out onto the balcony.

I'm gonna look at you when you drive to the forest,

Mary says.

Please Mary. I don't want anything to happen to you. You could fall in the snow on the balcony, I say.

Okay. I'll go inside, Mary replies.

Back inside the house, I take her to bed.

The fire alarm goes off when Mary is making candy on the stove. I had forgotten to turn off the fuse. She was able to turn on the burner and had poured sugar and cream in a pot that was creating black smoke all over the kitchen. I open the window and the balcony door to air out the smoke. I go to the store and get candy for Mary. When I give her the goodies she smiles for a second, and then lashes out on in rage:

WHERE IS MY SODA?

I didn't get any soda. Soda is not good for your teeth, I reply.

It's none of your business, Karl. They are my teeth. I do what I want? Mary says.

I don't want to get into another argument with Mary. I change the topic and start singing made up songs which Mary is backing up with her musical memory. Even if she has dementia, she can improvise musically. I'm moved emotionally by her. She is so gifted. I start crying inside and some happy tears come out. This is a beautiful moment. I appreciate Mary despite of her wild and intense behaviors.

This morning, Mary talks about the voices she used to have at the mental institution she was at:

I heard voices in the hospital. The voices got worse when I got out of the hospital.

These hallucinations frightened her. Mary looks distressed. I sit next to Mary listen to her and hold her hand. We have an early lunch.

The problem with you Karl is that you don't respect dead people, Mary says.

I respect dead people. I just think that dead people are dead, I reply.

Mary explains how it is:

They are alive. Ruby is dead and I talk to her on the

telephone. Dead people have muscles and things. They can have sex.

In heaven? I ask.

Yes! They can have more sex in heaven because they respect sex. It's not a common thing. When I go to heaven, I'm going to have a lot of sex. I don't have sex now. That's why God respects me. I want to have sex with all the men that I love. Jesus is going to decide what men I have sex with, Mary explains.

Mary keeps on talking about sex in heaven. I start cooking dinner. I make Jambalaya which is a Creole take on Spanish paella containing chicken, sausage, long-grain rice and the combination of onions, bell peppers and celery known as the trinity. I use chopped parsley, minced garlic cloves and red pepper. Mary gets up fast to come to the kitchen table when I say that the Jambalaya is ready.

We eat in holy silence. Mary looks overjoyed. After supper, I tuck her in. She keeps on talking about all the good sex she will have with her boyfriends in heaven.

Good night, Mary, I say.

Wow! Karl, you're a fantastic cook. The Jambalaya was delicious, Mary answers half-sleeping.

I'm leading a digital conference for youth workers. Mary asks me if I she can bring me some cheese sandwiches and milk. Last time Mary brought sandwiches and milk she fell onto one of the sofas and spilled the milk all over the living room.

No, I say.

Mary loses her balance. I excuse myself from the Zoom conference and run towards Mary. I'm able to catch her before she falls.

After the conference when I enter the kitchen Mary is preparing pancakes without eggs. There is flour everywhere. She has sliced cheese in the pancake batch and prepared twenty garlic cloves to put into the batch.

I used to have a boyfriend. We used to go to motels

to have sex, Mary says.

Okay, I reply.

I take out Mary's trumpet. Mary shows Heidi and I how she used to play it.

I wake up by hearing Mary opening the door to the snowy garden while waiting for her lover Mr. Johnson. Mary says that maybe he's not real. Maybe he is a shadow.

Mary is filled with anxiety. I help her inside and close the door behind me.

Would you like to see and talk to Mr. Johnson, Karl? Mary asks.

That's not possible. Did you see Mr. Johnson? Don't worry Mary. It will be alright, I reply.

Look, Karl. Mr. Johnson is coming. He comes here all the time. I have a raspberry cake for him, Mary says and laughs.

I think you better come and see Karl. Mr. Johnson is here, Mary says.

I brew some coffee and make oatmeal.

Would you like some coffee, Mary?

I want some coffee! Mary shouts with joy.

Mary and I talk during breakfast about the Swedish Migration Agency and that they have rejected her resident permit application and that she needs to go back to the United States very soon.

I want to stay in Sweden with you Karl. You're so sweet to me, Mary says.

Thank you, Mary, I reply.

We talk about the COVID-19 pandemic and the new UK variant in the US. We have coped with Covid by staying at home most of the time.

Surviving a severe coronavirus infection is hard. After the pandemic situation has calmed down a little bit it will be possible to fly back to Louisiana, I explain.

I want to live with my mama. We get along good together. Karl, you have an awful a lot of books. Do you read them all? Mary asks.

No but depending on what I write about I bring them out to my desk to look through. I love my books. I used to work in two bookshops. I got a lot of books then, I reply.

Mary has now been here in Sweden for almost three years. She likes Sweden and at the same time misses Louisiana.

I sing and dance for Mary during lunch.

Welcome to Karl's wild and crazy diner, a place that your mama said never to go to. That was long ago. I've been looking for a place. Do you ever wonder what kind of food Karl serves? I sing.

I smile with a red beat mouth. Mary laughs.

My only food is..., I say and smile with black olive teeth.

You're crazy, Karl! Mary says and laughs.

I keep on singing, let's have a fresh starter.

I smile with a broccoli mouth. Mary laughs so she is almost peeing on herself.

I heard you. You wanted some more? I sing.

I heard you, I say and smile with ginger fiber teeth hanging down on my lips.

Come with me to Karl's place. Come with me to Karl's place. Please don't think about your worries. Please come down to Karl's place, I sing.

I swirl around in funny dance moves. Mary enjoys her lunch.

20 SHADOW PEOPLE FOR SUPPER

West Sweden, February 2021

Mary continuously shifts from the world of the living to the dead.

Where were you? I went down the street and you weren't there, Mary asks.

I went for a walk in the forest, I reply.

Mary informs me that her husband Mr. Johnson and her sister are coming for supper. Mary calls them the shadow people. She believes that the shadow people are real. Mary gets ready by changing her clothes. It's cold in the house. Mary has put on a short jeans skirt to be attractive for her husband Mr. Johnson.

Karl, don't you think that I have pretty legs for an eighty-year-old woman? Mary asks.

Yes, I reply.

Mary lifts her skirt and pushes out her legs in front me and opens the front door to the snowy garden. The moonshine light up Mary's legs.

Ruby! Mr. Johnson! Mary shouts.

It's -9 degree Celsius. The chilly air fills the hallway. The dogs in the neighbor's garden bark.

Karl, what's for supper? You need to cook something good for our shadow guests, Mary says five minutes later.

I will go upstairs and prepare the supper, I tell Mary.

I start cooking a Valencian seafood paella. I invite Mary to the table. A steamy pan of paella is in front of us. I have cooked shrimp, lobster, mussels and cuttlefish with white rice, herbs, olive oil and salt. We sit in holy silence and eat.

What's for dessert, Karl? Mary asks.

I have baked delicious Portuguese custard tarts called *pastel de natas*.

Mm, Karl, you're an amazing chef. I love your food,

Mary says.

She is calm whilst eating. Twenty minutes later, Mary's mind is spiraling with heavy anxiety.

You better come up here. You are my husband Mr. Johnson. You come here right now. Are you coming? The food is ready. Please come! Mary screams to the shadow people.

She opens the front door again.

Let me open the door for you, she says.

WHERE ARE THEY, KARL? Mary screams.

Mary walks down the slope in the heavy snowfall.

They say if we don't see them we don't love them, Mary talks to her sister and her husband out loud in front me.

Mary, why do you look around for dead people? I'm here. I'm a real person, I reply.

Mary keeps on looking for her supper guests for another hour and comes back inside to go to bed.

Mary has a sense of humor even when she is having dementia and hallucinations. With Maria and the girls, I have been doing funny accents in Swedish and impressions to make them laugh. My sense of humor with Mary must be expanded to new levels including facial expressions and long wild dance routines to make Mary laugh. I often include Mary in the dance routines. Then she passes out smiling.

You are the only person who can make me laugh, baby, Mary tells me when we have supper.

I give her the largest spinach tooth smile I can. Mary laughs.

You're crazy Karl, she says.

She keeps on laughing until she goes to sleep.

Mary is sleeping. I go for a walk in the beautiful snow landscapes. When I return home, Mary has hung her wet clothes all over the hallway. I go upstairs to talk to her. When I enter the kitchen, the stove is pulled out from the wall. When I go for walks or leave the house, I routinely turn off the fuse to prevent any fires in case Mary decides to cook and goes to sleep. Mary has filled a pot with beans.

How are you, Mary? I ask.

Oh Karl, I went outside in the snow and fell. A nice lady neighbor helped me up. I was going to cook beans and rice, Mary says.

That was nice. I can cook the food, I say.

I'm peeing on myself, Mary says.

I support her when she goes to the bathroom. Then I tuck her in. Mary realizes that her daughter died after more than four months after Maria passing away. I didn't know that my little girl is dead. I didn't grieve her. I was so happy to have that little girl. She was a gifted child. I was so happy to give birth to my child. My husband was there with me every step of the way, Mary says.

Why did you hit Maria when she was sick with cancer? I ask Mary.

She needed that. I can hit her. I call Maria in heaven. Karl says that I hit you, Maria and you didn't like that, Mary replies.

The Covid-19 pandemic is going on in the United States. Mary doesn't have a place to stay in Louisiana. My plan is to travel back to Louisiana with Mary in the summer of 2021 in case we find a nursing home for her.

It's a beautiful winter morning with sunshine and magical snowfall. Mary opens the front door. Freezing air fills the house. She stands barefoot on the cold front steps.

My husband Mr. Johnson is coming. We're going to have sex. We can have sex in heaven too. Mr. Johnson when are you coming to get me? I'm ready. Oh, I need to go upstairs. If he comes please let him in, Mary says.

Okay, I say.

He said he's leaving his house now, Mary says.

She looks very aroused.

Mr. Johnson and his brother are going to have sex with me. I'm gonna sleep with them. You know all my

175

business, Karl. I'm waiting for them. They didn't come. I talked to them on the telephone all night. Karl, you're one of the sweetest men I know besides my husband Mr. Johnson, Mary says.

Snow clouds pass outside the kitchen window where Mary and I eat oatmeal.

I have good news. An investigator from the Swedish Migration Agency called me and said that she has taken over the case from the other officer. She said that she has seen that I have pushed myself to the limit to care for Maria, you, and the girls. Now the migration agency will do what they can to support me. She will talk to the border police service and work to organize to send you back to the United States, I tell Mary.

This call was an amazing relief for all of us. I hope everything works out. I can't keep going. I'm so dizzy all the time. I write an email message to the Swedish Migration Agency:

This is a cry for help regarding the American citizen Mary Jackson Guillory who was supposed to be expelled from Sweden on December 9, 2020. It's no longer working out to have Mary living with me because the level of care that she needs is so great that I no longer will be able to perform my full-time work at the university and support my two daughters. Both daughters experience massive stress when they contact me and hear Mary's anxiety filled screams. They feel bad for days after having experienced her behavior.

Mary needs help from the Swedish Migration Agency to return to the United States. The background is that my wife Maria Guillory Hedman passed away in 2020 after having had brain cancer. On November 11, 2020, the Migration Agency decided to expel Mary to the United States within four weeks. Mary has dementia, psychosis and unsteady walk making it dangerous for her to step outdoors without the constant support from another person. She has anxiety and manic behaviors. Her mental health has deteriorated lately. When I write this message it is 3:50 a.m. Mary has either been outside or been opening the door the entire night. She has let freezing cold air (-15 degree Celsius) into the house. She talks constantly about Jesus and two men that she will let into the house.

I have cared for Mary day and night 24/7 since June 12, 2018. At the same time, I have cared for my terminally brain cancer sick wife who passed away. I have cared for my daughters experiencing rage attacks by Mary. I work as a university professor on a full-time basis. When Mary is not letting me sleep at night due to her manic behavior I am not able to cope much longer. I need your help before I have a breakdown.

21 PULL MY NAIL OFF

West Sweden, February, 2021

It's a frosty morning. I had a lovely breakfast and feel calm. It's ten minutes before my lecture via Zoom. I feel totally prepared. My body tense up when I hear Mary's footsteps in the stairs. She bangs very hard on my bedroom door.

Please leave, Mary. I'm going to teach on the computer in a few minutes, I say.

Anxiety overtakes Mary.

PULL IT OFF AS HARD AS YOU CAN. PULL IT OFF AS HARD AS YOU CAN. PULL IT OFF AS HARD AS YOU CAN, Mary yells and bangs on the door.

Mary has had a very large nail on one of her big toes for as long as I remember. The nail is brown, thick, and nasty. It looks like a rotten moldy cheese that you forgot to eat for weeks on end. I look at Mary. I insist that I will assist her later today, but she doesn't give in. I don't want Mary to screaming about the toenail during my whole lecture. I'm an accommodating man. I run upstairs as quick as I can and put on plastic gloves.

PULL IT OFF! Mary shouts after me.

I jump run downstairs in a few seconds. When Mary sits comfortably, I lift her foot in the air and remove the toenail with my hand. It bleeds a lot. The floor is covered with blood residue. I clean her big toe with alcohol and the floor.

Thank you, Karl. Thank you, Karl. Thank you, Karl, Mary says.

You're welcome. Did it hurt? I ask and look at her.

No. I'm okay, Mary says and looks grateful and pleased.

Mary lays down on my bed behind my chair. I run to the desk, login and make it ten seconds before the lecture starts.

Good morning. Welcome to this lecture about crisis management, I say with a big smile.

After the lecture I think about my beloved daughters. They are my guardian angels. Bianca walks with me in nature. Heidi stands up for me as an advocate when I'm about to go under. I love to talk to and dance with them. We tell stories and play theatre. We're having so much together.

A few days ago, I wrote a letter to the Swedish Migration Service without a response. Heidi writes a support letter to the Swedish Migration Service. The subject of Heidi's message is *If my dad falls, I will fall*.

Hello. My name is Heidi Hedman. I'm nineteen years old and study information systems at the University of Gothenburg. I'm the daughter of Karl Hedman. On Sunday night, my dad sent another cry for help in a message regarding the acute situation we're in. I'm writing to support his message. Please help us to solve the situation with my grandmother Mary Guillory. Please help us with her expulsion to the United States. My dad has cared for Mary and the family 24/7 for many years. My now deceased mom Maria suffered a multitude of psychotic episodes and terminal brain cancer. She died in September 2020. My grandmother Mary has dementia and psychosis. She lives at home with my dad and because of her illness she exposes my dad to mental and physical abuse. Mary was refused a residence permit on November 11th, 2020. On December 9[th,] 2020, she was supposed to leave Sweden. Due to financial reasons, we cannot afford to pay for her return trip to the United States. There must be something that someone can do. My dad is incredibly strong, but there is only so much one human being can cope with and my dad has gone beyond that point a long time ago. Would it help if you got to know him a bit?

My dad loves black tea so strong that he always put two tea bags in the cup all the time. My dad loves to read. He always has a pile of books on the desk including poetry books, novels and other literature for his courses and research. My dad loves Spanish TV shows. We have the same favorite series *La Casa de Papel*. My dad has a full-time job as a university lecturer. He really enjoys this and is very passionate about his work. When he tells me about what research he is doing or when he interacts with his students I can see that he lights up. It hurts me so much to know that he risks losing this because no one can help him with Mary. My dad is what a parent should be.

My dad has always been there for me despite of these circumstances. He has shown what loyalty is. He has taught me to be curious, listen, and at the same time stand up for myself. Most of all he has taught me about love and care. Now it is my turn to be there for my dad. I ask for the same care that he has shown everyone else in his surroundings. Please help my dad. I plead one more time. There must be something that someone can do. We don't ask for much. We need support for a Swedish citizen in need. Why wait until it is too late? My dad is the only reason why I'm still healthy and sane. If he falls I don't know what I will do. I'm fully conscious that life is not fair, but sometimes there is room for justice. Sincerely, Heidi Hedman

I'm so proud of Heidi for writing this support letter.

I leave the house to go to a coffee shop with Bianca to have *Semla*, the wheat flour bun, flavored with cardamom, filled with almond paste, and whipped cream. The traditions of *semla* are rooted in Fat Tuesday when the buns were eaten at a last celebratory feast before the Christian fasting period of Lent. After this feast, I go to a group therapy session with a social worker.

When I return home it's freezing cold. I check the mailbox. I hear a scream. My first thought is that Mary is lying in the snow somewhere frozen half dead. I can't see her. I enter the house and call Mary's name. I hear her from the basement. I find Mary standing in the darkness shouting out through the small glass windows in the corner in the back of the wine cellar.

Thank God. Karl's leg is not broken, Mary says.

We go upstairs. Mary calls up Ruby with the toilet paper roll.

Ruby, are the two Marias there? Mary asks.

The migration service officer calls me. She says that they are planning to hand over Mary's case to the Swedish border police and to ask the border police to arrange a sick transport for Mary from Sweden to the United States. She says that she will call me back when she knows more. The officer asks for Mary's medication list.

I reply that I can ask Mary's Swedish doctor to print and sign Mary's medication list to bring to the United States. I also tell her that Mary needs a nursing home, care home or a shelter when she arrives in Louisiana. I inform her that Mary gets a pension that we have used for medications, doctor visits and hospital visits in Sweden.

Mary screams with a high pitch voice:
THERE'S A SNAKE!!
Mary stamps on the floor and shouts:
SNAKE! SNAKE! SNAKE!
I don't see a snake, I reply.
Mary screams:
THERE IT IS. SNAAAAKE!

Mary's migration service officer calls me. She says that a nurse from the border police will fly with Mary to Louisiana. On Thursday, I have an appointment with the Swedish Migration Agency. They ask me to bring Mary's passport, medication list, HMO Louisiana card, and all the other documentation for her trip which they will scan and send to the Swedish border police. The migration service officer says that she will find out if Mary needs to be tested for Covid and get the two vaccinations for Covid before she flies.

When we have supper Mary says that she is happy to go back to the United States with the nurse. She doesn't care if the nurse is a man or a woman. This means that Mary will return to Louisiana in the coming weeks. Caring for Mary the last three years was one of the most intense periods in my life. Psychologically it wears on me. Sooner or later I probably will have to pay for it with my health. Everyone is saying that I'm doing a great job. Even when I go to bed my mind goes on thinking about the possibility of Mary leaving the house freezing to death somewhere or walking on the road nearby getting hit by a car or a truck.

Bianca and I go sledding in the snow hills. We are laughing and giggling intensely. We are having so much fun.

Mary and I start the day with dancing to the dance song *Pump Up The Jam* by Technotronic.

Snow had fallen all night long. The bedroom door opens early in the morning. Mary is in her winter clothes when she cries to me:

I'm not going to any nursing home! I'm going to stay with my mama!

Mary goes outside and leaves the door open. An endless stream of beautiful snowflakes swirl to the ground. Mary slips and falls on the ice. I rescue her from a freezing death. Her body is cold. I look back at the mark where Mary fell. It looks like a snow angel.

It's freezing cold, Karl, Mary says.

I lift Mary. I bring her inside and help her to change her clothes. I light a fire.

Karl, what date am I going to the United States? Mary asks.

Soon, I reply.

How is the Corona situation in the United States? Mary asks.

The White House website states that the United

States had experienced more than 24 million confirmed COVID cases and more than 400,000 COVID deaths. You need to have a negative COVID test when you enter the United States.

Do I have the Corona virus, Karl? Mary asks.

No, I reply.

What symptoms do people get when they have Corona, Karl? Mary asks.

Most common symptoms are fever, dry cough, and tiredness. Serious symptoms are difficulty breathing or shortness of breath, chest pain or pressure, and loss of speech or movement, I reply.

Jesus. I don't have all of that, Mary says.

What do I do if I get the symptoms? Mary asks.

Seek immediate medical attention, I say.

Mary walks up to me and hugs me.

You will take care of that, Karl?

Yes, I will take care of that. Don't worry, Mary, I say.

22 WHISTLING THERAPY

West Sweden, February 2021

I foster a relationship with Mary to cope and to not go under. My main strategy is to whistle when I care for her. Whistling is my kind of therapy. I feel better when I whistle. When whistling I stay flexible to handle any situations with her.

Karl, you might become a famous whistler. You have a beautiful tone, she says.

Thank you, Mary, I reply.

Karl, have you ever thought about being a magician? Mary asks.

No, I reply.

People in mental health hospitals should have your whistling on tapes, Karl. Your whistling would soothe all of them, Mary says.

Thank you, Mary.

How do I look, Karl?

Mary shows off her newly brushed hair in waves on her shoulders.

You look great, I say.

We make a pot of gumbo with chicken and sausages.

Karl, you make things so happy. Look at the way he goes. That man can dance. You sure know how to party. Did your dad teach you that? Mary says.

I learnt how to party in Louisiana, I reply.

When I was in fifth grade, I was sick as a dog every day. Mami cooked a nice supper every day. It was ready at noon, Mary says.

A neighbor lady used to come to our house every Christmas and made us sit around the table. She said, I'm coming here for my Christmas dinner. I don't know if I'll be here next Christmas. One of us might not be here. I'm saying this because you might not remember, Mary says.

Mary enters my bedroom with a hot cup of coffee.

I burnt my tongue a little bit, she says.

Do you like coffee? I ask.

I love coffee. I drank it all, Mary replies.

Karl, I'm going to Baton Rouge. Mr. Johnson lives there. He's my husband. I'm gonna squeeze, hug, kiss and tell him, Hello my husband. I love you. He's going to be sweet to me. He's gonna say, You can do what you wanna do. I'm going kiss him on the mouth. I kiss him on the neck. They made him over and it's just like he is young. He's a lovely man. I'm going to have sex with him. He's a sexy man. He's going to show me how to have sex. We're going to be naked. We will hug and snuggle. I love that. Karl, do you want to come to our house when we have sex? I love to have sex with Mr. Johnson. You can sit in the bedroom. You can sit on the bed and look at us when we have sex. It might rock you too much, Karl.

No, thanks. I'm fine. I'll pass on that offer, I say.

Mr. Johnson wanted all the girls to like him when he was a teacher. Every time I saw him, I loved him. I think he was meant for me. He was the man that I first lay my eyes on. I smiled. My mama didn't like him. He wanted to marry my mama, but she didn't want to marry him. I could love his brother too.

The evening is crisp and cold. I cook Massaman curry for supper. It's a mild, tasty, and sweet curry spiced with cumin, cardamom, and cinnamon. I add coconut milk, meat, onions, potatoes, and roasted peanuts. After supper, I help Mary to change incontinence pads and tuck her in with seven blankets. She is very content. I improvise and make up a goodnight song for Mary.

It's going to be alright. Good night, sleep tight, I sing.

I think I'm falling in love with you, Karl, Mary says.

Thank you. Aren't you in love with Mr. Johnson? I ask.

Yes, I love him. He's my husband, Mary says.

23 VISITING THE OTHER SIDE

West Sweden, February 2021

Karl, you always work so fast and have so much energy, Mary says.

I don't always have a lot of energy. I become exhausted when you look for dead people outside the house in this intense way. Please don't spend all your time with dead people. I'm here and I'm alive. I'm a real person, I say.

How is he going to marry me if he's dead? They are alive like us. They drive cars like everyone else. Mr. Johnson and his brother were going to save me, Mary says.

How can dead people save you? I ask.

Some people believe that you're dead, Karl. And I'm dead too, Mary says.

Mary laughs.

Who said that? I'm not dead. I'm alive. I'm here with you, I say.

Mary giggles.

I'm just playing with you, Karl.

Mary and I do a coronavirus disease song and dance and laugh.

I'm peeing on myself laughing. I'm going to the bathroom, Mary says.

The nurse from the border police calls me. She says that she will contact the American Embassy in Stockholm to plan Mary's return trip to the United States.

Mary says, I thought about something today. I was about thirty years old. It was a school day. I was late for school. That's why I was going kind of fast. A boy ran in front of my car. He looked right at me. I slammed on the breaks so fast. I nearly hit him. He made it across the street. That was God protecting the little boy and me. I loved that boy so much. And that was all.

Mary yawns. I tuck her in with many warm blankets. She smiles at me like a little baby.

Darling. I love you Karl. We're two love birds, Mary says and goes to sleep.

Mary has been having one of her manic days. I feel overwhelmed. I'm always multitasking. Today I'm teaching my social work students via Zoom from home and caring for Mary as it is most days. Something is going to happen to my health if I continue to live like this.

In the afternoon, I stand next to Mary on the road outside the house. She refuses to go inside and looks around for Ruby anxiously. She looks like a racehorse ready to run off. We live very close to the highway. Even if I ask Mary to stay in the house, she runs out on the highway several times. Mary says that Ruby is coming and that she is going to catch a bus to pick her up. I leave my class several times and run out to the highway to help her back to the house and save her from getting hit by the passing trucks and cars driving with high speed. I really want Mary to make it to the United States alive.

At 3 a.m. Mary enters my bedroom. She turns on the light and is upset.

Karl, a man called Ruby bad things and bothered her. I don't know what he said. Karl, help Ruby, Mary says.

You can pray, I reply.

Yes. I can just pray. I'm taking in the spirit. Jesus, my sister... I'm so upset. Ruby is very upset too. There are some mean people in this world. I'm glad that you're nice Karl and can console me and Ruby, Mary says.

I start dancing silly dance moves with a jelly man style.

Mary, I want to know what is going on in your life... I sing.

I make up an improvised song and new wild dance movements. Mary is laughing so much that she is peeing on herself.

That's so cute Karl. I love when you dance funny. I'm going to calm myself down now. Karl, you're something boy, she says.

I clean up Mary's pee on the floor and give her new clothes.

Good morning, Mary. How're you doing? We're going to see your doctor this morning, I say.

I take Mary to the doctor. The Swedish border police, the American Embassy in Stockholm and the dementia care in Baton Rouge all want a recent assessment of Mary by a physician to plan her return trip to the United States and dementia care in Louisiana.

Is my doctor good looking? Mary asks.

Yes, he is handsome. I think you will like him, I say.

Two border police nurses visit Mary in the house to get to know to her before the return trip. Mary tells the police ladies that she attended a concert with the soul and rock'n'roll singer Jackie Wilson. Mary was dressed in a gorgeous red dress. Jackie shouted out, here is a song for the lady in the red dress. Mary screamed. She loved Jackie Wilson.

One of the police ladies asks me to create a music list for Mary for the return trip. Mary and I sit in my bedroom and listen to Jackie Wilson and Sam Cooke. When Sam Cooke sings *A Change is Gonna Come* I'm crying and break down. Tears run down my cheeks as signs of love and care for Mary. At the same time the tears are an expression of relief after caring for her day and night for almost three years. She has had high anxiety bursting out on me in screams and physical attacks. Finally, Bianca, Heidi and I will have an opportunity to live in peace and quiet.

Karl, I love you. Thanks for being so nice. Aren't you going with me to Louisiana? Mary says.

I will stay here with the girls, I reply.

Mary and I dance to electronic dance music.

Look at those lean hips shaking. You're blessed,

Karl. You're a good-looking man. Oh God Karl I'm gonna miss your muscular and sexy hips and you when I go to Baton Rouge. You wear me out. I got to rest sometimes. I got to go because you make me laugh all the time. Bye, bye darling, Mary shouts.

Mary looks out of the kitchen window down on the neighbors' gardens.

There are some strange people in this neighborhood. They may work witchcraft on us. Look they are working in the garden, Mary says.

I just see the neighbors working in their gardens, I reply.

Mary waits on the street outside for her lover.

Mary, please come inside, I say.

She follows me into the house. There is something on her mind, Karl, we have two problems. The principal doesn't want anyone blowing the nose in the office.

Okay, I'm not gonna do it. I promise. What's the other problem? I reply.

Do you think Mr. Johnson is going to leave me? Mary says.

I don't know, I reply.

Mary asks me:

Are you going to take the Corona shot or are you going to heaven right away? Are you ready to die from Corona? I don't care if you live or die. My daddy died. Ruby brought him back to life. I'm gonna have sex with Mr. Johnson. He works with God. God will help him to get up his penis. He has nothing to worry about. We're going to have hot sex, Mary says.

Mary is gone in the evening. I thought she was on the street outside the house, but she wasn't there. I start to run. I see her far away. She stands by the highway next to passing cars and trucks. She holds on to the road fence toward the river and the waterfall. It's several meters down to the river filled with large stones. Mary would die in case she falls on them. I run as fast as I can and finally reach her.

189

You don't have to take me home. I'm waiting for Mr. Johnson. I will kiss him when he comes. We will have sex when he gets here, Mary says.

You can't wait for him all night, I say.

I hold her hands and convince her to walk back with me to the house.

Mary enters my bedroom at 3 a.m. She looks at me.

Karl, what time is it? Mary asks.

What does your clock say? I respond.

It says three o'clock, but the time is wrong, Mary says.

No, it is 3 a.m., I say.

Can I come in and talk to you? Mary asks.

No, I'm sleeping. Please leave. I'll make oatmeal for us in the morning and then we can talk, I say.

Okay, Mary says.

I'm pouring my Assam tea when Mary enters my bedroom.

Are you ready? I'm going to Baton Rouge General to get the Corona shot so I won't die, she says.

Do you know that we're in Sweden? The Atlantic Ocean is between the United States and Europe, I say.

There are special roads to go to the hospital. Come on, Karl, Mary says and leaves the house.

Thirty minutes later, Mary returns to the house.

I didn't see them. I'm gonna rest for a while and walk to the corner. I'm kind of nervous. Oh God please help me. Can you walk with me? Mary says.

Okay, I say and help Mary upstairs to her bed.

After her nap, Mary and I go on a walk around the community. When we come back, she lies down to rest in my bed.

Bye Karl. I'm leaving, Mary says.

She kisses me on the cheek.

Bye Mary, I say.

I need to do my university work and stay in the house. I'm aware that Mary could walk out to the highway and get killed. Even if I know this, I need to take care of my work. I can't follow her around all the time. Mary returns to the house. The snow melts on the floor. Mary says:

Do you want me to tell you what happened? I went to the crazy lady's house. I don't know if she is crazy, but I call her crazy. I walked to her car and knocked on the window of the car. Nobody answered. Then I went to the next car at the next house. Nobody answered. Then I walked to the next house and knocked. Nobody answered. Finally, an old man answered. I went to the next house and knocked on the car window. Nobody answered. A voice told me I think it was Jesus. He told me to go home. Then you opened the door. What did you think about that?

I think our neighbors think that you're weird walking around to every house and car to knock on them, I reply.

Mary laughs.

I walk down the street and talk to the neighbors. One man says that Mary tried to push herself into his house. He didn't want that and closed the door on her. After that she knocked on his car door.

West Sweden, March 2021

I'm preparing to supervise two social work students. I hear Mary. She's very upset and is crying hard. Mary believes she will be having sex today, but she can't find her lover. She looks up at me with a sad facial expression and screams:

I HAVEN'T FOUND MY HUSBAND MR. JOHNSON. I WANT TO HAVE SEX WITH HIM. MY MOTHER LOVED HIM. MY GRANDMOTHER LOVED HIM. PLEASE KARL LET ME FIND MY HUSBAND. HELP ME FIND MY HUSBAND. PLEASE DARLING. FIND MY HUSBAND! I WANT TO HAVE SEX WITH HIM. I NEED HIM BAD. GET HIM HERE!

Mary leans over me when she is screaming in my right ear. Her saliva runs down on my shirt. She keeps on crying and shakes me roughly.

YOU DON'T EVEN CARE KARL. I THOUGHT YOU CARED ABOUT ME. YOU CAN HELP ME FIND HIM. I NEED HIM. GET HIM NOW KARL! Mary shouts.

She starts hitting me. I lead her out of my bedroom and lock the door. Mary takes her stick and hits the door until she gets tired. After a while I can hear her walking back upstairs.

Her mind is filled with forgetfulness. She returns to me and walks outside. When she comes inside, Mary says:

Mr. Johnson and his brother are coming soon. I hope they have some fried chicken for me. My favorite dish is fried chicken and potato salad.

Oh, it is, I reply.

Do I look pretty, Karl? Mary asks.

Yes, you look pretty, I reply.

I had excited myself. I wanted to have sex with him. I had sex with him. It was good sex. Good sex is when you love someone, and you have sex with him. Bad sex is when you are not in love with someone and just have sex to have sex. Do you know how we got together? Mary says.

No, I reply.

His uncle brought him to me. I fell in love with Mr. Johnson. I loved him more than I could ever say. I loved him because he looked like a cowboy. I love cowboys because they do wonderful things to people. I think cowboys are sexy. I love shirtless cowboys. I love sexy men. They are so sweet, gentle, and kind. They are handsome men more than I can say. Cowboys love me. All the men love me. They love me because I'm sweet and I'm gonna be kind to them, Mary says.

Mary is still in love in one of the men that she started thinking about lately. He was a university professor. She says that he was very attractive. She talks about the first time she came into his office. He talked to her and touched her hips and breasts. Mary says:

WHY DID YOU DO THAT MR. LONG? You knew that I was a nice girl and had never been kissed. Then later I was running for being the queen in a beauty contest. You told me that my dress wasn't fitted enough to see my hips. Why did I want the young men to look at my hips? They could see my beautiful face. I remember one day it snowed and you said sweetly thank God, the sun. This meant so much to me. You know that there was so much evil in your department. There were about three atheist professors. They almost destroyed my faith in God. I doubted about God so many times. These professors helped me because I started going to holy communion every day for three years. Then I went to holy communion when I got married because I had marital problems and I got pregnant and had a beautiful baby, Maria.

Mary is thinking about her upcoming return to

Louisiana:

My mama, sister, brother, and daddy can come and see me in Baton Rouge when I go back. I love the man that comes by every day with a salad at 10 o'clock. He has a horse. I don't like to ride horses. One time when I was riding, I was about to fall off the horse. That is why I don't like horses. I'm tired to talk, Karl. I'm going to bed.

Good night, Mary, I say.

Mary returns to me half an hour later and bangs on my bedroom door. She opens the door and is dressed in Maria's blue business suit.

I'm ready to get the shot. How do I look, Karl? Mary asks.

You look great Mary, I reply.

Karl, I didn't put makeup on. I was rushing so fast. I thought you were leaving me. Who are you? You, one of my boyfriends, when I was in the mental health hospital, Mr. Johnson, and his brother. I am on time. I don't want to make Mr. Johnson wait. I'm going to Baton Rouge General Hospital. We're getting the shots so people won't die. We don't want to die. We want to live. Do you want to die Karl?

No, I reply.

That is why we are getting the shots, so we won't die.

After the shots we can go to a street fair. I want to eat popcorn and drink a cold drink. I want to ride a pony. Ride the pony. Get on the pony and ride a horse. Bucket bucket it dooo. Hug me Karl, Mary says.

I hug Mary.

Thank you, Karl. You're the best man in the world. You have a good heart. It's so stressful to get ready for the ride, Mary says.

I'm reassuring Mary that she doesn't need to get the shot for Covid today. I tell her that the vice-consul at the American Embassy in Stockholm called me this morning and said that they are working with the American authorities to prepare for her return. He

194

said that the only requirement is that you get tested for Covid just before you travel.

Okay, Mary replies.

She relaxes in her face and sits down on the chair next to me for a while. After a few minutes she forgets what we talked about. Her face is filled with anxiety again.

Karl, where are my gloves and my hat. They are on the table in your bedroom, I say.

Thank you. I'm going upstairs to get them, Mary says.

She brings her rosary beads, starts praying and says:

When are we going to get my little daughter? We got to go to get her. I know that Maria is tired of waiting for us. I told her that we were coming today. She wants to see her husband and her mama. We're a lazy group of people aren't we? We're lazy to not get our little girl. I'm gonna call her now. Maria, I'm so sorry that we haven't come to get you. I told Karl that we are a lazy group of people. Karl cleans the kitchen and does things like that. He doesn't want the house to get too messy. You know that Karl is stupid of not being able to go now. Maria says that she knows that. Karl says that he came to your funeral, but you haven't died Maria. How can he go to the funeral? You have been talking to me all the time. Karl, how was the other woman that you are mixing my little girl with?

I close my eyes and cry inside.

Maria died from brain cancer in September last year, I say with tears in my eyes.

Maria says she didn't. I don't know what Karl is talking about. He's stupid. You're my little girl and you're alive. Your grandmother Juliet knows that you're alive. Maria says how is Juliet. She doesn't even know her. Bye Maria. I'm gonna call you tomorrow, Mary says.

Mary falls asleep in my bed.

She wakes up, goes upstairs, and returns with her

winter clothes on and says:

Karl, are you ready to pick up your little girl Maria? I'm ready. We're going now. CALL HER! CALL HER! You need to pick up your little girl. Do you know her address so you know where to go? If I had a little girl that was alive, I would be happy to pick her up. Juliet is ready for her to go home. She raised Maria.

Mary, calm yourself. Maria passed away in September, I say.

SHE DIDN'T PASS AWAY! MARIA DIDN'T DIE. SHE DIDN'T DIE. YOU SHOULD BE HAPPY THAT SHE'S ALIVE. YOU SHOULD BE HAPPY, Mary screams and looks at me with big anxious eyes.

I think to myself that this is madness. We're looking at one another.

Put on your hat, Karl! I have my hat on. I tell the American Embassy in Stockholm that Maria is alive. I'm so hot. It's hot in here. You have the heater so high so it's steamy hot. I don't know what to do. KARL, GET UP! KARL, YOU STUPID MAN. WE'RE GOING. GET THE CAR. YOU'RE STUPID. STUPID, Mary says.

Mary, would you like to have some water? I ask.

Yes, please, Mary replies.

When Mary says that she will get her rosary I walk out to the car and leave. I leave Mary stressing about Maria. I go to the grocery store to think about something else. It's been a difficult week at home. It's not easy to care for Mary. The intense pace of her worry and constant outbreaks makes me stay stressed as soon as I hear her footsteps, when she is close to me, and after she leaves. When I check my blood pressure when she is not around it's okay. When she approaches me with her squeaky and loud voice and her persona maxed with constant high anxiety, I feel tired and get headaches. When I check my blood pressure and Mary is present it's so high that the information text on the blood pressure machine states that I need to go to the emergency room.

Mary enters my bedroom dressed in her burgundy Smurf hat hanging down on the right side and her jacket unzipped. Her gaze is distressed.

Are you okay? I ask.

Karl, help me please with my jacket. Mr. Johnson is coming soon to get the shot. You're coming too aren't you? I love you so much Karl. You're a sweet and a wonderful gentleman. Today is the last day sir to get the shot. You don't want to die, Karl. Mr. Johnson ought to come up to get me, Mary says.

Mary looks out of the window for Mr. Johnson.

How do I look? Mary asks.

You look fabulous. I respond.

Are you hungry? I ask.

No, I have the pineapple pieces that you cut this morning. I could have a mandarin, Mary says.

I throw a mandarin in the air to Mary. She catches it and laughs out loud.

Please help me Karl. Give me a big hug! Mary says.

I hug Mary.

I'm enjoying my morning tea when Mary enters my bedroom. She calls it my office.

What date am I supposed to go back to the United States? Mary asks.

They called from the American embassy three days ago and said that they sent off the request of assistance to the American authorities. It will take a few weeks, I reply.

It's not gonna take a few weeks. I'm going back tomorrow. Ruby is supposed to come and get me, Mary explains.

Ruby is dead, I explain.

THAT'S NOT TRUE. SHE AIN'T DEAD. RUBY IS COMING TO GET ME. GIVE ME ONE REASON FOR RUBY NOT COMING TO GET ME? Mary shouts.

Ruby is dead, I repeat.

RUBY HAS A BRAIN AND WALKS AROUND! Mary

explains screamingly.

Karl, you're a darling man. What am I? A darling lady? Mary says.

Yeah, I reply.

The Vice-Consul at the U.S. Embassy in Sweden called me this morning. He said that the Health and Human Services accepted your case. You have been assigned a repatriation case manager. He has talked to the Swedish border police and collaborates both with them and the Health and Human Services.

Karl, are you gonna talk to Ruby and tell her that I will fly in my airplane? Ruby was going to pick me up here. I want you to go with me, Mary says.

I nod.

One night it's worse than usual. It's 1.30 a.m. I'm sleeping deeply. Mary wakes me up abruptly by repeatedly hitting me all over my body.

GET UP! GET UP! GET UP, KARL! Mary screams loudly.

It's 1.30 a.m. Mary. I was sleeping. Please go back to bed, I plead.

Mary keeps hitting my body.

GET UP NOW! GET MY SHOES! I'M GOING WITH MR. JOHNSON TO GET THE SHOT, Mary screams.

Please calm down, Mary. You don't need to scream, I say.

I get up and go upstairs to make Mary's bed.

There you go, Mary says.

When I'm upstairs Mary leaves the house and walks out on the street to look for Mr. Johnson. It's a cool night. I put on my clothes and walk outside.

I'm about to fall, Karl. Help me, Mary shouts.

I run to Mary and catches her before she falls.

Let's go inside the house and go back to bed. Please Mary, I beg her.

I'm staying here. Mr. Johnson is coming and we're going in his car to get the shot, Mary explains.

I hold Mary's hand and help her back into the house. I help her upstairs and tuck her in in her bed.

Five minutes later I hear Mary walking downstairs again. She opens the front door and goes outside again. Before I put on my shoes Mary has fallen into the well-pruned bushes and dropped her bible in the grass. I run out to help her up and lead her back into the house.

I can help you to your bed, I say.

I don't want to go to bed. I'm gonna sit her on the chair and read the bible, Mary says.

It's now 2 a.m. and I go back to bed. I hear Mary leaving the house again. I get back up and put on my shoes. I help Mary back inside.

Mary, please stay inside the house. If I fall asleep and you're back outside again you may fall on the ground and freeze to death, I say.

I'm just gonna read the bible here, Mary says.

Okay. Good night, I say.

I hear Mary turning the pages in the children's bible. My heart is beating fast. I'm on standby to help Mary if she goes back outside again.

It's 2.30 a.m. Mary is still reading the bible outside my bedroom door. I get up again.

Please go back upstairs and read in your bed or in the kitchen. Please don't go outside. I'm begging you. Please. There is a danger in case you fall on the street and freeze to death, I say.

Suppose I don't fall. I do what I want to do! Mary says.

Okay. Good night, I say.

I can't stay up all night long with Mary and go to the university to work in the morning. It's physically and psychologically impossible in the long run.

Goodnight, Mary says.

It's 3.15 a.m. I wake up because I hear someone screaming outside the house.

MR. JOHNSON, WHERE ARE YOU? WHERE ARE YOU? Mary screams in falsetto in the garden.

I help Mary back into the house. I help her upstairs. I warm milk and give it to her. She reads loudly from the bible about Moses. I listen to her for a few minutes. When I'm about to go back to bed Mary screams:

COME BACK, KARL. COME BACK. COME BACK.

I say nothing.

When I pass Heidi's room I see that Mary has pulled off the door. The door is hanging against the wall. I put it back. When I come back downstairs, I feel a cold breeze through the house. The front door to the street is fully open. I close it. The lights are on everywhere. Mary must have walked around the house when I went to sleep. It's now close to 4 a.m. Mary is preaching with a loud voice in the kitchen. My chest hurts. I feel worn out. I go to Mary in the kitchen. She has pulled out the cord from the Internet box and talks to it. I tuck her in and say goodnight. She holds her rosary and pray.

Everything feels out of control. I wake with a pounding headache after having stayed up with Mary during the night. I was so stressed out that I couldn't go to sleep until 6 a.m. and then just rest a little bit before I do my university work in the morning. I'm the examiner in an examination seminar today in the advanced course management in social work. Mary is just as intense today. She's going in and out of the house to find her Corona chauffeur to take her to get the Covid shot. I serve her meatballs, potatoes, and gravy. This is new fuel for Mary to run around the yard looking for the driver.

I'm working on the computer when one of the cats walk over the desk. A thick disgusting worm falls out of the cat butt and lands on the keyword. I can't take it anymore. I feel massively vulnerable and have low tolerance for worms from the cat behind. I clean of the keyboard with alcohol and drive to the pharmacy to get worm medicine for the cat.

Later in the afternoon, I'm feeling dizzy. It feels like I'm gonna faint. I lie down in the bed and close my eyes. Mary keeps on walking around on the second floor of the house. At least she's not outside. I really don't want to live with Mary anymore. I understand that she is multi-sick, but her intense and aggressive behavior is breaking me. When the sun sets Mary goes to her bed and for the first time in two manic days, I'm able to wind down. I enjoy a cup of Ceylon tea and assess the management students' papers. I'm still feeling lightheaded. I decide to go to bed early.

Heidi and I celebrate our birthdays today. Heidi is 20 and I'm 54. I pick up Bianca. We drive to Gothenburg where Heidi lives. It's wonderful to have a fun day with my beloved daughters after an intense period caring for Mary.

It must have been difficult for you, Karl. Maria is dead. I didn't see that before. I haven't supported your grief. I feel so sad. Maria is dead, Mary says.

She bursts out into noisy tears sounding like crocodile tears, but who am I to judge her.

I'm happy that you finally recognize that Maria died. Yes, you are right. You have denied Maria's passing and have not let me mourn in peace, I say.

I didn't go to the funeral, Mary says.

The funeral was six months ago. I'm trying to be patient and understanding with Mary.

You and I sat next to Maria's coffin in the church, I say.

I don't remember that. Maria would have been here with us if she was alive, Mary replies.

Yes, I say.

Less than five minutes later Mary and I start cooking crawfish étouffée for lunch.

Is Maria coming? Mary asks.

Maria is dead, I say.

MARIA AIN'T DEAD! Mary screams.

I think to myself that Mary already forgot that she said that Maria was dead a few minutes ago.

Karl, you know that I was in love with one of my instructors when I was in college? Mary asks.

Yes, I reply.

201

He came to my house and tried to put his hands inside my pants to touch my butt for three hours. He wanted to touch my behind! I didn't let him do it. Each time he tried to do it I jumped off the porch. I loved him, but I didn't want him to touch my behind. He didn't love me, Mary says.

Mary gets the urge to make eggnog. Mary beats eight egg yolks. She doesn't add any brandy and rum because she takes meds. She adds cream and well-beaten egg whites. Mary sprinkles with nutmeg to taste. She pours the eggnog in many glasses that she places on every shelf in the refrigerator. When she wants a glass of eggnog she usually pours out another glass with eggnog which means that I need to clean the entire refrigerator. I suggest to her that she can make less eggnog and drink it immediately to prevent any glasses from spilling out. Mary thinks that is a very bad idea. I finish dusting the nutmeg from the kitchen table and the floor. She takes out two eggnog drinks for us and we share a laugh.

It's 5 a.m. I'm sleeping. Mary opens the door to my bedroom. She is wearing outdoor clothes and says:

Karl, something happened tonight. My boyfriend and I had a sex date. We are having sex when some boys in the neighborhood come and disturb us. Ruby calls the police. They should put them in the penitentiary. This neighborhood is bad right. Two men have guns and threaten the drivers of the cars so they can't drive. People think they can do people. Be careful when you go walking. They can run your neighborhood.

Mary is very anxious. I tell Mary to calm herself and ask her if she wants an early breakfast. She would like that. I make oatmeal and boil eggs for us. We also have watermelon. Mary smiles when I serve her breakfast.

You make me breakfast in bed every day. Every day. You're the sweetest man, Karl. The sweetest man, Mary says.

Thank you, I reply.

A little later, I'm sitting in the bedroom reading a book. Mary enters and updates me about what is going on, Me and Mr. Johnson are going to go on a date to eat breakfast.

Mary leaves the house. Usually, I go to the window to see if she is okay. This morning I'm so sleepy and worn out after she has been awake for so many nights that I decide to stay in my chair. After a while Mary returns.

Ruby knows how to deal with those youngsters. It was good that she taught at the senior high school. These terrible rascal boys threatened me. They said they wanna go to my address. You shouldn't go with people you don't know, Mary says.

Mary looks confused.

Karl, where are my pads? Mary asks.

Your pads are in the closet in your bedroom, I reply.

Mary puts on a new pad and goes back to the garden. I can hear her talking to herself and laughing. Mary goes in and out of the house asking me every five minutes what time it is in a compulsive way saying:

My boyfriend Mr. Johnson is coming soon to take me to breakfast.

Mary returns inside when I'm whistling and dancing. She says smilingly, I love that pretty whistling. I love my Karl. You will always be my Karl. You're highly talented. You're a good dancer. You look so good. You're a good cook. You make delicious food.

You're a magnificent trumpet player and teacher, I say.

Mary kisses me on the cheek three times and touches my hair.

You have pretty hair, Karl. I'm going outside to my boyfriend again. Bye, Mary says.

Her nose is running. She smiles at me and asks, You have some tissues?

I give Mary some tissues.

Thank you, Karl. You have everything handy. Karl says here it is. It's too cold outside for me to go out there again.

Do you want some hot chocolate? I ask her.

Mary smiles and nods. I make her hot chocolate. She looks at me as she was a sweet and happy toddler getting her Saturday candy.

A little later, I think that Mary is in the garden when my mother calls. She says that our neighbor came to her and told her that Mary was walking next to the highway. I look outside and see Mary walking back to the house. She says cryingly, I can't find my mama. I'm gonna get the police to help me.

My mother knocks on the door. She is worried about Mary. I explain to her that I care for Mary day and night without any support:

I don't have the energy to follow Mary everywhere she goes. I'm dizzy after Mary has been waking me up several nights this week. Mary goes from manic to calm and calm to manic in seconds. Back and forth. Back and forth.

My mother says that she understands and leaves.

Can I sleep in your bed, Karl? Mary asks.

Okay, I reply.

Mary goes to sleep after a few minutes. Heidi calls me on Messenger and says that she's coming home from Gothenburg this afternoon. I'm looking forward to see Heidi.

Mary wakes up. She sits on the chair next to me.

I'm here for you, Mary I say.

She smiles. I cry inside. Caring for Mary is both beautiful and painful. I'm relatively stable and able to be there for her just a little bit more.

I have a surprise for you, Mary, I say.

WHAT?

I'll cook something yummy.

We go upstairs. I fry a reindeer steak for lunch.

Would you like to have some reindeer? I ask.

I don't wanna eat Rudolf, Karl, Mary says.

You can taste the reindeer. It's not dangerous, I reply.

Mary tastes the reindeer. She smiles approvingly.

Mary knows that she is dependent on me. She writes a list after supper with things she is dependent on and that I help her with.

Things Karl helps me with:

1. Drive me to the Dr.
2. Make appointments for the nurse and the doctor.
3. Give me medicine.
4. Bathe me and shower me.
5. Cook and serve me food.
6. Pick up medicine from the pharmacy.
7. Go shopping for clothes and food.
8. Wash clothes.

Mary thanks me for doing these things for her. I'm so impressed by her that she is so structured in her head. Some days she doesn't know where she is or what is going on. Today is a good day.

Heidi is home from Gothenburg this weekend. In the afternoon, she drives alone to a national park to enjoy the nature. I'm home alone with Mary who is screaming:

KARL! GET THE CAR! WE'RE GOING TO THE COURT HOUSE TO GET THE CORONA SHOT.

I asked the nurse if you can get the Covid shot, but they can't give it to you because you're not a Swedish resident. You will get the Covid vaccination when you go back to Louisiana, I say.

YOU STUPID MAN! WE'RE GOING. GET THE CAR, KARL! YOU'RE STUPID. STUPID. STUPID, Mary screams.

Please calm yourself down, I say.

I've put up with Mary's screaming and abuse in the house since June 2018. I had it. Usually I just stay calm, accept Mary's wild behaviors, and try to distract her to think about something else. I'm sick and tired of her. She screams almost all the time. It feels like she's ruined the lives of all of us. Maria is dead. The girls and I are nervous. I don't want to blame Mary because she's sick, but this time I can't stop myself. I yell back at her:

I'M SO TIRED OF YOU SCREAMING AT ME ALL THE TIME. I HELP YOU DAY AND NIGHT. YOU ALMOST SCREAMED THE ENTIRE TIME WHEN MARIA WAS DYING FROM CANCER. WHEN MARIA DIED YOU KEPT ON SCREAMING AT ME. YOU HAVE TOTALLY DENIED THAT MARIA DIED AND HAVE TRIED TO CONVINCE ME OVER AND OVER AGAIN THAT MARIA IS ALIVE AND IS A LITTLE GIRL LIVING IN BATON ROUGE. YOU STRESS OUT BIANCA AND HEIDI. I HAD IT WITH YOU!

I'm surprised that I yelled back. Usually, I just accept anything Mary says and does. Mary looks at me. She doesn't say anything. My heart is beating fast. I stood up to her. I know that I shouldn't scream at a person with dementia and mental illness, but it feels good to draw the line at some point.

Heidi returns home. Her face is smiling. She says that she had a good hike. I will go with her to her train back to Gothenburg. When I return home to the house, I cook chicken gumbo. Mary looks different. Her face is calm. I've not seen her face like that for years.

She says, Karl, I'm gonna change my ways from the old Mary to the new Mary. I'm making people mental with my screaming. I'm changing my lifestyle around. I have changed my makeup. Look, Karl. Don't you think I'm pretty?

Yes, you're pretty, Mary, I reply.

Karl, I have changed it back to conducting my own life. I have been talking all the time and not listened to you, she says.

Mary stops talking and listens to me. This is something new. Mary usually keeps on talking about all kinds of things without having eye contact with and listening to other people. Mary painted her fingernails when I drove Heidi. She's calm. I'm in shock. I look at her again and smile.

I care about you, I say.

Mary smiles at me.

I smile at her and say, I'm so happy. You really look and act as a changed person. You talk in a polite way to me. I can't believe it. You haven't screamed this evening. I'm so proud of you, Mary.

Karl, you say things that lift me and other people up. If I have everything I need I don't scream. When I scream can you lift your right finger? Mary says.

Okay, I say.

I lift my right finger and smile. I smell urine. Mary has peed on herself. She doesn't want to take a shower. I give her a washcloth with soap and water. She washes herself. I help her to change the clothes and give her a new pad. I change her bedclothes.

Thank you for keeping up with my clothes, Mary says and smiles with warm eyes.

No worries boo. It's my pleasure, I reply.

Mary beams.

Would you like to have some more gumbo? I ask.

I'm good, she replies.

After we finish the supper, I hug Mary goodnight. I can't believe it. It's a miracle. I hope it will last and that she will be calm tomorrow too. I feel so much more relaxed. I close my eyes and go to sleep early.

Oh, I have something to tell you, Karl. My mama told me that if you have a trace of black in you they would kill you or beat you up. You don't know down south what traces you have. She didn't say anything about herself at work. She wouldn't have any money to care for her babies and children. You know Karl, times were hard. They were glad to have a job, Mary says.

When Mary and I have supper, she talks about hips.

I'm thinking about Mr. Walker's hips. He got pretty hips. All women love his hips. Do you want to see his hips, Karl?

No, I reply.

You don't want to see his hips? What's wrong with you, Karl? Even Mr. Prude liked Mr. Walker's hips. Do you believe that I kissed Mr. Prude? I kissed his cheeks on the face like this, Mary says.

Mary is getting up to kiss my cheek.

Do you have Corona, Karl? Mary asks.

Maybe, I reply and smile.

Jesus! I'm not gonna kiss you anymore, Mary says and laughs big.

You're a crazy man, Karl.

Mary hits me three times on my arm and laughs. Mary likes to do things three times.

Can you calm me down, Karl? Mary asks in a hyperactive way.

Listen up. You need to calm down yourself. Are you alright? I ask.

Yes. I'm going to bed now. Good night, Mary says.

Good night, I say.

Mary is fully dressed in her winter jacket when she enters my bedroom at 5 a.m. saying:

I'm leaving my husband Mr. Johnson. He's a terrible man. He hid it. Karl, how do you leave a marriage?

You file for divorce, I reply.

I didn't even know it. He hurt me, Mary says.

Mary walks confidently with a big beauty queen smile and says:

I can get any man. I'm young and beautiful. I love you Karl one thousand times better than Mr. Johnson. You can do anything. You can cook, dance, sing and whistle. You're a fine gentleman. You got nice ways. You don't mind cooking for a woman and serving her. Women work too.

I make oatmeal and boil eggs for Mary and me early in the morning. I tell her that I'm going back to campus teaching.

I say the rosary for you baby, Mary says.

Thank you. I love you. Bye, I reply.

I have been teaching from home via Zoom since Maria passed away in September until now. Today I'm going back to in-person teaching on campus until June. This means that I will leave Mary alone at home during weekdays. I have informed the U.S. Embassy in Stockholm, Office of Aging and Adult Service, Louisiana Department of Health, and the Swedish border police and healthcare system that this means that Mary may walk to the highway close to the house and get killed. I don't feel good about this set up, but I need to think about my own mental health and job security. It has been cold lately so hopefully this fact will make Mary stay in the house until I return home after work.

After 16 months of Zoom teaching and meetings I'm super happy to do my classroom teaching. I'm leading a master's course about crisis leadership in social work. I'm going back to my dress code wearing a fine shirt and pants. The students are so engaged. They come from all over the world. We have fun and learn from each other.

I write a letter to the Office of Aging and Adult Service in Louisiana:

After my wife Maria died in September last year I've been home with Mary for six months teaching via Zoom. This week I started teaching on campus on weekdays in several courses that I'm leading until the end of June. This means that I'm leaving Mary alone after early breakfasts until late nights when I return home. It takes me about 90 minutes to drive to campus and then I teach for eight hours and sometimes supervise students after the teaching. This week when I have been gone Mary has been in acute life-threatening situations walking to the highway one minute away from the house. Neighbors have called me at work and said that she walks on or next to the highway. I don't have anyone to look after Mary. I can't stay home any longer because I'm teaching campus courses. Mary is delusional almost all the time believing that her mom, dad, sister, brother, and Maria are here. If I don't get them, she screams in rage at me. And I never get them because they are dead. When she is not screaming in rage she squeaks in falsetto which is extremely stressful. She is awake most of the time every night. I'm so worn out now that it affects my driving to work and teaching. I even have feelings of fainting every day. I'm worrying when I'm teaching that Mary may get killed any moment. When Mary is not screaming she is manic laughing very loud for 10-30 minutes at a time mixing that with loud preaching monologues with dead people. Her dementia is causing memory loss. She forgets about her latest rage outburst on me. I feel like an emotional wreck. With this background information about the acute situation here at home I'm asking for urgent help to find any temporary housing for her in Louisiana because I can't guarantee her safety here. Would it possible for her to be in a temporary housing so she can leave soon to the United States? I have also cared for my wife with regular psychotic episodes from 1997 to 2019 and when she had brain cancer from 2018 to 2020 and finally now Mary from 2018 to 2021. I need a break from Mary to prevent me from breaking down. Please help me.

The agency representative replies one hour later:

We have forwarded your request to the contacts we have in the State Department and with the repatriation office. We wish we could do more. Office of Aging and Adult Services, Louisiana Department of Health.

Mary is all pumped up. Tonight, is the night she has been waiting for. She feels excited. Mary has dumped principal Johnson. She has met a new, amazing man that she is going to marry tonight and have hot sex with. Mary's new man is Mr. Roberts who will be the new principal for an elementary school in Baton

210

Rouge next year.

Heidi is home from Gothenburg. We eat shrimp étouffée and apple pie. Mary doesn't want any supper because she is saving herself for the wedding dinner. She is really longing for the wedding and to cuddle with Mr. Roberts. She says that he is good at cuddling and smooshing. Mary gets started about these exciting things that are going to happen tonight. She is not going to sleep. She will have sex all night long.

Mary is pushing herself into Heidi's room.

Do you have any wedding shoes for me? Mary asks Heidi.

I live in Gothenburg now. I don't have any shoes here, Heidi replies.

Mary drools a big pile of saliva on Heidi's floor. Heidi thinks that disgusting.

Mary drools liked that on my sweaters and kisses my face with saliva every day, I say to comfort Heidi about the saliva pile.

Heidi laughs.

Mary walks down to my bedroom.

Can I get you something? I ask.

You can get Mr. Roberts. I want to have sex with him. Get him Karl, Mary replies.

I love that man. He's big and handsome like you, Karl. I don't want to talk about him too much because I want to see Mr. Roberts, Mary says.

We're gonna have sex. The sex is gonna heal us. I need sex. I haven't had sex for a long time. I had sex in 1955 or something and I haven't had sex with nobody since then. I'm gonna have sex with my husband tonight. I brushed my teeth and my tongue so I can kiss him. I'm so fresh. I put on deodorant. Ruby is going to bring a pair of shoes so don't worry. Will you help me to put on my wedding dress and zip it up, Karl? Mary asks.

Yes, I reply.

I found a wedding dress in the bedroom, Mary says

211

and looks at the picture of Maria on my bedroom wall.

My little girl died, right. What was it? Did she have a brain tumor? Mary asks.

Yes, I reply.

Jesus helps Maria and stays with her all day long. Maria was so happy. I'm gonna be sweet to Mr. Roberts. I'm gonna cook for that man. I'm gonna fry my chicken in cooking oil. I'm not gonna hit him. I'm not gonna put my pretty hands in his face. I hit another boyfriend one time. I slapped him. Guess what he did? He slapped me back. We kissed and made up. He was very sweet to me. My brother knew how sweet he was. I want to put deodorant on again. Then I want to put my wedding dress on. You're gonna help me right? Mary asks.

Yes, I reply.

I'm gonna dance with my husband. That fine man can dance. I love him. I know that you can dance, Karl. You're a beautiful dancer, Mary says.

Mary sits down on a chair in my bedroom and falls asleep after an hour. I let her sleep and wake her up to help her to her bed. I tuck her in.

Is Ruby coming with my wedding dress? Mary says and goes back to sleep.

Karl, we didn't have the wedding. We went to sleep. I'm so disappointed, she says when I make the oatmeal for her, Heidi, and myself.

I give Mary her oatmeal and orange juice in the morning.

You're so cute, Karl. I think I want to marry you instead of Mr. Roberts, Mary says.

It's snowing outside.

In case the wedding is not working out with Mr. Roberts I can marry you, Karl, Mary reassures me.

I love you, Karl. It's not sexual love. It's love from God. You're a sweet friend, Mary says.

I don't answer.

Mr. Roberts loves another woman at the school. He

will have sex with her too. He loves both of us. Isn't that sweet? He's gonna treat her and me nice. We are both sweet and beautiful teachers. We will have sex all the time. He doesn't want to marry her. He wants to marry me. I want him to have sex with his pretty little girlfriend. She's gonna come to my wedding with Mr. Roberts, Mary says.

It's now 11:30 p.m. It's Sunday night and I'm preparing myself mentally to teach next day and the entire week. Mary cleans herself and changes her clothes. I'm ready to go to sleep. Mary is sitting in winter clothes and a hat on a chair outside my bedroom. I can't relax when I know that Mary can leave the house and freeze to death when she is waiting for her husband.

Mary laughs and talks loud to herself. I finally go to sleep. I wake up several times during the night. Each time I hear Mary laughing and talking to herself throughout the night.

It's just after midnight. I'm sleeping when Mary storms into my bedroom.

GET UP! GET UP! GET UP KARL NOW! WHERE IS THE GROUND MEAT? Mary screams.

Please take a deep breath. Please calm down. We don't have any ground meat. Please go back to bed. I need to get up early in the morning to drive to the university to teach. It's in the middle of the night, I reply.

Mary grabs one of my legs and starts to pull it back and forth.

IT'S NOT THE NIGHT, KARL. IT'S IN THE MORNING AND YOU'RE GETTING UP NOW! I'M HUNGRY. I WANT FOOD NOW! Mary shouts and sits down on my legs and pulls one of my arms in a rough way.

Please calm down, Mary, I say tenderly.

I get up and make oatmeal for her. She smiles and looks very happy.

I go back to bed. My heart is pounding hard.

Mary and I eat another breakfast together in the morning. When I take my shower, I hear Mary crying out for help. I put on my clothes quickly. I take two steps at a time when running up the stairs. When I enter the kitchen, Mary is under the kitchen table unable to get up. She has peed on herself, and her pants are wet. There is a circle with pee around her on the floor. I remove the table and put a chair next to Mary so she can use the chair to pull herself up.

I grow increasingly concerned about Mary's wellbeing. She has feelings of disorientation. Sometimes she doesn't know where she is and is charming in the next moment. She lashes out in anger and is emotionally fragile. Nights and days are filled with chaos. Her wild presence controls and dominates my every waking moment at home. She hears the voices of Ruby, Juliet, and others. Her constant psychotic talk wears me out.

It's 2 a.m. I'm sleeping. Mary storms into my bedroom and hit my body. I wake up in shock. She screams aggressively:

GET UP! GET UP! GET UP, KARL! I'M HUNGRY.

You need to calm down, Mary, I say with a pleading voice.

I still feel shaken from Mary hitting me. I get up and make oatmeal for her. My heart beats fast. I go back to bed.

In the morning when I enter her bedroom with her washed clothes that she peed on yesterday she smiles and says:

I love you, Karl. You're so sweet. Where is Ruby?

Ruby passed away in 2013, I reply.

OH, YOU SHUT UP, KARL. YOU SHUT UP. YOU'RE STUPID, Mary screams.

I don't want to live in a toxic home with constant screaming and emotional abuse.

Why do you scream at me day and night? I ask Mary.

YOU SHUT UP, KARL. YOU'RE STUPIDER THAN I

THOUGHT, she screams.

I cook the breakfast and return to my bedroom to eat the food alone. This is my kind of mild resistance to her behavior. I want Mary to respect me. After breakfast I drive to the forest to walk along a beautiful waterfall and follow a creek deep into the forest. I breathe deeply and starts to relax. It's not easy to care for her. This destructive behavior will not stop until she leaves Sweden. I hope Mary will fly soon. I feel desperate. I just want to be alone.

American Citizens Services at the Embassy of the United States of America updates me that the police are looking at the first week of May for Mary's repatriation.

I cook in the kitchen.

Karl, do you know where my behind is? Mary asks.

No, I reply.

It's under my pants, Mary explains.

Oh, I say.

Karl, you're my sweet little macaroni man, she says with a voice of joy.

Me and Mr. Johnson are gonna have sex tonight. I want to love and kiss him. He's penis is gonna stick. He's gonna come inside of me. We're gonna have a baby. I need to have surgery first because my period doesn't come anymore, Mary says.

25 TURNING POINT

West Sweden, April 2021

Suddenly, it's a switch in the chain of events after dealing with crisis after crisis when caring for Mary. I'm walking and breathing fresh air in the forest. Spring has arrived. The birds are singing. For the first time in decades, I face a positive turning point in my life. Massive stress, psychic and physical pain, mental illness, and cancer have filled our lives in the family. I have done everything it takes to lift myself and my family members with patience and emotional resilience. It has sometimes ripped my soul into pieces. Maria has passed away. I have hardly had any moments to grieve and reflect about her passing. The tears pour down my face. I don't need to worry any more. I'm letting go.

Mary is leaving in a few days. I know that she has dementia and psychosis, but I never wanted to be locked up in the house with her the last years. Mary suffers from anxiety. I have had to deal with her fears and worries which have minimized my sleep and self-care. I decided a long time ago to see stressful and overwhelming pressures in my life with a hopeful, optimistic, and positive sense of humor. It has been challenging to cope with her dementia, mental illness and aggression hitting me and screaming in rage.

Today is a new day. I can't affect the past. I will learn from my experiences. I have sweet people around me. I feel hopeful about the future. I have a purpose in life. I will nurture myself, my daughters, and the closest friends I trust with love and care.

A phone call with the Swedish border police officer is uplifting. Mary will fly back to the United States in her own airplane with a physician, a nurse and two police officers. They will come to our house early in the morning of May 4th. When they arrive, the doctor will give Mary a Covid test and drive her to the airport if the test result is negative. I have already packed three suitcases. We are now waiting for the decision by the American Airport Administration for permission to land at John F. Kennedy International Airport in New York City. I'm so relieved and grateful.

It's another day in the house with a sex hungry 80-year-old lady.

I WANT TO HAVE SEX WITH MY HUSBAND! KARL, WHERE IS MY HUSBAND? Mary screams.

I don't know, I reply.

GET MY HUSBAND NOW! LET'S GO FIND HIM, OKAY, Mary shouts.

Okay, I reply.

Mary screams:

I DON'T WANT TO FLY WITH THOSE PEOPLE. YOU HEAR, KARL. I'M DRIVING TO BATON ROUGE WITH RUBY. If I fly will they call my people?

Who are your people? I ask.

My people are my sister Ruby, brother Claude, mother Juliet and my grandmother Willy B. Miles. Maria, my daughter is in heaven, Mary explains.

HOW CAN I TELL MY BABY MARIA WHEN I ARRIVE IN NEW ORLEANS? TELL ME, KARL. I want that little cat, Mary shouts and reaches out for the cat.

The cat runs away in fear from Mary.

I don't know how you can tell Maria, I say.

SHUT UP KARL. YOU CRAZY MAN. TELL ME NOW, Mary screams.

My stomach tightens and my heart starts beating fast. I begin deep breathing and try to calm down. I begin to whistle and dance to distract her. She says:

Your whistling is beautiful. You got a nice behind, Karl. You're so hot. See how you can dance.

Mary reaches out to touch my butt with her hands. She can't reach me. I continue dancing and whistling.

I don't remember how many hundreds of times I've

been groped from behind by Mary over the last three years. When I have bent down to get food for her in the refrigerator Mary has walked up to me to grab my bottom.

Later that evening when I'm in bed sleeping Mary enters my bedroom. I wake up.

Can you please go back to your bed? I ask Mary.

I'm gonna sit here, Mary replies.

I can't go back to sleep if you sit here. Please turn out the light when you leave, I say.

I STAY IF I WANT! Mary shouts. It smells musky in the bedroom.

I turn around and try to go back to sleep even with the lights on. Mary makes different sounds. I feel tense all over my body when she's here. I see Mary closing her eyes and is about to go to sleep sitting up.

Please go back to your room, I say.

Can you help me upstairs? Mary asks.

I get up and help her upstairs and tuck her into her bed. I go back to my bed.

Ten minutes later I hear Mary's footsteps again. She enters my bedroom again.

My bedroom is filled with a scent of Mary's urine. I have already changed her incontinence pads and clothes several times today and tonight. I'm really exhausted. I need to get up early to go and teach at the university.

I'm going to bed now, Karl. I love you. Goodnight, Mary says twenty minutes later.

Goodnight Mary. I love you, I reply.

You know where that man is that I'm married to, Karl? Mary asks.

No, I reply.

I've been looking all over the house for him. Where is he? I would give him sex three or four times per day if he came. I'm gonna marry you instead Karl. You got a nice stomach and behind, Mary says when she reaches out to touch my butt again.

I keep on walking in a way to avoid Mary's groping.

Mary storms into my bedroom at 2 a.m.

KARL, WAKE UP! YOU NEED TO FIX MY BED! Mary shouts.

What happened? I ask.

My pillow fell out of the bed. I was gonna get it when I fell, Mary explains.

I walk upstairs and make her bed. I find the pillow under her bed. She is very anxious after falling.

I'm scared, Karl, she says.

You're safe now, I say reassuringly.

I help her to go to the bathroom and tuck her in. Mary talks loud to dead people from her past. She tells stories and laugh so loud so it's echoing all over the house. When I'm back in my bed I hear Mary laughing. I can't go back to sleep until 4 a.m. when she starts to calm down.

Mary returns to my bedroom at 4.40 a.m.

I need some pens and paper, Karl. I need to figure out something, Mary says.

I get up and give her some pens and paper.

She writes 2000-1995=1005.

I don't ask any questions. I just go back to bed.

I sleep for one hour before my alarm rings. When I get up to make breakfast I'm dizzy. I see stars and almost collapse. I still need to get up because I need to supervise my social work students. I'm longing for May 4th when Mary is leaving so I can sleep peacefully every night.

Outside the kitchen window spring clouds are drifting by.

I love you, Karl, Mary says.

I love you too, Mary, I reply.

I'm peeing on myself. I'm peeing right now, Mary says.

I help her out of bed and to the bathroom, give her a new incontinence pad, new underwear, and pants. She smiles.

You're the best Karl, she says.

I'm going to the heart clinic today to do an

ultrasound examination of my heart, I say.

If you die Karl it will be alright. I'm going back to Baton Rouge soon anyway. Bianca and Heidi can take care of the house when you die, Mary says in a reassuring way.

Okay. Thank you. Yes. Death happens to all of us. Thank you for caring about me, I reply.

Karl, give me the rosary. I'll pray for you when you go to the heart clinic, she says.

The cardiologist tells me that my blood pressure and electrocardiogram values are normal. He does an ultrasound examination on me. I lie on my left side on the hospital bed. He puts liquid on my chest and moves the ultrasound stick over my heart. Images of a moving heart are visible on the screen.

Your heart looks better than other men in your age. I will send you a new invitation to visit me in a couple of years, the cardiologist says.

I'm so happy and relieved to have a good heart. I don't want to drive back to Mary. I order shrimp and vegetables from the Thai restaurant close to Bianca's apartment and walk to her.

After we enjoy the lunch, we drive to the beach and listen to the waves. Nine years ago, our family visited a desolate wilderness wetland. Bianca and I decide to drive through wild forests and return to this nature reserve. At the vast peatland we experience nature's magnificence and strong winds. This area is one of southern Sweden's largest wetland areas, with different birds and a luxuriant flora. We walk along boardwalks over the bog, various types of moorland, wetland, forests, and land islets. The highland moor, with its gently raised contour, is one of the most highly developed landscapes of the type in Europe. Bianca and I climb up to the bird tower and look at the view.

26 FREEZING TO DEATH

April 2021

Mary and I have a quiet and peaceful day together. When I make the reindeer dinner, she says that she will speak in a calm way after I went to the see the cardiologist. I feel happy for a few minutes that Mary has had this realization to take it easy at home. Five minutes later, Mary is anxious getting ready to drive over the Atlantic Ocean to get her Covid shot in Baton Rouge.

You're flying back to the United States just in a few days when you can get your shot in Louisiana, I say.

I'm not going with those people in the airplane. Mr. Johnson is going to take me in his car to the courthouse in Baton Rouge to get the shot this evening, Mary explains.

We have had this discussion so many times before the last months. I show Mary a map of Europe and the United States and point out the Atlantic Ocean. I explain that it's impossible to drive to the United States from Europe. Mary doesn't understand me.

She goes upstairs to get her winter jacket. Mary opens the front door and leaves the house. It's chilly outside. She walks to the bus stop and awaits the arrival of her Corona ride. Mary looks anxiously back and forth for her ride.

That was that. I had the opportunity to relax for a few minutes. I go outside to Mary and ask her to come back with me inside. She insists on waiting for the Corona ride. The stress is building up inside of me. She promised me earlier to start taking it easy to support my health too, but that didn't last long. I'm not disappointed, but I need a break.

Mary stands on the street screaming and hollering: JESUS! JESUS! JESUS! KARL, GET MY RIDE NOW. KARL, FIND MR. JOHNSON. HE'S GONNA TAKE ME. KARL, FIND HIM NOW.

Mary, take a deep breath. Mary, breath. Breath with me. Breath with me. Would you like to have hot chocolate? I ask.

NO! Mary screams.

Mary yells on the street for another half-an-hour and returns inside. I've made her bed. I say goodnight informing her that I need to get up early in the morning to drive to the university. It's not a good night. After a few minutes she is back in my bedroom just as anxious as she was before.

Mary screams, KARL, YOU NEED TO HELP ME NOW TO FIND MY RIDE. MR. JOHNSON IS COMING TONIGHT TO GET ME. WE'RE GONNA GET THE SHOT!

The cat that is lying in my bed jump down on the floor and run away when she hears Mary shouting. When she finally returns to her bed several hours later she laughs in a loud and totally bizarre way. I'm so tired of her. Mary wears me out. I'm an incredibly resilient person, but I have pushed myself to the limit so many times now the last years that I need a break. I'm feeling overwhelmed. Five minutes after I thought that she was going to rest Mary is back asking for help to find her Corona ride. She is wearing her winter jacket, a hat, and her purse over one of her shoulders. My heart pounds nervously. She opens the front door and lets in the cold air. Mary goes outside again. I close the door. Another hour has passed. She returns inside and goes upstairs. Ten minutes later she goes outside again. She has her tunnel vision to wait for her corona ride. In the dark street Mary experiences the cold winter winds. I really want to go to sleep and not wait up for her all night long.

Mary comes back inside to get her packed suitcases. She insists that the corona ride is coming tonight. After five hours of Mary going in and out of the house it's freezing inside the house. I've locked my bedroom door. Mary repeatedly bangs hard on my door. She's full of rage.

OPEN UP KARL NOW! OPEN UP KARL NOW! Mary screams.

I try to calm myself down.

Karl, you're my only hope and my only friend. If they come, do you want to go with us? I talked to mama, my brother and sister. They didn't die, Mary says.

I open the door for Mary. She talks about that they are all going to get the Covid shot tonight and the shot for eternal life. She keeps on talking for an hour. It's after midnight.

Please go to bed Mary, I plead.

Okay. I'll go to bed. You don't think they are coming to get me tonight? Mary says.

No, please go to bed, I say.

Mary goes upstairs. I tuck her in.

Goodnight, I say.

Goodnight darling, she says.

Late at night, Mary leaves the house again and walks out to the street.

After a while I wake up. I don't hear her. Usually, she talks or sings loud at night. I jump out of bed and walk upstairs to see if she is in her bed. She is not there. I look outside. She is not on the street. I put my clothes on and run to the highway. I can't see her anywhere. Perhaps she walked to the waterfall and the river. Maybe she drowned. After I have scanned the area around the highway I walk in the opposite direction. There is a starry sky. The air is very cold. I stop and listen. Somewhere there is a weak sound from someone. I keep on walking and see a shadow moving. Mary lies still on the grass in a garden. Is she dead?

Mary, I say.

Who is it? Mary asks in a quiet way.

It's Karl. I'm gonna help you home, I say.

Mary is cold. Her hat is on the grass. Her jacket is not zipped. She had brought a banana and a pear.

Her voice is weak and affected by the cold air. She is shivering and can't hardly walk. I rescue her from freezing to death.

Oh Karl. You saved my life. It's so cold. I was gonna die, Mary says.

She leans on me, and we take many breaks. Mary leans on lamp posts and mailboxes. I carry her in the end to the house. When we return home, I help her upstairs. She is so worried. Mary shakes and squeaks at the same time.

I know that you had a rough night, Mary. I can help you to your bed so you can rest now, I say.

Thank you, Karl. You're so sweet. You take of me. I'm your baby, Mary replies.

Yes, you're my baby, Mary, I say.

I help Mary to the bed and tuck her in.

Please pray. It's gonna be alright, I reassure Mary.

Our father... Mary prays.

It's been five intense hours of Mary's corona ride activity. I'm really going to sleep now. I hope that she won't go back outside. 5 a.m. in the morning Mary bangs hard on my locked bedroom door.

Open the door, Karl. I want to kiss you before I go with Mr. Johnson, Mary says.

I get up to make oatmeal for Mary and me. I feel dizzy because I have only slept a little bit. Mary has been manic.

I appreciate you to the highest, Karl. You saved my life last night, she says.

Mary kisses me on my cheek. She goes out and in out of the house. She is worried and waits for Mr. Johnson to give her a ride to the Corona shot center in Baton Rouge. She explains that Mr. Johnson flew here last night. She is hyper and all dressed. Mary has her big suitcases ready.

I'm dancing in the bedroom to let go of my stress and worries. I think that it's going to be alright soon. It feels so good to dance and feel the music. Dancing gives me energy and helps me in my self-care.

I'm getting ready to drive to the university. Mary sits on the chair next to me.

Do you want the Corona stick to put on your shoes? Mary says and points to the shoehorn.

Do you want some tea? I can go upstairs and get you a tea bag? Mary says.

No, thanks. I'm fine, I reply.

I'm getting into the car to drive to the university. Mary is inside the house. I have informed the embassy of the United States, the Swedish border police, and other agencies many times that I need to do my work. I've been caring for Mary at home and taught via Zoom at the same time. Now I'm driving to the university campus knowing that Mary might be killed in traffic. It's eight days before her planned departure to Louisiana.

When I'm driving to campus a neighbor calls me. He says that Mary is outside on the street again. I explain the situation and say that I will write to the Swedish border police to ask if Mary can be admitted before she leaves on May 4th to save her life. At the campus other neighbors call me and say that she is back on the highway.

I write a letter to the Swedish Migration Service:

Hello. I'm writing to inform you that Mary has been manic since 6 p.m. last night going in and out of the house all night long. I'm writing to ask you to admit her before the departure on May 4th to save her life. I saved her in the middle of the freezing night when she had walked down the street and had fallen on the ground. When I found her she was lying in the frost with her face down. My heart was racing. She leaned on me, and I carried her gently home. Mary had been exposed to cold temperatures. Being out in the freezing night lying on the ground affected her. When I talked to her, she was unable to think clearly or move well. Mary had inadequate clothing to be lying on the ground in the freezing temperatures. She was shivering, exhausted and felt very tired. Mary was confused. She forgot that she fell outside. She had slurred speech. I got Mary into her warm bed with many blankets. I made warm milk to help her to increase her body temperature. Please help me. Kind regards, Karl Hedman

Mary says, Last night when I was about to freeze to death Mr. Johnson never came. Ruby parked too far away. The only one that came was you Karl. You saved my life. Now I'm so glad I got my sweet boyfriend David back. He's gonna pick me up tonight. We're going to a chicken place. David, do you remember when you used to visit me at the mental health hospital?

Mary keeps on talking about David. She laughs loud to herself telling different stories about her relationship with David. Both my mama and Mami didn't mind that I had sex with him because he was sweet as a saint. He was a holy man. My mama didn't want me to have sex with bad men.

The social services, psychiatry or home care are not able to help me to support Mary in any way before her departure. I talk to the deacon in the Swedish Church. She says that she will visit Mary which I'm so grateful for. My mom will go with the deacon when she is visiting Mary tomorrow.

David gets me everything I want. If I want to get chicken he goes and get it. Isn't that a sweet man? Mary says.

Yes, I reply.

We used to have sex. He was my man, Mary says.

He's a wonderful gentleman. He can take care of me. He thinks that women need things. He could do anything. He knew that mama needed her house fixed and he got a man to fix it. He told the man to fix the house the way the woman wants. David did it without charge. We gave the other man 500 dollars. I bought the material. David had a truck. He brought the lumber. He fixed up my mama's whole house. He paid for all the molding on the house. We paid him back later. He got cement to my little darling Maria's swing. He was sweet. David loved me so much, Mary says.

27 ROCK'N'ROLL PARTY

West Sweden, April 2021

Mary and I have just finished the honey glazed salmon and asparagus supper.

I'm so glad that you have that beautiful music. That Fats Domino singing. Isn't that him? Mary asks.

Yes, I reply.

Thank you God for Fats Domino, Mary exclaims.

I start whistling to the music and Mary smiles.

Karl, when you go to heaven God can put you on television when you whistle. You're the sweetest man I know, Mary says.

I invite Mary to a Karl Hedman rock'n'roll choreographed partnered dance which is age adapted and improvised.

Are you ready to rock'n'roll, Mary? I ask.

Yes, Sir, Mary says.

Our rock'n'roll moves are mixed with the Swing dance Lindy Hop. Our dancing is not acrobatic. It still requires a lot of skill and stamina. Mary and I do kicks and low lifts. I don't throw Mary in the air. I do my own jumps. We skip the flips. We do the original 6-basic step and the modern 9-basic step in our dance that lasts about thirty minutes. Mary looks exhausted and sits down.

I'm stopping because I'm so tired. I'm a little human being. I'm going back to bed. I'm so sleepy, Mary says.

I help Mary back to bed. She smiles. I stay with her until she falls asleep. This was my farewell gift to Mary. I love her even if she's the wildest old lady I ever met in life. Tears run all over my face. An era will end on Tuesday. It's a little bit sad, but I need some time for myself and my daughters without Mary.

After breakfast, I drive to the university. During the day, the deacon visits Mary with my mom. She prays and sits with her. Mary was grateful for the lovely visit by the deacon. She was surprised that the deacon was a woman. She is used to have male Catholic deacons in Louisiana. When I return home from the university, Mary shows empathy and acknowledges that I grieve.

Where is Maria? Mary asks.

Maria passed away last year, I say.

How did she die? Mary asks.

She died from brain cancer, I say.

You must sure feel sad Karl, Mary says.

Yes, I feel sad, I reply.

Mary says, I brought your little girl Maria to you. She came down from heaven. I guess she's going back to heaven now. She doesn't want to sit down too long. Maria is so beautiful with a pretty dress. She's coming back tomorrow. Maria loves you so much.

I think of Kramer in Seinfeld when Mary storms into my bedroom at 4.30 a.m. She is mixed up. My eyes haven't yet opened.

Where is that man? I'm going outside to see if he is there. Mr. Johnson is going to pick me up to go to the courthouse in Baton Rouge to get the Corona shot, Mary says anxiously and goes outside.

I get up and look outside. Mary stands by the road in her winter jacket.

Breakfast is ready, I tell Mary from the balcony. Today I'm supervising two social work students when Mary enters the bedroom. She is pushy and leans over me. She grabs one of my arms and looks furious. She screams and threatens to kill me in front of my students on the Zoom screen:

WHERE IS THAT MAN? I'M GONNA KILL YOU KARL IF YOU DON'T FIND HIM! I'M GONNA KILL YOU IF YOU DON'T FIND HIM!

I look at the students' uncomfortable faces. I tell Mary with a calm voice that I'm supervising and ask her to calm down.

Mary shouts with a high-pitched voice:

I DON'T CARE! I DON'T CARE! I DON'T CARE!

I explain to the students that I'll be back in a few minutes and that I need to care for Mary. The students say that they understand. I think that they have seen her before when we have had supervision meetings via Zoom, but this is the first time when they see her in rage. I run up to her bedroom and get her rosary beads. When I return to my bedroom Mary sits on the chair. I give her the rosary. She smiles and prays quietly. Mary gets up and sits back on the bed. After a while, she lies down on my bed and says with a gentle voice:

Karl, you are the sweetest man. I want to marry you.

I'm about to have another supervision meeting via Zoom. I have walked into the living room to have peace before the next meeting when Mary storms in. I take a deep breath when my heart beats fast. She screams:

Tell the people at your work that your wife is not dead. SHE AIN'T DEAD! MY DAUGHTER IS ALIVE! I'm going to call the school board. The people haven't come yet. I'm going to go to the place where they said that she died. ARE YOU COMING, KARL?

I will supervise another student in a few minutes, I respond.

I'LL GO ALONE TO THE PEOPLE. THEY'RE COMING SOON, Mary shouts.

I tense up knowing that my next Zoom meeting will not be peaceful.

My daughter is still alive. I told you so. I wonder where my mama is. Do you know where she is, Karl? Mary asks.

No, I reply. Mary continues her manic behavior and worries all evening long. She sits outside in a garden chair for several hours until it gets dark.

Mary, I'm going to bed now. I'm so sleepy. Please come inside. I don't want you to freeze to death if I fall asleep, I say.

Mary walks inside.

Good night, I say.

Good night, Karl, Mary says.

It wasn't a good night. Mary worries a lot. I can hear that she is awake in the living room when I'm about to fall asleep. I wake up two hours later at 1 a.m. when I hear a noise from the living room. It takes some time before I'm able to get up. Mary is passing my bedroom door and goes upstairs.

When she is passing she tells me:

Mama says that I need to turn around left to find something.

Mary turns around left in a circle in the hallway.

I plead with a low voice:

Please go to bed, Mary. I'm not feeling well.

Mary is turning left around and around and around...

I have been there for Mary the last three years. I feel like a nervous wreck with her. The madness at home never stops. She says that she loves me so much. At the same time, she abuses me day and night. I know that she's sick. I can't do this anymore. I just need to have peace in my own home. I don't want to be here anymore. I want to travel to other countries again. I don't want to be with Mary. Everything is about her.

The next day, I see a family therapist to talk about my burdens. The family therapist is a man in my age. We talk about what the problems are in my life. He asks me what I do to relax and about exercise. I tell him that I go on soothing nature walks.

28 BOOK TORNADO

West Sweden, May 2021

When I finally get up later that night and walk into the living room to see what happened I'm a little bit shocked. I'm used to seeing wild things living with Mary for three years. This time, she has pulled out hundreds of books from the bookcases. The books lie in a chaotic tornado pile on the floor. That must have been the noise that I heard last night. Some of the books have been damaged when Mary pulled them out. I put the books back into the bookcases. I go to her bedroom to see if she's inside the house. She is in her bed. She exclaims and licks one of her fingers:

I did it. I'm so happy.

I saw that all the books were pulled out and were lying on the floor in the living room. What did you do? I ask.

I did it, Mary says happily.

I'm silent. What can I say? If she's happy about pulling out all the books I'm accepting it. Mary is leaving in four days. I'll let her do whatever she feels like doing until then. I don't want to cramp her style. I smile with Mary and dance and whistle a story for her. She smiles.

You're crazy Karl. I love you, Mary says.

Yes, I'm crazy. I love you too Mary, I reply.

Mary keeps on talking loud to herself and to dead family members all night long.

I had a minimal and bad night's sleep. I had a nightmare about Mary. I can hear her laughing and telling stories to herself. I go to the kitchen to make the breakfast.

Good morning Mary. What are you laughing about? I ask.

I'm laughing about how foolish Ruby was. She was a mess, Karl. She wanted to date the beautiful men and wanted me to have the ugly men. Why? Mary says

233

and continues to laugh.

I just want men to be kind and spiritual like you Karl, Mary says.

I want to talk about what happened last night when I was sleeping. Can you explain again why you pulled out all the books? I ask.

I had a terrible time. I never gonna get into that fix again. I pulled out all the books so I could walk. Who is going to pick up all the books? Mary says.

I picked up the books already last night, I reply.

You're so sweet Karl. Thank you for doing that. You're my sweet boyfriend fixing everything in my life. You cook for me, you help me in the bathroom, you clean up after me and you're the best whistler, Mary says.

Why is there a table leg here? I ask Mary.

I brought that leg last night when I walked back upstairs. I used it as a stick, Mary explains.

You're so creative. You never stop to surprise me, I reply.

Mary smiles.

The winter is over. It's the spring again. I'm walking peacefully in the forest. The lights have changed. I breath in fresh air and drink the sun. I'm sitting among beautiful hepatica flowers and listen to the waterfalls around me. A rabbit runs above the falls. I whistle. I close my eyes the last hour. I'm sitting down quietly meditating on the soft moss surrounded by sweet music of flowing creek water. I love life.

I feel happy and relaxed the last days before Mary's departure. I have endured so much. This is a breath of promise on something new. I peel an orange for Mary.

The devil tried to take my orange from me. Is that true, Karl? Mary asks.

I don't think that's true, I say.

The man that is over it says it's true, Mary says.

Is that God that you are talking about? I ask.

I don't know who it is? Mary replies.

I'll make some coffee. Would you like some? I ask.

I'd like that very much, she says and smiles.

After the coffee, I help Mary to her bed. She takes a nap. After resting, she jumps out of bed and asks:

Karl, when do I fly back?

In two days, I reply.

What is the doctor gonna ask me? Mary asks.

He will give you a Corona test, I reply.

How do you do the Corona test? Mary asks.

The doctor will get a sample from your nose and throat, I explain.

That's easy, Mary says.

I believe it's gonna be alright. In Louisiana, you'll meet your best friend Alice, I say.

Oh, I love Alice so much, Mary says.

I smile.

Mary, do you have any other questions about your flight? I ask.

Not really. I can't think of any. Do you tell me who to live with? Can I live with my sister, brother, mother, and grandmother in Baton Rouge? Mary replies.

First you will stay at a hospital so they can assess you.

Then you will move to a nursing home, I say.

Karl, I want to stay with my mama, Mary says.

I don't know what to say.

Karl, can you help me to put on my shoes? Mary asks.

When I help Mary with her shoes I find a urine filled pad.

Look what I found, I say.

I put the pad in a plastic bag and place it in the garbage can outside the house.

A PAD IN MY PANTS, Mary says and laughs.

Karl, you're the sweetest gentleman I have ever seen. I have seen many gentlemen, but you're the sweetest and kindest gentleman. That made it easier for me to live in this foreign country, Mary says.

The light is coming in through the window warming our faces.

Karl, have you ever seen the aftermath of a storm? I don't remember what hurricane it was. The sunshine was so bright in the sky. I'm so glad that God showed me this beautiful aftermath of a storm. What is the aftermath of the winter in Sweden? Mary says.

It's these beautiful blooming spring flowers and the beautiful light, I say and point to the garden flowers.

Karl, I want you to come upstairs with me now and see me brushing my teeth because it's a beautiful sight to see, Mary says.

Okay. I'll come and look at you, I say.

Mary smiles.

Where is your little girl, Maria? Mary asks.

Maria died, I reply sorrowful and sit down.

SHE AIN'T DEAD! SHE'S ALIVE! CALL THE HOSPITAL! ASK THEM IF MARIA GUILLORY IS LIVING OR IS DEAD? Mary screams and shakes me.

My stomach aches and my heart beats fast. Mary is restless.

Why are you not crying if she's dead? Mary asks.

Because she died seven months ago, I reply.

Why do you think that all these people are dead? Maria, mama, Mami, Ruby and Claude are alive, Mary says.

I'm really looking forward to Mary leaving. I have survived through perseverance and that I have been able to laugh at myself and Mary.

The morning is clear and cold. I make oatmeal when Mary wakes up.

Is this the day when I fly back? Mary asks.

No, it's tomorrow, I reply.

How long is it I've been in Sweden? Mary asks.

You have been here for almost three years, I reply.

One of my contacts at the American embassy calls me. I give him an update about Mary. Later, I talk to one of the border police contacts. She says that the physician will do an assessment of Mary when he comes to the house and give Mary a Covid test tomorrow morning. Mary's friend Alice and the nurse Ann from the Alzheimer organization in Baton Rouge write that they look forward to seeing Mary in person in Louisiana.

I go to the church and light a candle for Mary and the other passengers that the flight to New York City will be alright. I go for a long walk in the forest after that. I stroll along the river in the pouring spring rain. Cranes fly over me among thousands of hepatica flowers. A squirrel climbs in a tree close to me. Water steam is rising from the grass under the wild apple trees.

29 THE FAREWELL

West Sweden, May 2021

I wake up Mary at 4.30 a.m. to get her ready for the flight. Mary and I get along all right. We say a prayer that she and the other passengers will have a good flight. I'm happy to make the breakfast for Mary and give her the morning medication. She puts on her finest clothes and looks energized. Mary is looking forward to the flight in a few hours. We say goodbye before her flight companions arrive to the house.

I love you so very much, Mary says when kissing one of my cheeks.

I love you, Mary, I reply.

I guess I'll see you around, Mary says.

I'll visit you in Louisiana, I reply.

A physician, a nurse, two security officers from the Swedish Prison and Probation Service and two police inspectors come to the house at 5 a.m. The physician does a Covid test on Mary with a Q tip in her nose. She is sleepy now. I help her downstairs to the van. We walk beside one another. Mary walks slowly. I lift her into the van. The physician sits next to Mary. He will examine her on the way to the airport. Mary and I hug each other.

I love you, Mary. I wish you a lovely flight home. Take good care, I say.

I love you, Karl, Mary says. Mary is squeezing my hand hard. We wave goodbye.

I feel peace within and such a rush of relief in the moment when they drive off. I have been feeling overwhelmed for such a long time after the massive emotional distress the last years. I walk inside the house. I take a long and hot shower and close my eyes. It's wonderfully soothing. My sense of self is coming back.

This is the beginning of a new life chapter. I feel grateful for the support I have received from Bianca and Heidi, close friends, and the Swedish and American government officials, without whom I never would have been able to help Mary to return to Louisiana. I put the kettle on and make black tea. I close my eyes. I did it. I got out from being a prisoner in the Mary world.

One of the border police inspectors calls me from the airport. She says that Mary is doing well. The ride went very well. Mary got along with the doctor. She says that Mary's eyes and face were shining when she saw all the security men at the security counter. Mary tested negative. She is ready to fly. I'm at peace. It's my turn to live a quiet life. I think about Maria's song *It's my shining moment*. It's my way to live...

It's 9 a.m. when 80-year-old Mary flies back to America. She will have a little part of my heart. I pray to God that she and the other passengers will have a safe flight to New York City where she will be met by the American authorities. The border police inspector calls me again in the evening. She says that Mary's flight to New York City was alright. The Swedish physician has handed over Mary to the American physician.

I'm relieved. I close my eyes and smile. Bianca, Heidi, and I have gone through suffering and struggles. We did it together. We're a team and trust each other. With empathy and hope we will grow as a family without Mary. I'm letting go of her and I live for my beloved daughters.

30 COMING HOME TO AMERICA

New York City, May 2021

I'm happy for Mary. She snuggles up next to her physician. The police inspector has prepared the playlist with her favorite music. Mary feels safe and goes to sleep. She wakes up in New York City. She's home again in the United States. Mary survived three years in the cold country of Sweden experiencing midnight sun, wolves, moose, and living in one of the villages where the Vikings came from. She has missed the people and the food in Louisiana.

Baton Rouge, May 2021

Mary's contact at the Office of Aging and Adult Services in Louisiana writes that Mary arrived safely and was admitted to the emergency room in Baton Rouge. Her mood varied quite a lot from distressed to calm in the time she spent with her. Mary described me as a very nice man who brought her breakfast in bed every day. The hospital is planning to send her to a behavioral health unit in LaComb north of New Orleans. The unit is known for its specialization in geriatric care.

 Two walks later, the receptionist at the behavioral health unit in LaComb says that the staff have already fallen in love with Mary because she is so cute. They will do whatever she tells them to. After the geriatric care clinic, Mary goes to live in a nursing home in St. Francisville north of Baton Rouge. St. Francisville is a lush and quiet small town with antebellum homes and seven plantation homes including the Myrtles Plantation, which is rumored to be haunted. The bald-cypress tree which is the largest tree in North America east of the California Redwoods can be found in the area. Close to St. Francisville is The Angola Louisiana State

Penitentiary Museum, which was built on the site of a former plantation home and was the nation's largest maximum-security facility.

Towards the end of her life, Mary has a blood clot in one of her legs. She is admitted to a hospital in Baton Rouge. Mary is weak. Her closest friend Alice is by her side in the last days of her life. Mary passes away on October 12, 2021.

Maria's close friend Laura leads the funeral service preparations with me. Laura organizes all the local funeral work in Louisiana. I write the obituary for Mary with help from Laura:

MARY ALICE JACKSON GUILLORY
1940 – 2021

Graveside Service
St. George Catholic Church
November 2, 1 p.m.

To everything there is a season, and a time to every purpose under the heaven.

Ecclesiastes 3:1

Mary Alice Jackson Guillory, of St. Francisville, went home to be with God on October 12, 2021, at the age of 80. Born December 17, 1940, in Baton Rouge, she was the youngest child of Juliet Aguillard Jackson and Claude N. Jackson, II.

Her pursuit of learning was evident throughout her life. Mary received an M Ed. Degree in Elementary Education and an M Ed. Degree in Guidance and Counseling from Southern University. She did her graduate studies in education and certification in reading at Louisiana State University. Mary did graduate work at the University of Minnesota in educational psychology.

Mary worked as an educator in Baton Rouge. When she retired she was active in the senior citizen activities at the Dr. Leo S. Butler Community Center coordinated by her closest friend, Alice Toombs. A devout Catholic, Mary worshipped at St. George Catholic Church for many years and believed in studying as well as living the Word.

Mary was married to Anthony Guillory. Through this union was born one daughter, Maria. Maria married university professor Karl Hedman and moved to Sweden, his home country, where they had two daughters. Mary lived with her daughter's family in Sweden for three years when Maria was diagnosed with terminal brain cancer. Maria passed away in 2020, and Mary moved back to Louisiana, settling in St. Francisville.

Mary was preceded in death by her parents Juliet and Claude, daughter Maria, brother Claude III, and sister Ruby. She leaves to cherish her memory her son-in-law Karl and granddaughters Bianca and Heidi.

In all the world there was no one like Mary. She is in God's heart. No one can replace her. A graveside service will take place Monday, November 2, at 1:00pm at the St. George Catholic Church cemetery. Officiant is Father Paul Yi.

Four days after Mary died, Bianca and Heidi come to visit me over the weekend. We light candles for Mary and talk about what she meant to us. We have enjoyed fun moments with Mary when she sang and danced to Louisiana songs. She has taught us to pray and appreciate higher learning. I listen to the gentle fall rain when I go to sleep.

Mary is buried at St. George Cemetery in Baton Rouge. It's a beautiful day. Father Paul leads the peaceful prayer service with Laura, Ann from the Alzheimer's Services of the Capital Area and Carolyn from St. George. They say farewell and pray for Mary and the family. The birds sing all around. Her grave is surrounded by shading oak trees. In Sweden, Bianca, Heidi, and I light candles for Mary and cherish her memory.

Mary has come to the end of the road. She spreads her angel wings to reunite with Maria and Juliet in heaven. I think about her in the arms of Maria and Juliet. Mary lets go of the guilt and shame she has carried around in life after not being able to care for Maria in her girlhood when she was admitted to the mental health hospitals. God bless you, Mary.

I have loved and supported Maria and Mary for twenty-five years. They have lived with psychotic struggles and mental illness. They perceived or interpreted reality differently from Bianca, Heidi, and I. Maria and Mary hallucinated, heard voices, had visions and delusions as paranoia and delusions of grandeur. Their psychotic behaviors have forced Bianca, Heidi, and I to experience their confused thinking, excessive fears or worries, extreme mood changes of highs and lows, inabilities to cope with daily problems or stress, troubles understanding and relating to situations and to people, excessive anger, hostility, violence, and suicidal thinking. The psychotic behaviors have caused parental abduction, family conflicts, relationship difficulties, social isolation, legal and financial problems, poverty, and homelessness.

Mental illness can lead to self-blame and guilt. Recovery for persons with mental illness or their loved ones can include having insights about blaming someone for their mental illness. Mental illness isn't someone's fault. Mental illness is experienced. It is not who the person is. They don't do anything to cause it. Recovery is about letting go of self-blame, shame, and stop blaming people with mental illnesses. We are all valuable as human beings.

Bianca, Heidi, my mother, and I visit Maria's grave in Sweden. We light candles of love and watch them burn bright with hope. We pray for Maria and holding hands in heaven. We ask questions about their souls and go on existing without them. We remember the times when we danced and laughed together. We are here to warm you and hold your hands when you are cold and worried, always around, to love and care.

I make pancakes when Heidi and Bianca visit me on Father's Day. We go for a walk to a coffee shop next to the library. I love them with all my heart and soul. I'll always be there for them.

READING GROUP QUESTIONS

1. How do you think you would respond in these different situations that Karl and his family were faced with?
2. What resources might have been more helpful to him and them during these times?
3. What did you like best about this book?
4. What did you like least about this book?
5. Which scene has stuck with you the most?
6. What surprised you most about the book?
7. How did the book impact you?
8. If you could ask the author anything, what would it be?
9. Which characters in the book did you like best?
10. Which characters did you like least?
11. What emotions did this book evoke for you?
12. What did you learn?
13. What questions do you still have?
14. Has this book affected the way you go about your life? If so, in what way?

ACKNOWLEDGEMENTS

I am immensely grateful to my beloved daughters Bianca and Heidi for contributing to the book by sharing perspectives on what happened in the family. Heartfelt gratitude to Malinee Bheenick and Mary McCall who read the book and gave invaluable comments. I want to express appreciation to Miriam Childs, Regardt Ferreira, Nina Gunnarsson, Laura Larkin, and Heather Perlis, for helpful support and feedback. Thank you to you, my dear readers.

Karl Hedman

Borås, Sweden
November 2021

AUTHOR'S NOTE

As a dear friend of mine said, mental illness is a natural part of the human condition. There is so much negative stigma around mental illness. So many of us are touched by mental illness either directly or via a loved one. We all need to experience liberation. This book is written for anyone touched by mental illness and/or dementia, either through a loved one or in themselves. I hope readers will find comfort and acceptance whilst reading this piece. That is my humble attempt.

Karl Hedman

ABOUT THE AUTHOR

DR. KARL HEDMAN was born in Sweden in 1967. He moved to Los Angeles for his graduate studies at UCLA. After earning his Doctor of Philosophy degree and working as a university professor Karl pursued his lifelong dream of becoming an author. He lives in Sweden.

For more information about Karl Hedman and keep up to date with what he's doing:

Website: http://karlhedman.com

Twitter: @KarlHedman

Instagram: instagram.com/drkarlhedman/

Facebook: OfficialKarlHedman

Karl Hedman

The Louisiana Beauty Queen

The Louisiana Beauty Queen unveils a tearful love story with heartbreaking tenderness.

1970: Mary is a Louisiana beauty queen and teacher with many sexy boyfriends. She gives birth to the baby girl Maria. Her world falls apart after a second divorce. She is admitted to mental health hospitals for years leaving Maria with her grandmother. Mary plans to commit suicide and take Maria too along.

1995: After falling in love in Los Angeles and romancing in France Maria and I get married in Stockholm and have two daughters.

2000: Maria is diagnosed with paranoid schizophrenia. During a psychotic attack Maria abducts our daughters, hiding them in from myself and the police for months. I begin a breathless chase to find the girls.

2018: Mary is evicted in Louisiana and moves to the family in Sweden. She has dementia coupled with mental illness, manic outbursts, and sex fantasies. Her behavior pushes the already frail family unit to its limits. Most days turn into a wild roller coaster ride, and I can barely catch my breath.

2019: Maria is diagnosed with terminal brain cancer foreshadowing a darker family tragedy to come.

Made in the USA
Las Vegas, NV
26 November 2021

35332261R00144